Praise for *A Hat Full of Sky*:

'Oodles of dry wit, imagination and shrewdly observed characters . . . As always, Pratchett is effortlessly amusing' *Independent on Sunday*

'In this sequel to *The Wee Free Men*, Pratchett approaches an even more perfect union of domestic and epic fantasy, and the humour similarly races from cerebral to burlesque without dropping a stitch' *The Horn Book (USA)*

'Pratchett's ear for dialogue is superb' *The Times*

'The kind of book adults will enjoy and be delighted for their children to read' *Starburst*

'All ends well – but not before the reader has been hurtled through a series of hilarious scenarios with a carefully devised blend of wit and the simple wisdom of a clear-cut moral line' *Books for Keeps*

'The message throughout is one of self-empowerment and self-improvement . . . [this book] will be relished by children . . . as well as adults' *INIS*

'This gravitas, together with the crackling energy of his ideas and style and his delicious subversion of traditional fairytales, makes *A Hat Full of Sky* a perfect read' *Times Educational Supplement*

'Pratchett weaves a tale that isn't afraid to detour into biting satire . . . By turns hilarious and achingly beautiful, this *be* just right' *Kirkus Reviews, USA*

'The story comes with all of Pratchett's unique comic inimitability and moves with page-turning insistence to its surprising, satisfying conclusion' *The School Librarian*

'Fantastically inventive and humorous fantasy adventure. Fans will be sky high' *Sunday Times*

Books by Terry Pratchett

THE WEE FREE MEN*

THE AMAZING MAURICE AND HIS EDUCATED RODENTS*

THE AMAZING MAURICE AND HIS EDUCATED RODENTS
playscript (adapted by Stephen Briggs)✻

THE BROMELIAD TRILOGY
(containing TRUCKERS, DIGGERS and WINGS)

TRUCKERS*

DIGGERS*

WINGS*

THE CARPET PEOPLE*

THE JOHNNY MAXWELL TRILOGY
(containing ONLY YOU CAN SAVE MANKIND, JOHNNY AND THE DEAD and JOHNNY AND THE BOMB)

ONLY YOU CAN SAVE MANKIND*

JOHNNY AND THE DEAD*

JOHNNY AND THE BOMB*

JOHNNY AND THE DEAD
playscript (adapted by Stephen Briggs)✻

For adults of all ages

The *Discworld*® series

THE COLOUR OF MAGIC*

THE LIGHT FANTASTIC*

EQUAL RITES*

MORT*

SOURCERY*

WYRD SISTERS*

PYRAMIDS*

GUARDS! GUARDS!*

ERIC*¥

MOVING PICTURES*

REAPER MAN*

WITCHES ABROAD*

SMALL GODS*

LORDS AND LADIES*

MEN AT ARMS*

SOUL MUSIC*

INTERESTING TIMES*

MASKERADE*

FEET OF CLAY*

HOGFATHER*

JINGO*

THE LAST CONTINENT*

CARPE JUGULUM*

THE FIFTH ELEPHANT*

THE TRUTH*

THIEF OF TIME*

NIGHT WATCH*

MONSTROUS REGIMENT*

GOING POSTAL*

THE COLOUR OF MAGIC – GRAPHIC NOVEL

THE LIGHT FANTASTIC – GRAPHIC NOVEL

MORT: A DISCWORLD BIG COMIC (illustrated by Graham Higgins)¥

GUARDS! GUARDS!: A DISCWORLD BIG COMIC
(adapted by Stephen Briggs, illustrated by Graham Higgins)¥

SOUL MUSIC: THE ILLUSTRATED SCREENPLAY

WYRD SISTERS: THE ILLUSTRATED SCREENPLAY

MORT – THE PLAY (adapted by Stephen Briggs)

WYRD SISTERS – THE PLAY (adapted by Stephen Briggs)

MEN AT ARMS – THE PLAY (adapted by Stephen Briggs)

GUARDS! GUARDS! – THE PLAY (adapted by Stephen Briggs)

MASKERADE (adapted for the stage by Stephen Briggs)❖

CARPE JUGULUM (adapted for the stage by Stephen Briggs)❖

LORDS AND LADIES (adapted for the stage by Irana Brown)❖

INTERESTING TIMES (adapted by Stephen Briggs)◆

THE FIFTH ELEPHANT (adapted by Stephen Briggs)◆

THE TRUTH (adapted by Stephen Briggs)◆

THE SCIENCE OF DISCWORLD (with Ian Stewart and Jack Cohen)✪

THE SCIENCE OF DISCWORLD II: THE GLOBE
(with Ian Stewart and Jack Cohen)✪

THE DISCWORLD COMPANION (with Stephen Briggs)¥

THE STREETS OF ANKH-MORPORK (with Stephen Briggs)

THE DISCWORLD MAPP (with Stephen Briggs)

A TOURIST GUIDE TO LANCRE – A DISCWORLD MAPP
(with Stephen Briggs and Paul Kidby)

DEATH'S DOMAIN (with Paul Kidby)

NANNY OGG'S COOKBOOK

THE PRATCHETT PORTFOLIO (with Paul Kidby)¥

THE LAST HERO (with Paul Kidby)¥

GOOD OMENS
(with Neil Gaiman)

STRATA

THE DARK SIDE OF THE SUN

THE UNADULTERATED CAT (illustrated by Gray Jolliffe)¥

* also available in audio ¥ published by Victor Gollancz

❖ published by Samuel French ◆ published by Methuen Drama

✪ published by Ebury Press ❉ published by Oxford University Press

TERRY

PRATCHETT

A Hat Full of Sky

A STORY OF DISCWORLD

CORGI BOOKS

A HAT FULL OF SKY
A CORGI BOOK 0552 551449

First published in Great Britain by Doubleday,
an imprint of Random House Children's Books

Doubleday edition published 2004
Corgi edition published 2005

1 3 5 7 9 10 8 6 4 2

Papers used by Random House Children's Books are natural, recyclable products made from wood grown in sustainable forests. The manufacturing processes conform to the environmental regulations of the country of origin.

Corgi Books are published by Random House Children's Books,
61–63 Uxbridge Road, London W5 5SA,
a division of The Random House Group Ltd,
in Australia by Random House Australia (Pty) Ltd,
20 Alfred Street, Milsons Point, Sydney, NSW 2061, Australia,
in New Zealand by Random House New Zealand Ltd,
18 Poland Road, Glenfield, Auckland 10, New Zealand,
and in South Africa by Random House (Pty) Ltd,
Endulini, 5A Jubilee Road, Parktown 2193, South Africa

THE RANDOM HOUSE GROUP Limited Reg. No. 954009
www.**kidsatrandomhouse**.co.uk

A CIP catalogue record for this book is available from the British Library.

Printed and bound in Great Britain by
Cox & Wyman Ltd, Reading, Berkshire.

A Hat Full of Sky

Introduction

From 'Fairies and How to Avoid Them' by Miss Perspicacia Tick:

The Nac Mac Feegle
(also called Pictsies, the Wee Free Men, the Little Men and 'Person or Persons Unknown, Believed to Be Armed')

The Nac Mac Feegle are the most dangerous of the fairy races, particularly when drunk. They love drinking, fighting and stealing, and will in fact steal anything that is not nailed down. If it *is* nailed down, they will steal the nails as well.

Nevertheless, those who have managed to get to know them, and survive, say that they are also amazingly loyal, strong, dogged, brave and, in their own way, quite moral. (For example, they won't steal from people who don't have anything.)

The average Feegle man (Feegle women are rare – *see later*) is about six inches high, red-haired, his skin turned blue with tattoos and the dye called woad and, since you're this close, he's probably about to hit you.

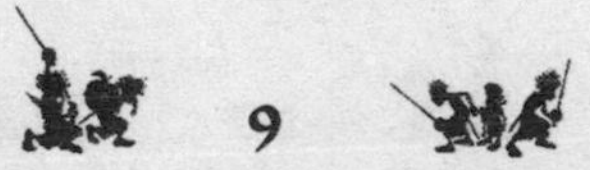

He'll wear a kilt made of any old material, because amongst the Feegles the clan allegiance is shown by the tattoos. He may wear a rabbit-skull helmet, and Feegles often decorate their beards and hair with feathers, beads and anything else that takes their fancy. He will almost certainly carry a sword, although it is mainly for show, the Feegles' preferred method of fighting being with the boot and the head.

History and Religion

The origin of the Nac Mac Feegle is lost in the famous Mists of Time. They say that they were thrown out of Fairyland by the Queen of the Fairies because they objected to her spiteful and tyrannical rule. Others say they were just thrown out for being drunk.

Little is known about their religion, if any, save for one fact: they think they are dead. They like our world, with its sunshine and mountains and blue skies and things to fight. An amazing world like this couldn't be open to just *anybody*, they say. It must be some kind of a heaven or Valhalla, where brave warriors go when they are dead. So, they reason, they have already been alive somewhere else, and then died and were allowed to come here because they have been so *good*.

This is a *quite* incorrect and fanciful notion because, as we know, the truth is exactly the other way round.

There is not a great deal of mourning when a Feegle dies, and it's only because his brothers are sad that he's not spent more time with them before going back to the land of the living, which they also call 'The Last World'.

Habits and Habitat
For choice, the clans of the Nac Mac Feegle live in the burial mounds of ancient kings, where they hollow out a cosy cavern amongst the gold. Generally there will be one or two thorn or elder trees growing on it – the Feegles particularly like old, hollow elder trees, which become chimneys for their fires. And there will, of course, be a rabbit hole. It will look just like a rabbit hole. There will be rabbit droppings around it, and maybe even a few bits of rabbit fur if the Feegles are feeling particularly creative.

Down below, the world of the Feegle is a bit like a beehive, but with a lot less honey and a lot more sting.

The reason for this is that females are very rare among the Feegle. And, perhaps because of this, Feegle women give birth to lots of babies, very often and very quickly. They're about the size of peas when born but grow extremely fast if they're fed well (Feegles like to live near humans so that they can steal milk from cows and sheep for this purpose).

The 'queen' of the clan is called the Kelda, who as she gets older becomes the mother of most of it. Her husband is known as The Big Man. When a girl child is born – and it doesn't often happen – she stays with her mother to learn the *hiddlins*, which are the secrets of keldaring. When she is old enough to be married, *she must leave the clan*, taking a few of her brothers with her as a bodyguard on her long journey.

Often she'll travel to a clan which has no kelda. Very, very rarely, if there is no clan without a kelda, she'll meet with Feegles from several clans and form a completely new clan, with a new name and a mound of its own. She will also choose her husband. And from then on, while her word is absolute law among her clan and must be obeyed, she'll seldom go more than a little distance from the mound. She is both its queen and its prisoner.

But once, for a few days, there was a kelda who was a human girl . . .

A Feegle Glossary, adjusted for those of a delicate disposition

Bigjobs: human beings

Blethers: rubbish, nonsense

Carlin: old woman

Cludgie: the privy

Crivens!: a general exclamation that can mean anything from 'My goodness!' to 'I've just lost my temper and there is going to be trouble.'

Dree your/my/his/her weird: facing the fate that is in store for you/me/him/her

Geas: a very important obligation, backed up by tradition and magic. Not a bird.

Eldritch: weird, strange. Sometimes means oblong, too, for some reason.

Hag: a witch, of any age

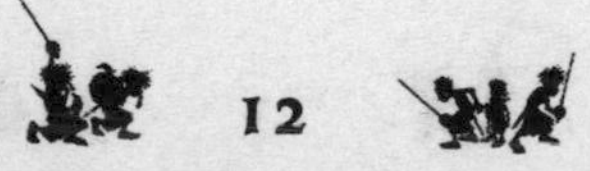

Hagging/Haggling: anything a witch does

Hiddlins: secrets

Mudlin: useless person

Pished: I am *assured* that this means 'tired'.

Scunner: a generally unpleasant person

Scuggan: a *really* unpleasant person

Ships: woolly things that eat grass and go baa. Easily confused with the other kind.

Spavie: see *Mudlin*

Special Sheep Liniment: probably moonshine whisky, I am very sorry to say. No one knows what it'd do to sheep, but it is said that a drop of it is good for shepherds on a cold winter's night and for Feegles at any time at all. Do not try to make this at home.

Waily: a general cry of despair

Chapter 1

Leaving

It came crackling over the hills, like an invisible fog. Movement without a body tired it, and it drifted very slowly. It wasn't thinking now. It had been months since it had last thought, because the brain that was doing the thinking for it had died. They always died. So now it was naked again, and frightened.

It could hide in one of the blobby white creatures that baa'd nervously as it crawled over the turf. But they had useless brains, capable of thinking only about grass and making other things that went baa. No. They would not do. It needed, needed *something better, a strong mind, a mind with power, a mind that could keep it safe.*

It searched . . .

The new boots were all wrong. They were stiff and shiny. Shiny boots! That was disgraceful. Clean boots, that was different. There was nothing wrong with putting a bit of a polish on boots to keep the wet

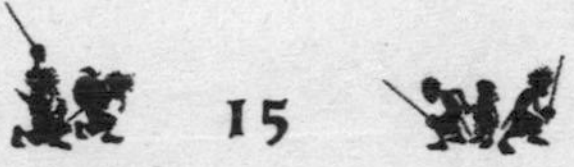

out. But boots had to work for a living. They shouldn't *shine*.

Tiffany Aching, standing on the rug in her bedroom, shook her head. She'd have to scuff the things as soon as possible.

Then there was the new straw hat, with a ribbon on it. She had some doubts about that, too.

She tried to look at herself in the mirror, which wasn't easy because the mirror was not much bigger than her hand, and cracked and blotchy. She had to move it around to try and see as much of herself as possible and remember how the bits fitted together.

But today . . . well, she didn't usually do this sort of thing in the house, but it was important to look smart today, and since no one was around . . .

She put the mirror down on the rickety table by the bed, stood in the middle of the threadbare rug, shut her eyes and said:

'See me.'

And away on the hills something, a thing with no body and no mind but a terrible hunger and a bottomless fear, felt the power.

It would have sniffed the air, if it had a nose.

It searched.

It found.

Such a strange mind, like a lot of minds inside one another, getting smaller and smaller! So strong! So close!

It changed direction slightly, and went a little faster. As it moved, it made a noise like a swarm of flies.

The sheep, nervous for a moment about something they couldn't see, hear or smell, baa'd . . .

. . . and went back to chewing grass.

Tiffany opened her eyes. There she was, a few feet away from herself. She could see the back of her own head.

Carefully, she moved around the room, not looking down at the 'her' that was moving, because she found that if she did that then the trick was over.

It was quite difficult, moving like that, but at last she was in front of herself and looking herself up and down.

Brown hair to match brown eyes . . . there was nothing she could do about that. At least her hair was clean and she'd washed her face.

She had a new dress on, which improved things a bit. It was so unusual to buy new clothes in the Aching family that, of course, it was bought big so that she'd 'grow into it'. But at least it was pale green, and it didn't actually touch the floor. With the shiny new boots and the straw hat she looked . . . like a farmer's daughter, quite respectable, going off to her first job. It'd have to do.

From here she could see the pointy hat on her head, but she had to look hard for it. It was like a glint in the air, gone as soon as you saw it. That's why she'd been worried about the new straw hat, but it had simply gone through it as if the new hat wasn't there.

This was because, in a way, it wasn't. It was invisible, except in the rain. Sun and wind went straight through, but rain and snow somehow saw it, and treated it as if it were real.

She'd been given it by the greatest witch in the world, a real witch with a black dress and a black hat and eyes that could go through you like turpentine goes through a sick sheep. It had been a kind of reward. Tiffany had done magic, serious magic. Before she had done it she hadn't known that she could; when she had been doing it she hadn't known that she was; and after she had done it she hadn't known how she had. Now she had to *learn* how.

'See me not,' she said. The vision of her . . . or whatever it was, because she was not exactly sure about this trick . . . vanished.

It had been a shock, the first time she'd done this. But she'd *always* found it easy to see herself, at least in her head. All her memories were like little pictures of herself doing things or watching things, rather than the view from the two holes in the front of her head. There was a part of her that was always watching her.

Miss Tick – another witch, but one who was easier to talk to than the witch who'd given Tiffany the hat – had said that a witch had to know how to 'stand apart', and that she'd find out more when her talent grew, so Tiffany supposed the 'see me' was part of this.

Sometimes Tiffany thought she ought to talk to

Miss Tick about 'see me'. It felt as if she was stepping out of her body, but still had a sort of ghost body that could walk around. It all worked as long as her ghost eyes didn't look down and see that she *was* just a ghost body. If that happened, some part of her panicked and she found herself back in her solid body immediately. Tiffany had, in the end, decided to keep this to herself. You didn't have to tell a teacher *everything*. Anyway, it was a good trick for when you didn't have a mirror.

Miss Tick was a sort of witch-finder. That seemed to be how witchcraft worked. Some witches kept a magical lookout for girls who showed promise, and found them an older witch to help them along. They didn't teach you how to do it. They taught you how to know what you were doing.

Witches were a bit like cats. They didn't much like one another's company, but they *did* like to know where all the other witches *were*, just in case they needed them. And what you might need them for was to tell you, as a friend, that you were beginning to cackle.

Witches didn't fear much, Miss Tick had said, but what the powerful ones were afraid of, even if they didn't talk about it, was what they called '*going to the bad*'. It was too easy to slip into careless little cruelties because you had power and other people hadn't, too easy to think other people didn't matter much, too easy to think that ideas like right and wrong didn't apply to *you*. At the end of *that* road was you dribbling and cackling to yourself all alone in a gingerbread house, growing warts on your nose.

Witches needed to know other witches were watching them.

And that, Tiffany thought, was why the hat was there. She could touch it any time, provided she shut her eyes. It was a kind of reminder . . .

'Tiffany!' her mother shouted up the stairs. 'Miss Tick's here!'

Yesterday, Tiffany had said goodbye to Granny Aching . . .

The iron wheels of the old shepherding hut were half buried in the turf, high up on the hills. The pot-bellied stove, which still stood lopsided in the grass, was red with rust. The chalk hills were taking them, just like they'd taken the bones of Granny Aching.

The rest of the hut had been burned on the day she'd been buried. No shepherd would have dared to use it, let alone spend the night there. Granny Aching had been too big in people's minds, too hard to replace. Night and day, in all seasons, she *was* the Chalk country: its best shepherd, its wisest woman, and its memory. It was as if the green downland had a soul that walked about in old boots and a sacking apron and smoked a foul old pipe and dosed sheep with turpentine.

The shepherds said that Granny Aching had cussed the sky blue. They called the fluffy little white clouds of summer 'Granny Aching's little lambs'. And although they laughed when they said these things, part of them was not joking.

No shepherd would have dared presume to live in that hut, no shepherd at all.

So they had cut the turf and buried Granny Aching in the Chalk, watered the turf afterwards to leave no mark, then they burned her hut.

Sheep's wool, Jolly Sailor tobacco and turpentine . . .

. . . had been the smells of the shepherding hut, and the smell of Granny Aching. Such things have a hold on people that goes right to the heart. Tiffany only had to smell them now to be back there, in the warmth and silence and safety of the hut. It was the place she had gone to when she was upset, and the place she had gone to when she was happy. And Granny Aching would always smile and make tea and say nothing. And nothing bad could happen in the shepherding hut. It was a fort against the world. Even now, after Granny had gone, Tiffany still liked to go up there.

Tiffany stood there, while the wind blew over the turf and sheep bells *clonked* in the distance.

'I've got . . .' She cleared her throat. 'I've got to go away. I . . . I've got to learn proper witching, and there's no one here now to teach me, you see. I've got to . . . to look after the hills like you did. I can . . . *do* things but I don't *know* things, and Miss Tick says what you don't know can kill you. I want to be as good as you were. I will come back! I will come back soon! I promise I will come back, better than I went!'

A blue butterfly, blown off course by a gust, settled

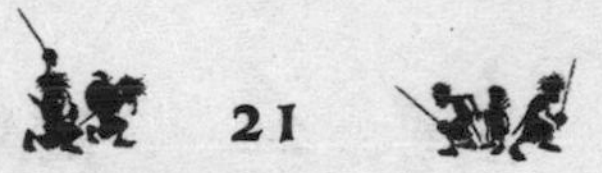

on Tiffany's shoulder, opened and shut its wings once or twice, then fluttered away.

Granny Aching had never been at home with words. She collected silence like other people collected string. But she had a way of saying nothing that said it all.

Tiffany stayed for a while, until her tears had dried, and then went off back down the hill, leaving the everlasting wind to curl around the wheels and whistle down the chimney of the pot-bellied stove. Life went on.

It wasn't unusual for girls as young as Tiffany to go 'into service'. It meant working as a maid somewhere. Traditionally, you started by helping an old lady who lived by herself; she wouldn't be able to pay much, but since this was your first job you probably weren't worth much, either.

In fact Tiffany practically ran Home Farm's dairy by herself, if someone helped her lift the big milk churns, and her parents had been surprised she had wanted to go into service at all. But as Tiffany said, it was something everyone did. You got out into the world a little bit. You met new people. You never knew what it could lead to.

That, rather cunningly, got her mother on her side. Her mother's rich aunt had gone off to be a scullery maid, and then a parlour maid, and had worked her way up until she was a housekeeper and married to a butler and lived in a fine house. It wasn't *her* fine house, and she only lived in a bit of it, but she was practically a *lady*.

Tiffany didn't intend to be a lady. This was all a ruse, anyway. And Miss Tick was in on it.

You weren't allowed to charge money for the witching, so all witches did some other job as well. Miss Tick was basically a witch disguised as a teacher. She travelled around with the other wandering teachers who went in bands from place to place teaching anything to anybody in exchange for food or old clothes.

It was a good way to get around, because people in the chalk country didn't trust witches. They thought they danced around on moonlit nights without their drawers on. (Tiffany had made enquiries about this, and had been slightly relieved to find out that you didn't have to do this to be a witch. You could if you wanted to, but only if you were certain where all the nettles, thistles and hedgehogs were.)

But if it came to it, people were a bit wary of the wandering teachers, too. They were said to pinch chickens and steal away children (which was true, in a way) and they went from village to village with their gaudy carts and wore long robes with leather pads on the sleeves and strange flat hats and talked amongst themselves using heathen lingo no one could understand, like '*Alea jacta est*' and '*Quid pro quo*'. It was quite easy for Miss Tick to lurk amongst them. *Her* pointy hat was a stealth version, which looked just like a black straw hat with paper flowers on it until you pressed the secret spring.

Over the last year or so Tiffany's mother had been quite surprised, and a little worried, at Tiffany's sudden thirst for education, which people in the village thought was a good thing in moderation but if taken unwisely could lead to restlessness.

Then a month ago, the message had come: *Be ready*.

Miss Tick, in her flowery hat, had visited the farm and had explained to Mr and Mrs Aching that an elderly lady up in the mountains had heard of Tiffany's *excellent* prowess with cheese and was willing to offer her the post of maid at four dollars a month, one day off a week, her own bed and a week's holiday at Hogswatch.

Tiffany knew her parents. Three dollars a month was a bit low, and five dollars would be suspiciously high, but prowess with cheese was worth the extra dollar. And a bed all to yourself was a very nice perk. Before most of Tiffany's sisters had left home, sleeping two sisters to a bed had been normal. It was a *good* offer.

Her parents had been impressed and slightly scared of Miss Tick, but they had been brought up to believe that people who knew more than you and used long words were quite important, so they'd agreed.

Tiffany accidentally heard them discussing it after she had gone to bed that night. It's quite easy to accidentally overhear people talking downstairs if you hold an upturned glass to the floorboards and accidentally put your ear to it.

She heard her father say that Tiffany didn't have to go away at all.

She heard her mother say that all girls wondered what was out there in the world, so it was best to get it out of her system. Besides, she was a very capable girl with a good head on her shoulders. Why, with hard work there was no reason why one day she couldn't be a servant to someone quite important, like Aunt Hetty had been, and live in a house with an inside privy.

Her father said she'd find that scrubbing floors was the same everywhere.

Her mother said, well, in that case she'd get bored and come back home after the year was up and, by the way, what did 'prowess' mean?

'Superior skill', thought Tiffany to herself. They did have an old dictionary in the house, but her mother never opened it because the sight of all those words upset her. Tiffany had read it all the way through.

And that was it, and suddenly here she was, a month later, wrapping her old boots, which'd been worn by all her sisters before her, in a piece of clean rag and putting them in the second-hand suitcase her mother had bought her, which looked as if it was made of bad cardboard or pressed grape pips mixed with ear wax, and had to be held together with string.

There were goodbyes. She cried a bit, and her mother cried a lot, and her little brother Wentworth cried as well just in case he could get a sweet for doing so. Tiffany's father didn't cry but gave her a silver dollar and rather gruffly told her to be sure to write home every week, which is a man's way of crying. She said goodbye to the cheeses in the dairy and the sheep in the paddock and even to Ratbag the cat.

Then everyone apart from the cheeses and the cat stood at the gate and waved to her and Miss Tick – well, except for the sheep, too – until they'd gone nearly all the way down the chalky-white lane to the village.

And then there was silence except for the sound of their boots on the flinty surface and the endless song of the skylarks overhead. It was late August, and very hot, and the new boots pinched.

'I should take them off, if I was you,' said Miss Tick after a while.

Tiffany sat down by the side of the lane and got her old boots out of the case. She didn't bother to ask how Miss Tick knew about the tight new boots. Witches paid attention. The old boots, even though she had to wear several pairs of socks with them, were much more comfortable and really easy to walk in. They had been walking since long before Tiffany was born, and knew how to do it.

'And are we going to see any . . . little men today?' Miss Tick went on, once they were walking again.

'I don't know, Miss Tick,' said Tiffany. 'I told them

a month ago I was leaving. They're very busy at this time of year. But there's *always* one or two of them watching me.'

Miss Tick looked around quickly. 'I can't see anything,' she said. 'Or hear anything.'

'No, that's how you can tell they're there,' said Tiffany. 'It's always a bit quieter if they're watching me. But they won't show themselves while you're with me. They're a bit frightened of hags – that's their word for witches,' she added quickly. 'It's nothing personal.'

Miss Tick sighed. 'When I was a little girl I'd have loved to see the pictsies,' she said. 'I used to put out little saucers of milk. Of course, later on I realized that wasn't quite the thing to do.'

'No, you should have used strong licker,' said Tiffany.

She glanced at the hedge and thought she saw, just for the snap of a second, a flash of red hair. And she smiled, a little nervously.

Tiffany had been, if only for a few days, the nearest a human being can be to a queen of the fairies. Admittedly, she'd been called a *kelda* rather than a queen, and the Nac Mac Feegle should only be called fairies to their face if you were looking for a fight. On the other hand the Nac Mac Feegle were *always* looking for a fight, in a cheerful sort of way, and when they had no one to fight they fought one another, and if one was all by himself he'd kick his own nose just to keep in practice.

Technically, they *had* lived in Fairyland, but had been thrown out, probably for being drunk. And now, because if you'd ever been their kelda they never forgot you . . .

. . . they were always there.

There was always one somewhere on the farm, or circling on a buzzard high over the chalk downs. And they watched her, to help and protect her, whether she wanted them to or not. Tiffany had been as polite as possible about this. She'd hidden her diary right at the back of a drawer and blocked up the cracks in the privy with wadded paper, and done her best with the gaps in her bedroom floorboards, too. They were little *men*, after all. She was sure they tried to remain unseen so as not to disturb her, but she'd got very good at spotting them.

They granted wishes – not the magical fairytale three wishes, the ones that always go wrong in the end, but ordinary, everyday ones. The Nac Mac Feegle were immensely strong and fearless and incredibly fast, but they weren't good at understanding that what people *said* often wasn't what they *meant*. One day, in the dairy, Tiffany had said, 'I wish I had a sharper knife to cut this cheese,' and her mother's sharpest knife was quivering in the table beside her almost before she'd got the words out.

'I wish this rain would clear up' was probably OK, because the Feegles couldn't do actual magic, but she had learned to be careful not to wish for anything that might be achievable by some small, determined, strong, fearless and fast men who were also not above giving someone a good kicking if they felt like it.

Wishes needed thought. She was never likely to say, out loud, 'I wish that I could marry a handsome prince,' but knowing that if you did you'd probably open the door to find a stunned prince, a tied-up priest and a Nac Mac Feegle grinning cheerfully and ready to act as Best Man definitely made you watch what you said. But they could be helpful, in a haphazard way, and she'd taken to leaving out for them things that the family didn't need but might be useful to little people, like tiny mustard spoons, pins, a soup bowl that would make a nice bath for a Feegle and, in case they didn't get the message, some soap. They didn't steal the soap.

Her last visit to the ancient burial mound high on the chalk down where the pictsies lived had been to attend the wedding of Rob Anybody, the Big Man of the clan, to Jeannie of the Long Lake. She was going to be the new kelda and spend most of the rest of her life in the mound, having babies like a queen bee.

Feegles from other clans had all turned up for the celebration, because if there's one thing a Feegle likes more than a party, it's a bigger party, and if there's anything better than a bigger party, it's a bigger party with someone else paying for the drink. To be honest, Tiffany had felt a bit out of place, being ten times as tall as the next tallest person there, but she'd been treated very well and Rob Anybody had made a long speech about her, calling her 'our fine big wee young hag' before falling face first into the pudding. It had all been very hot, and very loud, but she'd joined in the cheer when Jeannie had carried Rob Anybody over a tiny broomstick that had been laid on the floor. Traditionally, both the bride and the groom should jump over the broomstick but, equally traditionally, no self-respecting Feegle would be sober on his wedding day.

She'd been warned that it would be a good idea to leave then, because of the traditional fight between the bride's clan and the groom's clan, which could take until Friday.

Tiffany had bowed to Jeannie, because that's what hags did, and had a good look at her. She was small and sweet and very pretty. She also had a glint in her eye and a certain proud lift to her chin. Nac Mac Feegle girls were very rare and they grew up knowing they were going to be keldas one day, and Tiffany had a definite feeling that Rob Anybody was going to find married life trickier than he thought.

She was going to be sorry to leave them behind, but not *terribly* sorry. They were nice in a way but they could, after a while, get on your nerves. Anyway, she was eleven now, and had a feeling that after a certain age you shouldn't slide down holes in the ground to talk to little men.

Besides, the look that Jeannie had given her, just for a moment, had been pure poison. Tiffany had read its meaning without having to try. Tiffany had been the kelda of the clan, even if it was only for a short time. She had also been engaged to be married to Rob Anybody, even if that had only been a sort of political trick. Jeannie knew all that. And the look had said: *He is mine. This place is mine. I do not want you here! Keep out!*

A pool of silence followed Tiffany and Miss Tick down the lane, since the usual things that rustle in hedges tended to keep very quiet when the Nac Mac Feegle were around.

They reached the little village green and sat down to wait for the carrier's cart that went just a bit faster than walking pace and would take five hours to get to the village of Twoshirts, where – Tiffany's parents thought – they'd get the big coach that ran all the way to the distant mountains and beyond.

Tiffany could actually see it coming up the road when she heard the hoofbeats across the green. She turned, and her heart seemed to leap and sink at the same time.

It was Roland, the Baron's son, on a fine black horse. He leaped down before the horse had stopped, and then stood there looking embarrassed.

'Ah, I see a very fine and interesting example of a . . . a . . . a big stone over there,' said Miss Tick in a sticky-sweet voice. 'I'll just go and have a look at it, shall I?'

Tiffany could have *pinched* her for that.

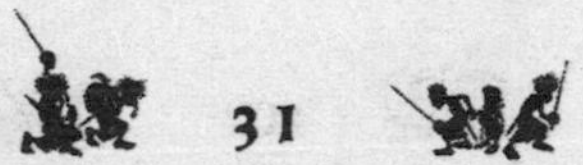

'Er, you're going, then,' said Roland as Miss Tick hurried away.

'Yes,' said Tiffany.

Roland looked as though he was going to explode with nervousness.

'I got this for you,' he said. 'I had it made by a man, er, over in Yelp.' He held out a package wrapped in soft paper.

Tiffany took it and put it carefully in her pocket.

'Thank you,' she said, and dropped a small curtsy. Strictly speaking that's what you had to do when you met a nobleman, but it just made Roland blush and stutter.

'O-open it later on,' said Roland. 'Er, I hope you'll like it.'

'Thank you,' said Tiffany sweetly.

'Here's the cart. Er . . . you don't want to miss it.'

'Thank you,' said Tiffany, and curtsied again, because of the effect it had. It was a little bit cruel, but sometimes you had to be.

Anyway, it would be very hard to miss the cart. If you ran fast, you could easily overtake it. It was so slow that 'stop' never came as a surprise.

There were no seats. The carrier went around the villages every other day, picking up packages and, sometimes, people. You just found a place where you could get comfortable among the boxes of fruit and rolls of cloth.

Tiffany sat on the back of the cart, her old boots dangling over the edge, swaying backwards and forwards as the cart lurched away on the rough road.

Miss Tick sat beside her, her black dress soon covered in chalk dust to the knees.

Tiffany noticed that Roland didn't get back on his horse until the cart was nearly out of sight.

And she knew Miss Tick. By now she would be just *bursting* to ask a question, because witches hate not knowing things. And, sure enough, when the village was left behind, Miss Tick said, after a lot of shifting and clearing her throat:

'Aren't you going to open it?'

'Open what?' said Tiffany, not looking at her.

'He gave you a present,' said Miss Tick.

'I thought you were examining an interesting stone, Miss Tick,' said Tiffany accusingly.

'Well, it was only *fairly* interesting,' said Miss Tick, completely unembarrassed. 'So . . . are you?'

'I'll wait until later,' said Tiffany. She didn't want a discussion about Roland at this point or, really, at all.

She didn't actually *dislike* him. She'd found him in the land of the Queen of the Fairies and had sort of rescued him, although he had been unconscious most of the time. A sudden meeting with the Nac Mac Feegle when they're feeling edgy can do that to a person. *Of course,* without anyone actually lying, everyone at home had come to believe that *he* had rescued *her*. A nine-year-old girl armed with a frying pan couldn't possibly have rescued a thirteen-year-old boy who'd got a sword.

Tiffany hadn't minded that. It stopped people asking too many questions she didn't want to answer or even know how to. But he'd taken to . . . hanging around. She kept accidentally running into him on walks more often than was really possible, and he always seemed to be at the same village events she went to. He was always polite, but she couldn't stand the way he kept looking like a spaniel that had been kicked.

Admittedly – and it took some admitting – he was a lot less of a twit than he had been. On the other hand, there had been such of lot of twit to begin with.

And then she thought, Horse, and wondered why until she realized that her eyes had been watching the landscape while her brain stared at the past . . .

'I've never seen that before,' said Miss Tick.

Tiffany welcomed it as an old friend. The Chalk rose out of the plains quite suddenly on this side of the hills. There was a little valley cupped into the fall of the down, and there was a carving in the curve it made. Turf had been cut away in long flowing lines so that the bare chalk made the shape of an animal.

'It's the White Horse,' said Tiffany.

'Why do they call it that?' said Miss Tick.

Tiffany looked at her. 'Because the chalk is white?' she suggested, trying not to suggest that Miss Tick was being a bit dense.

'No, I meant why do they call it a horse? It doesn't *look* like a horse. It's just . . . flowing lines . . .'

. . . that look as if they're moving, Tiffany thought.

It had been cut out of the turf right back in the old days, people said, by the folk who'd built the stone circles and buried their kind in big earth mounds. And they'd cut out the Horse at one end of this little green valley, ten times bigger than a real horse and, if you didn't look at it with your mind right, the wrong shape, too. Yet they must have known horses, owned horses, seen them every day, and they weren't stupid people just because they lived a long time ago.

Tiffany had once asked her father about the look of the Horse, when they'd come all the way over here for a sheep fair, and he told her what Granny Aching had told him, too, when he was a little boy. He passed on what she said word for word, and Tiffany did the same now.

''Taint what a horse *looks* like,' said Tiffany. 'It's what a horse *be*.'

'Oh,' said Miss Tick. But because she was a teacher as well as a witch, and probably couldn't help herself, she added, 'The funny thing is, of course, that officially there is no such thing as a white horse. They're called grey.'*

'Yes, I know,' said Tiffany. 'This one's white,' she added, flatly.

*She had to say that, because she was a witch and a teacher and that's a terrible combination. They want things to be *right*. They like things to be *correct*. If you want to upset a witch you don't have to mess around with charms and spells, you just have to put her in a room with a picture that's hung slightly crooked and watch her squirm.

That quietened Miss Tick down, for a while, but she seemed to have something on her mind.

'I expect you're upset about leaving the Chalk, aren't you?' she said as the cart rattled on.

'No,' said Tiffany.

'It's OK to be,' said Miss Tick.

'Thank you, but I'm not really,' said Tiffany.

'If you want to have a bit of a cry, you don't have to pretend you've got some grit in your eye or anything—'

'I'm all right, actually,' said Tiffany. 'Honestly.'

'You see, if you bottle that sort of thing up it can cause terrible damage later on.'

'I'm not bottling, Miss Tick.'

In fact, Tiffany was a bit surprised at not crying, but she wasn't going to tell Miss Tick that. She left a sort of space in her head to burst into tears in, but it wasn't filling up. Perhaps it was because she'd wrapped up all those feelings and doubts and left them up on the hill by the pot-bellied stove.

'And if of course you were feeling a bit downcast at the moment, I'm sure you could open the present he—' Miss Tick tried.

'Tell me about Miss Level,' Tiffany said quickly. The name and address was all she knew about the lady she was going to stay with, but an address like 'Miss Level, Cottage in the Woods near the dead oak tree in Lost Man's Lane, High Overhang, If Out Leave Letters in Old Boot by Door' sounded promising.

'Miss Level, yes,' said Miss Tick, defeated. 'Er, yes.

She's not really very old but she says she'll be happy to have a third pair of hands around the place.'

You couldn't slip words past Tiffany, not even if you were Miss Tick.

'So there's someone else there already?' she said.

'Er . . . no. Not exactly,' said Miss Tick.

'Then she's got four arms?' said Tiffany. Miss Tick had sounded like someone trying to avoid a subject.

Miss Tick sighed. It was difficult to talk to someone who paid attention all the time. It put you off.

'It's best if you wait until you meet her,' she said. 'Anything I tell you will only give you the wrong idea. I'm sure you'll get along with her. She's very good with people, and in her spare time she's a research witch. She keeps bees – and goats, the milk of which, I believe, is very good indeed owing to homogenized fats.'

'What does a research witch do?' Tiffany asked.

'Oh, it's a very ancient craft. She tries to find new spells by learning how old ones were really done. You know all that stuff about "ear of bat and toe of frog"? They never work, but Miss Level thinks it's because we don't know exactly what *kind* of frog, or which toe—'

'I'm sorry, but I'm not going to help anyone chop up innocent frogs and bats,' said Tiffany firmly.

'Oh, no, she never kills any!' said Miss Tick hurriedly. 'She only uses creatures that have died naturally or been run over or committed suicide. Frogs can get quite depressed at times.'

The cart rolled on, down the white, dusty road, until it was lost from view.

Nothing happened. Skylarks sang, so high up they were invisible. Grass seeds filled the air. Sheep baa'd, high up on the Chalk.

And then something came along the road. It moved like a little slow whirlwind, so it could be seen only by the dust it stirred up. As it went past, it made a noise like a swarm of flies.

Then it, too, disappeared down the hill . . .

After a while a voice, low down in the long grass, said: 'Ach, *crivens*! And it's on her trail, right enough!'

A second voice said: 'Surely the old hag will spot it?'

'Whut? The teachin' hag? She's nae a proper hag!'

'She's got the pointy hat under all them flowers, Big Yan,' said the second voice, a bit reproachfully. 'I seen it. She presses a wee spring an' the point comes up!'

'Oh, aye, Hamish, an' I daresay she does the readin' and the writin' well enough, but she disnae ken aboot stuff that's no' in books. An' I'm no' showin' meself while she's aroond. She's the kind of a body that'd write things doon about a man! C'mon, let's go and find the kelda!'

The Nac Mac Feegle of the Chalk hated writing for all kinds of reasons, but the biggest one was this: writing *stays*. It fastens words down. A man can speak his mind and some nasty wee *scuggan* will write it down and who knows what he'll do with those words? Ye might as weel nail a man's shadow tae the wall!

But now they had a new kelda, and a new kelda brings new ideas. That's how it's supposed to *work*. It stopped a clan getting too set in its ways. Kelda Jeannie was from the Long Lake clan, up in the mountains – and they *did* write things down.

She didn't see why her husband shouldn't, either. And Rob Anybody was finding out that Jeannie was definitely a kelda.

Sweat was dripping off his forehead. He'd once fought a wolf all by himself, and he'd cheerfully do it again with his eyes shut and one hand tied behind him rather than do what he was doing now.

He had mastered the first two rules of writing, as he understood them.

1) Steal some paper.

2) Steal a pencil.

Unfortunately there was more to it than that.

Now he held the stump of pencil in front of him in both hands, and leaned backwards as two of his brothers pushed him towards the piece of paper pinned up on the chamber wall (it was an old bill for sheep bells, stolen from the farm). The rest of the clan watched, in fascinated horror, from the galleries around the walls.

'Mebbe I could kind o' *ease* my way inta it gently,' he protested as his heels left little grooves in the packed-earth floor of the mound. 'Mebbe I could just do one o' they commeras or full stoppies—'

'You're the Big Man, Rob Anybody, so it's fittin' ye should be the first tae do the writin',' said Jeannie. 'I canna hae a husband who canna even write his ain name. I showed you the letters, did I not?'

'Aye, wumman, the nasty, loopy, bendy things!' growled Rob. 'I dinnae trust that Q, that's a letter that has it in for a man. That's a letter with a sting, that one!'

'You just hold the pencil on the paper and I'll tell ye what marks to make,' said Jeannie, folding her arms.

'Aye, but 'tis a bushel of trouble, writin',' said Rob. 'A word writ doon can hang a man!'

'Wheest, now, stop that! 'Tis easy!' snapped Jeannie. 'Bigjob babbies can do it, and you're a full growed Feegle!'

'An' writin' even goes on sayin' a man's wurds after he's *deid*!' said Rob Anybody, waving the pencil as if trying to ward off evil spirits. 'Ye cannae tell me that's right!'

'Oh, so you're *afeared* o' the letters, is that it?' said Jeannie, artfully. 'Ach, that's fine. All big men fear something. Take the pencil off'f him, Wullie. Ye cannae ask a man to face his fears.'

There was silence in the mound as Daft Wullie nervously took the pencil stub from his brother. Every beady eye was turned to Rob Anybody. His hands opened and shut. He started to breathe heavily, still glaring at the blank paper. He stuck out his chin.

'Ach, ye're a harrrrd wumman, Jeannie Mac

Feegle!' he said at last. He spat on his hands and snatched back the pencil stub from Daft Wullie. 'Gimme that tool o' perdition! Them letters won't know whut's hit them!'

'There's my brave lad!' said Jeannie as Rob squared up to the paper. 'Right, then. The first letter is an R. That's the one that looks like a fat man walking, remember?'

The assembled pictsies watched as Rob Anybody, grunting fiercely and with his tongue sticking out of the corner of his mouth, dragged the pencil through the curves and lines of the letters. He looked at the kelda expectantly after each one.

'That's it,' she said, at last. 'A bonny effort!'

Rob Anybody stood back and looked critically at the paper.

'That's it?' he said.

'Aye,' said Jeannie. 'Ye've writ your ain name, Rob Anybody!'

Rob stared at the letters again. 'I'm gonna go to pris'n noo?' he said.

There was a polite cough from beside Jeannie. It had belonged to the Toad. He had no other name, because toads don't go in for names. Despite sinister forces that would have people think differently, no toad has ever been called Tommy the Toad, for example. It's just not something that happens.

This toad had once been a lawyer (a human lawyer; toads manage without them) who'd been turned into a toad by a fairy godmother who'd *intended* to turn him into a frog but had been a bit hazy on the difference. Now he lived in the Feegle mound, where he ate worms and helped them out with the difficult thinking.

'I've told you, Mr Anybody, that *just* having your name written down is no problem at all,' he said. 'There's nothing illegal about the words "Rob Anybody". Unless, of course,' and the toad gave a little legal laugh, 'it's meant as an instruction!'

None of the Feegles laughed. They liked their humour to be a bit, well, funnier.

Rob Anybody stared at his very shaky writing. 'That's my name, aye?'

'It certainly is, Mr Anybody.'

'An' nothin' bad's happenin' at a',' Rob noted. He looked closer. 'How can you tell it's my name?'

'Ah, that'll be the readin' side o' things,' said Jeannie.

'That's where the lettery things make a sound in yer heid?' said Rob.

'That's the bunny,' said the toad. 'But we thought you'd like to start with the more *physical* aspect of the procedure.'

'Could I no' mebbe just learn the writin' and leave the readin' to someone else?' Rob asked, without much hope.

'No, my man's got to do both,' said Jeannie, folding her arms. When a female Feegle does that, there's no hope left.

'Ach, it's a terrible thing for a man when his

wumman gangs up on him wi' a toad,' said Rob, shaking his head. But, when he turned to look at the grubby paper, there was just a hint of pride in his face.

'Still, that's my name, right?' he said, grinning.

Jeannie nodded.

'Just there, all by itself and no' on a Wanted poster or anything. My name, drawn by me.'

'Yes, Rob,' said the kelda.

'*My* name, under my thumb. No scunner can do anythin' aboot it? *I've* got my name, nice and safe?'

Jeannie looked at the toad, who shrugged. It was generally held by those who knew them that most of the brains in the Nac Mac Feegle clans ended up in the women.

'A man's a man o' some standin' when he's got his own name where no one can touch it,' said Rob Anybody. 'That's serious magic, that is—'

'The R is the wrong way roond and you left the A and a Y out of "Anybody",' said Jeannie, because it is a wife's job to stop her husband actually exploding with pride.

'Ach, wumman, I didna' ken which way the fat man wuz walking',' said Rob, airily waving a hand. 'Ye canna trust the fat man. That's the kind of thing us nat'ral writin' folk knows about. One day he might walk this way, next day he might walk *that* way.'

He beamed at his name:

ЯOB NyЬO D

'And I reckon you got it wrong wi' them Y's,' he went on. 'I reckon it should be N E Bo D. That's Enn . . . eee . . . bor . . . dee, see? That's *sense*!'

He stuck the pencil into his hair, and gave her a defiant look.

Jeannie sighed. She'd grown up with seven hundred brothers and knew how they thought, which was often quite fast while being totally in the wrong direction. And if they couldn't bend their thinking around the world, they bent the world around their thinking. Usually, her mother had told her, it was best not to argue.

Actually, only half a dozen Feegles in the Long Lake clan could read and write very well. They were considered odd, strange hobbies. After all, what – when you got out of bed in the morning – were they good for? You didn't need to know them to wrestle a trout or mug a rabbit or get drunk. The wind couldn't be read and you couldn't write on water.

But things written down lasted. They were the voices of Feegles who'd died long ago, who'd seen strange things, who'd made strange discoveries. Whether you approved of that depended on how creepy you thought it was. The Long Lake clan approved. Jeannie wanted the best for her new clan, too.

It wasn't easy, being a young kelda. You came to a new clan, with only a few of your brothers as a bodyguard, where you married a husband and ended up with hundreds of brothers-in-law. It could be troubling if you let your mind dwell on it. At least back on the island in the Long Lake she'd had her mother to talk to, but a kelda never went home again.

Except for her bodyguard brothers, a kelda was all alone.

Jeannie was homesick and lonely and frightened of the future, which is why she was about to get things wrong . . .

'Rob!'

Hamish and Big Yan came tumbling through the fake rabbit hole that was the entrance to the mound.

Rob Anybody glared at them. 'We wuz engaged in a lit'try enterprise,' he said.

'Yes, Rob, but we watched the big wee young hag safe awa', like you said, but there's a hiver after her!' Hamish blurted out.

'Are ye sure?' said Rob, dropping his pencil. 'I never heard o' one of them in this world!'

'Oh, aye,' said Big Yan. 'Its buzzin' fair made my teeths ache!'

'So did you no' tell her, ye daftie?' said Rob.

'There's that other hag wi' her, Rob,' said Big Yan. 'The educatin' hag.'

'Miss Tick?' said the toad.

'Aye, the one wi' a face like a yard o' yoghurt,' said Big Yan. 'An' you said we wuzna' to show ourselves, Rob.'

'Aye, weel, this is different—' Rob Anybody began, but stopped.

He hadn't been a husband for very long, but upon marriage men get a whole lot of extra senses bolted into their brain, and one is there to tell a man that he's suddenly neck deep in real trouble.

Jeannie was tapping her foot. Her arms were still folded. She had the special smile women learn about when they marry, too, which seems to say 'Yes, you're in big trouble but I'm going to let you dig yourself in even more deeply.'

'What's this about the big wee hag?' she said, her voice as small and meek as a mouse trained at the Rodent College of Assassins.

'Oh, ah, ach, weel, aye . . .' Rob began, his face falling. 'Do ye not bring her to mind, dear? She was at oor wedding, aye. She was oor kelda for a day or two, ye ken. The Old One made her swear to that just afore she went back to the Land o' the Livin',' he added, in case mentioning the wishes of the last kelda would deflect whatever storm was coming. 'It's as well tae keep an eye on her, ye ken, her being oor hag and a' . . .'

Rob Anybody's voice trailed away in the face of Jeannie's look.

'A true kelda has tae marry the Big Man,' said Jeannie. 'Just like I married ye, Rob Anybody Feegle, and am I no' a good wife tae ye?'

'Oh, fine, fine,' Rob burbled. 'But—'

'And ye cannae be married to two wives, because

that would be bigamy, would it not?' said Jeannie, her voice dangerously sweet.

'Ach, it wasnae *that* big,' said Rob Anybody, desperately looking around for a way of escape. 'And it wuz only temp'ry, an' she's but a lass, an' she wuz good at thinkin'—'

'*I'm* good at thinking, Rob Anybody, and I am the kelda o' this clan, am I no'? There can only be one, is that not so? And I am thinking that there will be no more chasin' after this big wee girl. Shame on ye, anyway. She'll no' want the like o' Big Yan a-gawpin' at her all the time, I'm sure.'

Rob Anybody hung his head. 'Aye . . . but . . . ,' he said.

'But what?'

'A hiver's chasin' the puir wee lass.'

There was a long pause before Jeannie said, 'Are ye sure?'

'Aye, Kelda,' said Big Yan. 'Once you hear that buzzin' ye never forget it.'

Jeannie bit her lip. Then, looking a little pale, she said, 'Ye said she's got the makin's o' a powerful hag, Rob?'

'Aye, but nae one in his'try has survived a hiver! Ye cannae kill it, ye cannae stop it, ye cannae—'

'But wuz ye no' tellin' me how the big wee girl even fought the Quin and won?' said Jeannie. 'Wanged her wi' a skillet, ye said. That means she's good, aye? If she is a true hag, she'll find a way hersel'. We all ha' to dree our weird. Whatever's out there, she's got to face it. If she cannae, she's no true hag.'

'Aye, but a hiver's worse than—' Rob began.

'She's off to learn hagglin' from other hags,' said Jeannie. 'An' I must learn keldarin' all by myself. Ye must hope she learns as fast as me, Rob Anybody.'

Chapter 2

Twoshirts and Two Noses

Twoshirts was just a bend in the road, with a name. There was nothing there but an inn for the coaches, a blacksmith's shop, and a small store with the word SOUVENIRS written optimistically on a scrap of cardboard in the window. And that was it. Around the place, separated by fields and scraps of woodland, were the houses of people for whom Twoshirts was, presumably, the big city. Every world is full of places like Twoshirts. They are places for people to come from, not go to.

It sat and baked silently in the hot afternoon sunlight. Right in the middle of the road an elderly spaniel, mottled brown and white, dozed in the dust.

Twoshirts was bigger than the village back home and Tiffany had never seen souvenirs before. She went into the store and spent half a penny on a small wood carving of two shirts on a washing line, and two postcards entitled 'View of Twoshirts' which showed the souvenir shop and what was quite probably the same dog sleeping in the road. The little old lady behind the counter called her 'young lady' and said that Twoshirts was very popular later in the year, when people came from up to a milc around for the Cabbage-Macerating Festival.

When Tiffany came out she found Miss Tick standing next to the sleeping dog, frowning back the way they'd come.

'Is there something the matter?' said Tiffany.

'What?' said Miss Tick, as if she'd forgotten that Tiffany existed. 'Oh . . . no. I just . . . I thought I . . . look, shall we go and have something to eat?'

It took a while to find someone in the inn, but Miss Tick wandered into the kitchens and found a woman who promised them some scones and a cup of tea. She was actually quite surprised she'd promised that, since she hadn't intended to, it strictly speaking being her afternoon free until the coach came, but Miss Tick had a way of asking questions that got the answers she wanted.

Miss Tick also asked for a fresh egg, not cooked, in its shell. Witches were also good at asking questions that weren't followed by the other person saying 'Why?'

They sat and ate in the sun, on the bench outside the inn. Then Tiffany took out her diary.

She had one in the dairy too, but that was for cheese and butter records. This one was personal. She'd bought it off a pedlar, cheap, because it was last year's. But, as he said, it had the same number of days.

It also had a lock, a little brass thing on a leather flap. It had its own tiny key. It was the lock that had attracted Tiffany. At a certain age, you see the point of locks.

She wrote down 'Twoshirts', and spent some time thinking before adding 'a bend in the road'.

Miss Tick kept staring at the road.

'Is there something wrong, Miss Tick?' Tiffany asked again, looking up.

'I'm . . . not sure. Is anyone watching us?'

Tiffany looked around. Twoshirts slept in the heat. There was no one watching.

'No, Miss Tick.'

The teacher removed her hat and took from inside it a couple of pieces of wood and a reel of black thread. She rolled up her sleeves, looking around quickly in case Twoshirts had sprouted a population, then broke off a length of the thread and picked up the egg.

Egg, thread and fingers blurred for a few seconds and there was the egg, hanging from Miss Tick's fingers in a neat little black net.

Tiffany was impressed.

But Miss Tick hadn't finished. She began to draw things from her pockets, and a witch generally has a lot of pockets. There were some beads, a couple of feathers, a glass lens and one or two strips of coloured paper. These all got threaded into the tangle of wood and cotton.

'What is that?' said Tiffany.

'It's a shamble,' said Miss Tick, concentrating.

'Is it magic?'

'Not exactly. It's *trickery*.'

Miss Tick lifted her left hand. Feathers and beads and egg and pocket junk spun in the web of threads.

'Hmm,' she said. 'Now let me see what I can see . . .'

She pushed the fingers of her right hand into the spiderwork of threads and *pulled* . . .

Egg and glass and beads and feathers danced through the tangle, and Tiffany was sure that at one point one thread had passed straight through another.

'Oh,' she said. 'It's like Cat's Cradle!'

'You've played that, have you?' said Miss Tick vaguely, still concentrating.

'I can do all the common shapes,' said Tiffany. 'The Jewels and The Cradle and The House and The Flock and The Three Old Ladies, One With A Squint, Carrying The Bucket Of Fish To Market When They Meet The Donkey . . . although you need two people for that one, and I only ever did it once, and Betsy Tupper scratched her nose at the wrong moment and I had to get some scissors to cut her loose . . .'

Miss Tick's fingers worked like a loom.

'Funny it should be a children's toy now,' she said. 'Aha . . .' She stared into the complex web she had created.

'Can you see anything?' said Tiffany.

'If I may be allowed to concentrate, child? *Thank* you . . .'

Out in the road the sleeping dog woke, yawned and pulled itself to its feet. It ambled over to the bench the two of them were sitting on, gave Tiffany a reproachful look and then curled up by her feet. It smelled of old damp carpets.

'There's . . . *something* . . .' said Miss Tick, very quietly.

Panic gripped Tiffany.

Sunlight reflected off the white dust of the road and the stone wall opposite. Bees hummed between the little yellow flowers that grew on top of the wall. By Tiffany's feet, the spaniel snorted and farted occasionally.

But it was all *wrong*. She could feel the pressure bearing down on her, pushing at her, pushing at the landscape, *squeezing* it under the bright light of day. Miss Tick and her cradle of threads were motionless beside her, frozen in the moment of bright horror.

Only the threads moved, by themselves. The egg danced, the glass glinted, the beads slid and jumped from string to string—

The egg burst.

The coach rolled in.

It arrived dragging the world behind it, in a cloud of dust and noise and hooves. It blotted out the sun. Doors opened. Harness jingled. Horses steamed. The spaniel sat up and wagged its tail hopefully.

The pressure went – no, it *fled*.

Beside Tiffany, Miss Tick pulled out a handkerchief and started to wipe egg off her dress. The rest of the shamble had disappeared into a pocket with remarkable speed.

She smiled at Tiffany, and kept the smile as she spoke, making herself look slightly mad.

'Don't get up, don't do anything, just be as quiet as a little mouse,' she said.

Tiffany felt in no state to do anything but sit still; she felt like you feel when you wake up after a nightmare.

The richer passengers got out of the coach, and the poorer ones climbed down from the roof. Grumbling and stamping their feet, trailing road dust behind them, they disappeared.

'Now,' said Miss Tick, when the inn door had swung shut, 'we're . . . we're going to go for a – a stroll. See that little wood up there? That's where we're heading. And when Mr Crabber the carter sees your father tomorrow he'll say he – he dropped you off here just before the coach arrived and – and – and everyone will be happy and no one will have lied. That's important.'

'Miss Tick?' said Tiffany, picking up the suitcase.

'Yes?'

'What happened just now?'

'I don't know,' said the witch. 'Do you feel all right?'

'Er . . . yes. You've got some yolk on your hat.' And you're very nervous, Tiffany thought. That was the most worrying part. 'I'm sorry about your dress,' she added.

'It's seen a lot worse,' said Miss Tick. 'Let's go.'

'Miss Tick?' said Tiffany again as they trudged away.

'Er, yes?'

'You are *very* nervous,' said Tiffany. 'If you told me why, that means there's two of us, which is only half the nervousness each.'

Miss Tick sighed. 'It was probably nothing,' she said.

'Miss Tick, the egg exploded!'

'Yes. Um. A shamble, you see, can be used as a simple magic detector and amplifier. It's actually very crude, but it's always useful to make one in times of distress and confusion. I think I . . . probably didn't make it right. And sometimes you do get big discharges of random magic.'

'You made it because you were worried,' said Tiffany.

'Worried? Certainly not. I am *never* worried!' snapped Miss Tick. 'However, since you raise the subject, I *was* concerned. Something was making me uneasy. Something close, I think. It was probably nothing. In fact I feel a lot better now we're leaving.'

But you don't look it, Tiffany thought. And I was wrong. Two people means *twice* as much nervousness each.

But she was sure there was nothing magical about Twoshirts. It was just a bend in the road.

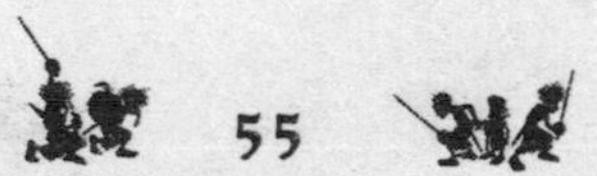

* * *

Twenty minutes later the passengers came out to get into the coach. The coachman did notice that the horses were sweating, and wondered why he could hear a swarm of flies when there were no flies to be seen.

The dog that had been lying in the road was found later cowering in one of the inn's stables, whimpering.

The wood was about half an hour's walk away, with Miss Tick and Tiffany taking turns to carry the suitcase. It was nothing special, as woods go, being mostly full-grown beech, although once you know that beech drips unpleasant poisons on the ground beneath it to keep it clear it's not quite the timber you thought it was.

They sat on a log and waited for sunset. Miss Tick told Tiffany about shambles.

'They're not magical then?' said Tiffany.

'No. They're something to be magical through.'

'You mean like spectacles help you see but don't see for you?'

'That's right, well done! Is a telescope magical? Certainly not. It's just glass in a tube, but with one you could count the dragons on the moon. And . . . well, have you ever used a bow? No, probably not. But a shamble can act like a bow, too. A bow stores up muscle power as the archer draws it, and sends a heavy arrow much further than the archer could actually *throw* it. You can make one out of anything, so long as it . . . looks right.'

'And then you can tell if magic is happening?'

'Yes, if that's what you're looking for. When you're good at it you can use it to help you do magic yourself, to really focus on what you have to do. You can use it for protection, like a curse-net, or to send a spell, or . . . well, it's like those expensive penknives, you know? The ones with the tiny saw and the scissors and the toothpick? Except that I don't think any witch has ever used a shamble as a toothpick, ha ha. All young witches should learn how to make a shamble. Miss Level will help you.'

Tiffany looked around the wood. The shadows were growing longer, but they didn't worry her. Bits of Miss Tick's teachings floated through her head: *Always face what you fear. Have just enough money, never too much, and some string. Even if it's not your fault it's your responsibility. Witches deal with things. Never stand between two mirrors. Never cackle. Do what you must do. Never lie, but you don't always have to be honest. Never wish. Especially don't wish upon a star, which is astronomically stupid. Open your eyes, and then open your eyes again.*

'Miss Level has got long grey hair, has she?' she said.

'Oh, yes.'

'And she's quite a tall lady, just a bit fat, and she wears quite a lot of necklaces,' Tiffany went on. 'And glasses on a chain. And surprisingly high-heeled boots.'

Miss Tick wasn't a fool. She looked around the clearing.

'Where is she?' she said.

'Standing by the tree over there,' said Tiffany.

Even so, Miss Tick had to squint. What Tiffany had noticed was that witches filled space. In a way that was almost impossible to describe, they seemed to be more real than others around them. They just showed up more. But if they didn't want to be seen, they became amazingly hard to notice. They didn't hide, they didn't magically fade away, although it might seem like that, but if you had to describe the room afterwards you'd swear there hadn't been a witch in it. They just seemed to let themselves get lost.

'Ah yes, well done,' said Miss Tick. 'I was wondering when you'd notice.'

Ha! thought Tiffany.

Miss Level got realer as she walked towards them. She was all in black, but clattered slightly as she walked because of all the black jewellery she wore, and she did have glasses, too, which struck Tiffany as odd for a witch. Miss Level reminded Tiffany of a happy hen. And she had two arms, the normal number.

'Ah, Miss Tick,' she said. 'And you must be Tiffany Aching.'

Tiffany knew enough to bow; witches don't curtsy (unless they want to embarrass Roland).

'I'd just like to have a word with Miss Level, Tiffany, if you *don't* mind,' said Miss Tick, meaningfully. 'Senior witch business.'

Ha! thought Tiffany again, because she liked the sound of it.

'I'll just go and have a look at a tree then, shall I?' she said with what she hoped was withering sarcasm.

'I should use the bushes if I was you, dear,' Miss Level called after her. 'I don't like stopping once we're airborne.'

There *were* some holly bushes that made a decent screen, but after being talked to as though she were ten years old Tiffany would rather have allowed her bladder to explode.

I beat the Queen of the Fairies! she thought as she wandered into the wood. All right, I'm not sure how, because it's all like a dream now, but I did do it!

She was angry at being sent away like that. A *little* respect wouldn't hurt, would it? That's what the old witch Mistress Weatherwax had said, wasn't it? 'I show you respect, *as you in turn will respect me.*' Mistress Weatherwax, the witch who all the other witches secretly wanted to be like, had showed her *respect*, so you'd think the others could make a bit of effort in that department.

She said: 'See me.'

. . . and stepped out of herself and walked away towards Miss Tick and Miss Level, in her invisible ghost body. She didn't dare look down, in case she saw her feet weren't there. When she turned and looked back at her solid body, she saw it standing demurely by the holly bushes, clearly too far away to be listening to anyone's conversation.

As Tiffany stealthily drew nearer she heard Miss Tick say:

'– but quite frighteningly precocious.'

'Oh dear. I've never got on very well with clever people,' said Miss Level.

'Oh, she's a good child at heart,' said Miss Tick, which annoyed Tiffany rather more than 'frighteningly precocious' had.

'Of course, you know my situation,' said Miss Level as the invisible Tiffany inched closer.

'Yes, Miss Level, but your work does you great credit. That's why Mistress Weatherwax suggested you.'

'But I am afraid I'm getting a bit absent-minded,' Miss Level worried. *'It was terrible flying down here, because like a big silly I left my long-distance spectacles on my other nose . . .'*

Her *other* nose? thought Tiffany.

Both witches froze, at exactly the same time.

'I'm without an egg!' said Miss Tick.

'I have a beetle in a matchbox against just such an emergency!' squeaked Miss Level.

Their hands flew to their pockets and pulled out string and feathers and bits of coloured cloth—

They know I'm here! thought Tiffany, and whispered, 'See me not!'

She blinked and rocked on her heels as she arrived back in the patient little figure by the holly bushes. In the distance, Miss Level was frantically making a shamble and Miss Tick was staring around the wood.

'Tiffany, come here at once!' she shouted.

'Yes, Miss Tick,' said Tiffany, trotting forward like a good girl.

They spotted me somehow, she thought. Well, they *are* witches, after all, even if in my opinion they're not very good ones—

Then the pressure came. It seemed to squash the wood flat and filled it with the horrible feeling that something is standing right behind you. Tiffany sank to her knees with her hands over her ears and a pain like the worst earache squeezing her head.

'Finished!' shouted Miss Level. She held up a shamble. It was quite different from Miss Tick's, and made up of string and crow feathers and glittery black beads and, in the middle, an ordinary matchbox.

Tiffany yelled. The pain was like red-hot needles and her ears filled with the buzz of flies.

The matchbox exploded.

And then there was silence, and birdsong, and nothing to show that anything had happened apart from a few pieces of matchbox spiralling down, along with an iridescent fragment of wing case.

'Oh dear,' said Miss Level. 'He was quite a good beetle, as beetles go . . .'

'Tiffany, are you all right?' said Miss Tick.

Tiffany blinked. The pain had gone as fast as it had arrived, leaving only a burning memory. She scrambled to her feet. 'I think so, Miss Tick!'

'Then a word, if you please!' said Miss Tick, marching over to a tree and standing there looking stern.

'Yes, Miss Tick?' said Tiffany.

'Did you . . . *do* anything?' said Miss Tick. 'You haven't been summoning things, have you?'

'No! Anyway, I don't know how to!' said Tiffany.

'It's not your little men then, is it?' said Miss Tick doubtfully.

'They're not mine, Miss Tick. And they don't do that sort of thing. They just shout "Crivens!" and then start kicking people on the ankle. You definitely know it's them.'

'Well, whatever it was, it seems to have gone,' said Miss Level. 'And we should go, too, otherwise we'll be flying all night.' She reached behind another tree and picked up a bundle of firewood. At least, it looked exactly like that, because it was supposed to. 'My own invention,' she said, modestly. 'One never knows down here on the plains, does one? And the handle shoots out by means of this button— Oh, I'm so sorry, it sometimes does that. Did anyone see where it went?'

The handle was located in a bush, and screwed back in.

Tiffany, a girl who *listened* to what people said, watched Miss Level closely. She definitely had only one nose on her face, and it was sort of uncomfortable to imagine where anyone might have another one and what they'd use it for.

Then Miss Level pulled some rope out of her

pocket and passed it to someone who wasn't there.

That's what she did, Tiffany was sure. She didn't drop it, she didn't throw it, she just held it out and let go, as though she'd thought she was hanging it on an invisible hook.

It landed in a coil on the moss. Miss Level looked down, then saw Tiffany staring at her and laughed nervously.

'Silly me,' she said. 'I thought I was over there! I'll forget my own head next!'

'Well . . . if it's the one on top of your neck,' said Tiffany cautiously, still thinking about the other nose, 'you've still got it.'

The old suitcase was roped to the bristle end of the broomstick, which now floated calmly a few feet above the ground.

'There, that'll make a nice comfy seat,' said Miss Level, now the bag of nerves that most people turned into when they felt Tiffany staring at them. 'If you'd just hang on behind me. Er. That's what I normally do.'

'You normally hang on *behind* you?' said Tiffany. 'How can—?'

'Tiffany, I've always encouraged your forthright way of asking questions,' said Miss Tick loudly. 'And now, please, I would love to congratulate you on your mastery of silence! Do climb on behind Miss Level, I'm sure she'll want to leave while you've still got some daylight.'

The stick bobbed a little as Miss Level climbed onto it. She patted it, invitingly.

'You're not frightened of heights, are you, dear?' she said as Tiffany climbed on.

'No,' said Tiffany.

'I shall drop in when I come up for the Witch Trials,' said Miss Tick as Tiffany felt the stick rise gently under her. 'Take care!'

It turned out that when Miss Level had asked Tiffany if she was scared of heights, it had been the wrong question. Tiffany was not afraid of heights at all. She could walk past tall trees without batting an eyelid. Looking up at huge towering mountains didn't bother her a bit.

What she *was* afraid of, although she hadn't realized it up until this point, was depths. She was afraid of dropping such a long way out of the sky that she'd have time to run out of breath screaming before hitting the rocks so hard that she'd turn to a sort of jelly and all her bones would break into dust. She was, in fact, afraid of the ground. Miss Level should have thought before asking the question.

Tiffany clung to Miss Level's belt and stared at the cloth of her dress.

'Have you ever flown before, Tiffany?' asked the witch as they rose.

'Gnf!' squeaked Tiffany.

'If you like, I could take us round in a little circle,' said Miss Level. 'We should have a fine view of your country from up here.'

The air was rushing past Tiffany now. It was a lot colder. She kept her eyes fixed firmly on the cloth.

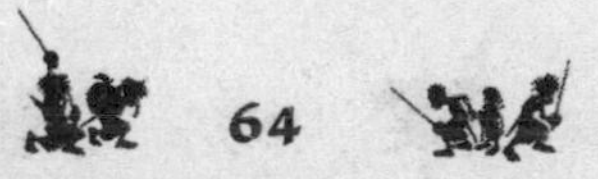

'Would you like that?' said Miss Level, raising her voice as the wind grew louder. 'It won't take a moment!'

Tiffany didn't have time to say no, and in any case was sure she'd be sick if she opened her mouth. The stick lurched under her and the world went sideways.

She didn't want to look, but remembered that a witch is always inquisitive to the point of nosiness. To stay a witch, she *had* to look.

She risked a glance and saw the world under her. The red-gold light of sunset was flowing across the land, and down there were the long shadows of Twoshirts and, further away, the woods and villages all the way back to the long curved hill of the Chalk –

– which glowed red, and the white carving of the chalk Horse burned gold like some giant's pendant. Tiffany stared at it; in the fading light of the afternoon, with the shadows racing away from the sliding sun, it looked alive.

At that moment she wanted to jump off, fly back, get there by closing her eyes and clicking her heels together, do *anything*—

No! She'd bundled those thoughts away, hadn't she? She had to learn, and there was no one on the hills to teach her!

But the Chalk was her world. She walked on it every day. She could feel its ancient life under her feet. The land was in her bones, just as Granny Aching had said. It was in her name, too; in the old language of the Nac Mac Feegle her name sounded like 'Land Under Wave', and in the eye of her mind she'd walked in those deep prehistoric seas when the Chalk had been formed, in a million-year rain made of the shells of tiny creatures. She trod a land made of life, and breathed it in, and listened to it, and thought its thoughts for it. To see it now, small, alone, in a landscape that stretched to the end of the world, was too much. She had to go back to it—

For a moment the stick wobbled in the air.

No! I know I must go!

It jerked back, and there was a sickening feeling in her stomach as the stick curved away towards the mountains.

'A little bit of turbulence there, I think,' said Miss Level over her shoulder. 'By the way, did Miss Tick warn you about the thick woolly pants, dear?'

Tiffany, still shocked, mumbled something which managed to sound like 'no'. Miss Tick had mentioned the pants, and how a sensible witch wore at least three pairs to stop ice forming, but she had forgotten about them.

'Oh dear,' said Miss Level. 'Then we'd better hedge-hop.'

The stick dropped like a stone.

Tiffany never forgot that ride, though she often tried to. They flew just above the ground, which was the blur just below her feet. Every time they came to a fence or a hedge Miss Level would jump it with a cry of 'Here we go!' or 'Upsadaisy!' which was probably meant to make Tiffany feel better. It didn't. She threw up twice.

Miss Level flew with her head bent so far down as to be almost level with the stick, thus getting the maximum aerodynamic advantage from the pointy hat. It was quite a stubby one, only about nine inches high, rather like a clown hat without the bobbles; Tiffany found out later that this was so that she didn't have to take it off when entering low-ceilinged cottages.

After a while – an eternity from Tiffany's point of view – they left the farmlands behind and started to fly through foothills. Before long they'd left trees behind, too, and the stick was flying above the fast white waters of a wide river, studded with boulders. Spray splashed over their boots.

She heard Miss Level yell above the roar of the river and the rush of the wind: 'Would you mind leaning back? This bit's a little tricky!'

Tiffany risked peeking over the witch's shoulder, and gasped.

There was not much water on the Chalk, except for the little streams that people called bournes, which flowed down the valleys in late winter and dried up completely in the summer. Big rivers flowed around it, of course, but they were slow and tame.

The water ahead wasn't slow and tame. It was *vertical*.

The river ran up into the dark blue sky, soared up to the early stars. The broom followed it.

Tiffany leaned back and screamed, and went on screaming as the broomstick tilted in the air and climbed up the waterfall. She'd known the *word,* certainly, but the word hadn't been so big, so wet, and above all it hadn't been so *loud.*

The mist of it drenched her. The noise pounded on her ears. She held onto Miss Level's belt as they climbed through spray and thunder and felt that she'd slip at any minute –

– and then she was thrown forward, and the noise of the fall died away behind her as the stick, now once again going 'along' rather than 'up', sped across the surface of a river that, while still leaping and foaming, at least had the decency to do it on the ground.

There was a bridge high above, and walls of cold rock hemmed in the river on either side, but the walls got lower and the river got slower and the air got warmer again until the broomstick skimmed across calm flat water that probably didn't know what was going to happen to it. Silver fish zigzagged away as they passed over the surface.

After a while Miss Level sent them curving up across new fields, smaller and greener than the ones at home. There were trees again, and little woods in deep valleys. But the last of the sunlight was draining away and, soon, all there was below was darkness.

Tiffany must have dozed off, clinging onto Miss Level, because she felt herself jerk awake as the broomstick stopped in mid-air. The ground was some way below, but someone had set out a ring of what turned out to be candle ends, burning in old jars.

Delicately, turning slowly, the stick settled down until it stopped just above the grass.

At this point Tiffany's legs decided to untwist, and she fell off.

'Up we get!' said Miss Level cheerfully, picking her up. 'You did very well!'

'Sorry about screaming and being sick . . .' Tiffany mumbled, tripping over one of the jars and knocking the candle out. She tried to make out anything in the dark, but her head was spinning. 'Who lit candles, Miss Level?'

'I did. Let's get inside, it's getting chilly—' Miss Level began.

'Oh, by magic,' said Tiffany, still dizzy.

'Well, it *can* be done by magic, yes,' said Miss Level. 'But I prefer matches, which are of course a lot less effort and quite magical in themselves, when you come to think about it.' She untied the suitcase from the stick and said: 'Here we are, then! I do hope you'll like it here!'

There was that cheerfulness again. Even when she felt sick and dizzy, and quite interested in knowing where the privy was as soon as possible, Tiffany still had ears that worked and a mind that, however much she tried, wouldn't stop thinking. And it thought: That cheerfulness has got cracks around the edges. Something isn't right here . . .

Chapter 3

A Single-Minded Lady

There was a cottage, but Tiffany couldn't see much in the gloom. Apple trees crowded in around it. Something hanging from a branch brushed against her as, walking unsteadily, she followed Miss Level. It swung away with a tinkling sound. There was the sound of rushing water, too, some way away.

Miss Level was opening a door. It led into a small, brightly lit and amazingly tidy kitchen. A fire was burning briskly in the iron stove.

'Um . . . I'm supposed to be the apprentice,' said Tiffany, still groggy from the flight. 'I'll make something to drink if you show me where things are—'

'No!' Miss Level burst out, raising her hands. The shout seemed to have shocked her, because she was shaking when she lowered them. 'No – I – I wouldn't dream of it,' she said in a more normal voice, trying to smile. 'You've had a long day. I'll show you to your room and where things are, and I'll bring you

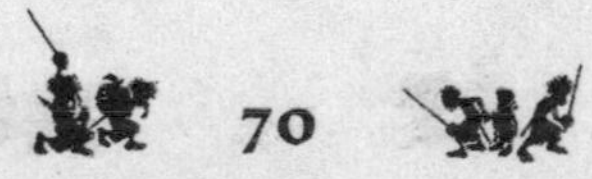

up some stew, and you can be an apprentice tomorrow. No rush.'

Tiffany looked at the bubbling pot on the iron stove, and the loaf on the table. It was fresh baked bread, she could smell that.

The trouble with Tiffany was her Third Thoughts.* They thought: She lives by herself. Who lit the fire? A bubbling pot needs stirring from time to time. Who stirred it? And someone lit the candles. Who?

'Is there anyone else staying here, Miss Level?' she said.

Miss Level looked desperately at the pot and the loaf and back to Tiffany.

'No, there's only me,' she said, and somehow Tiffany knew she was telling the truth. Or *a* truth, anyway.

'In the morning?' said Miss Level, almost pleading. She looked so forlorn that Tiffany actually felt sorry for her.

She smiled. 'Of course, Miss Level,' she said.

There was a brief tour by candlelight. There was a privy not far from the cottage; it was a two-holer, which Tiffany thought was a bit odd but, of course, maybe other people had lived here once. There was

*First Thoughts are the everyday thoughts. Everyone has those. Second Thoughts are the thoughts you think about the *way* you think. People who enjoy thinking have those. Third Thoughts are thoughts that watch the world and think all by themselves. They're rare, and often troublesome. Listening to them is part of witchcraft.

also a room just for a bath, a terrible waste of space by the standards of Home Farm. It had its own pump and a big boiler for heating the water. This was definitely posh.

Her bedroom was a . . . nice room. Nice was a very good word. Everything had frills. Anything that could have a cover on it was covered. Some attempt had been made to make the room . . . jolly, as if being a bedroom was a jolly wonderful thing to be. Tiffany's room back on the farm had a rag rug on the floor, a water jug and basin on a stand, a big wooden box for clothes, an ancient dolls' house and some old calico curtains and that was pretty much it. On the farm, bedrooms were for shutting your eyes in.

This room had a chest of drawers. The contents of Tiffany's suitcase filled one drawer easily.

The bed made no sound when Tiffany sat on it. Her old bed had a mattress so old that it had a comfy hollow in it, and the springs all made different noises; if she couldn't sleep she could move various parts of her body and play *The Bells of St Ungulants* on the springs – cling twing glong, gling ping bloyinnng, dlink plang dyonnng, ding *ploink*.

This room smelled different, too. It smelled of spare rooms, and other people's soap.

At the bottom of her suitcase was a small box that Mr Block the farm's carpenter had made for her. He did not go in for delicate work, and it was quite heavy. In it, she kept . . . keepsakes. There was a piece of chalk with a fossil in it, which was quite rare, and her personal butter stamp (which showed a witch on a broomstick) in case she got a chance to make butter here, and a dobby stone, which was supposed to be lucky because it had a hole in it. (She'd been told that when she was seven, and had picked it up. She couldn't quite see how the hole made it lucky, but since it had spent a lot of time in her pocket, and then safe and sound in the box, it probably *was* more fortunate than most stones, which got kicked around and run over by carts and so on.)

There was also a blue-and-yellow wrapper from an old packet of Jolly Sailor tobacco, and a buzzard feather, and an ancient flint arrowhead wrapped up carefully in a piece of sheep's wool. There were plenty of these on the Chalk. The Nac Mac Feegle used them for spear points.

She lined these up neatly on the top of the chest of drawers, alongside her diary, but they didn't make the place look more homely. They just looked lonely.

Tiffany picked up the old wrapper and the sheep's wool and sniffed them. They weren't *quite* the smell of the shepherding hut, but they were close enough to it to bring tears to her eyes.

She had never spent a night away from the Chalk before. She knew the word 'homesickness' and wondered whether this cold, thin feeling growing inside her was what it felt like—

Someone knocked at the door.

'It's me,' said a muffled voice.

Tiffany jumped off the bed and opened the door.

Miss Level came in with a tray that held a bowl of beef stew and some bread. She put it down on the little table by the bed.

'If you put it outside the door when you're finished, I'll take it down later,' she said.

'Thank you very much,' said Tiffany.

Miss Level paused at the door. 'It's going to be so nice having someone to talk to, apart from myself,' she said. 'I do hope you won't want to leave, Tiffany.'

Tiffany gave her a happy little smile, then waited until the door had shut and she'd heard Miss Level's footsteps go downstairs before tiptoeing to the window and checking there were no bars in it.

There had been something scary about Miss Level's expression. It was sort of hungry and hopeful and pleading and frightened, all at once.

Tiffany also checked that she could bolt the bedroom door on the inside.

The beef stew tasted, indeed, just like beef stew and not, just to take an example *completely* and *totally* at random, stew made out of the last poor girl who'd worked here.

To be a witch, you have to have a very good imagination. Just now, Tiffany was wishing that hers wasn't *quite* so good. But Mistress Weatherwax and Miss Tick wouldn't have let her come here if it was dangerous, would they? Well, would they?

They might. They just might. Witches didn't believe in making things too easy. They assumed you used your brains. If you didn't use your brains, you had no business being a witch. The world doesn't make things easy, they'd say. Learn how to learn fast.

But . . . they'd give her a chance, wouldn't they?

Of course they would.

Probably.

She'd nearly finished the not-made-of-people-at-all-honestly stew when something tried to take the bowl out of her hand. It was the gentlest of tugs, and when she automatically pulled it back, the tugging stopped immediately.

O-K, she thought. Another strange thing. Well, this *is* a witch's cottage.

Something pulled at the spoon but, again, stopped as soon as she tugged back.

Tiffany put the empty bowl and spoon back on the tray.

'All right,' she said, hoping she sounded not scared at all. 'I've finished.'

The tray rose into the air and drifted gently towards the door where it landed with a faint tinkle.

Up on the door, the bolt slid back.

The door opened.

The tray rose up and sailed through the doorway.

The door shut.

The bolt slid across.

Tiffany heard the rattle of the spoon as, somewhere on the dark landing, the tray moved on.

It seemed to Tiffany that it was vitally important that she *thought* before doing anything. And so she thought: It would be stupid to run around screaming because your tray had been taken away. After all, whatever had done it had even had the decency to bolt the door after itself, which meant that it respected her privacy, even while it ignored it.

She cleaned her teeth at the washstand, got into her night-gown and slid into the bed. She blew out the candle.

After a moment she got up, re-lit the candle and with some effort dragged the chest of drawers in front of the door. She wasn't quite certain why, but she felt better for doing it.

She lay back in the dark again.

Tiffany was used to sleeping while, outside on the downland, sheep baa'd and sheep bells occasionally went *tonk*.

Up here, there were no sheep to baa and no bells to tonk and, every time one didn't, she woke up thinking, What was that?

But she did get to sleep eventually, because she remembered waking up in the middle of the night to hear the chest of drawers very slowly slide back to its original position.

Tiffany woke up, still alive and not chopped up, when the dawn was just turning grey. Unfamiliar birds were singing.

There were no sounds in the cottage, and she thought: I'm the apprentice, aren't I? *I'm* the one who should be cleaning up and getting the fire lit. I know how this is supposed to go.

She sat up and looked around the room.

Her old clothes had been neatly folded on top of the chest of drawers. The fossil and the lucky stone and the other things had gone, and it was only after a frantic search that she found them back in the box in her suitcase.

'Now, *look,*' she said to the room in general. 'I *am* a hag, you know. If there are any Nac Mac Feegle here, step out this minute!'

Nothing happened. She hadn't expected anything to happen. The Nac Mac Feegle weren't particularly interested in tidying things up, anyway.

As an experiment she took the candlestick off the bedside table, put it on the chest of drawers and stood back. More nothing happened.

She turned to look out of the window and, as she did so, there was a faint *blint* noise.

When she spun round, the candlestick was back on the table.

Well . . . today was going to be a day when she got *answers*. Tiffany enjoyed the slightly angry feeling. It stopped her thinking about how much she wanted to go home.

She went to put her dress on and realized that there was something soft yet crackly in a pocket.

Oh, how could she have forgotten? But it had been a busy day, a very busy day, and maybe she'd wanted to forget, anyway.

She pulled out Roland's present and opened the white tissue paper carefully.

It was a necklace.

It was the Horse.

Tiffany stared at it.

Not what a horse looks like, but what a horse be . . . It had been carved in the turf back before history began, by people who had managed to convey in a few flowing lines everything a horse was: strength, grace, beauty and speed, straining to break free of the hill.

And now someone – someone clever and, therefore, probably also someone expensive – had made it out of silver. It was flat, just like it was on the hillside and, just like the Horse on the hillside, some parts of it were not joined to the rest of the body. The craftsman, though, had joined these carefully together with tiny silver chain, so that when Tiffany held it up in astonishment it was all there, moving-while-standing-still in the morning light.

She had to put it on. And . . . there was no mirror, not even a tiny hand one. Oh, well . . .

'See me,' said Tiffany.

And far away, down on the plains, something that had lost the trail awoke. Nothing happened for a moment, and then the mist on the fields parted as something invisible started to move, making a noise like a swarm of flies . . .

Tiffany shut her eyes, took a couple of small steps sideways, a few steps forward, turned round and carefully opened her eyes again. There she stood, in front of her, as still as a picture. The Horse looked very well on the new dress, silver against green.

She wondered how much it must have cost Roland. She wondered *why*.

'See me not,' she said. Slowly she took the necklace off, wrapped it up again in its tissue paper and put it in the box with the other things from home. Then she found one of the postcards from Twoshirts, and a pencil, and with care and attention, wrote Roland a short thank-you note. After a flash of guilt she carefully used the other postcard to tell her parents that she was completely still alive.

Then, thoughtfully, she went downstairs.

It had been dark last night, so she hadn't noticed the posters stuck up all down the stairs. They were from circuses, and were covered with clowns and animals and that old-fashioned poster lettering where no two lines of type are the same.

They said things like:

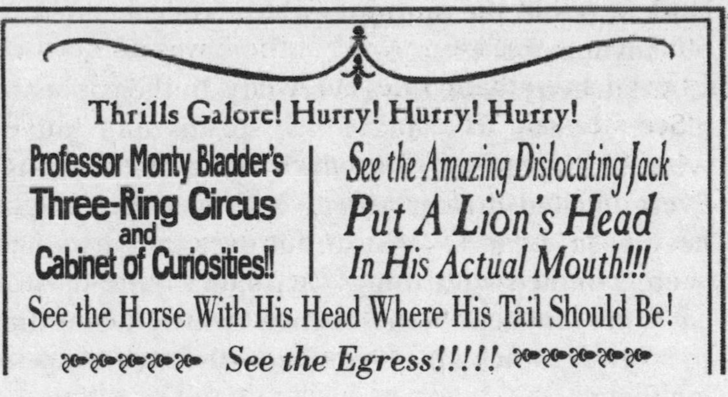

And so it went on, right down to tiny print. They were strange, bright things to find in a little cottage in the woods.

She found her way into the kitchen. It was cold and quiet, except for the ticking of a clock on the wall. Both the hands had fallen off the clock face, and lay at the bottom of the glass cover, so while the clock was still measuring time it wasn't inclined to tell anyone about it.

As kitchens went, it was very tidy. In the cupboard drawer beside the sink, forks, spoons and knives were all in neat sections, which was a bit worrying. Every kitchen drawer Tiffany had ever seen might have been *meant* to be neat but over the years had been crammed with things that didn't quite fit, like big ladles and bent bottle-openers, which meant that they always stuck unless you knew the trick of opening them.

Experimentally she took a spoon out of the spoon section, dropped it amongst the forks and shut the drawer. Then she turned her back.

There was a sliding noise and a tinkle exactly like the tinkle a spoon makes when it's put back amongst the other spoons, who have missed it and are anxious to hear its tales of life amongst the frighteningly pointy people.

This time she put a knife in with the forks, shut the drawer – and leaned on it.

Nothing happened for a while, and then she heard the cutlery rattling. The noise got louder. The drawer began to shake. The whole sink began to tremble—

'All right,' said Tiffany, jumping back. 'Have it your way!'

The drawer burst open, the knife jumped from section to section like a fish and the drawer slammed back.

Silence.

'Who *are* you?' said Tiffany. No one replied. But she didn't like the feeling in the air. Someone was upset with her now. It had been a silly trick, anyway.

She went out into the garden, quickly. The rushing noise she had heard last night had been made by a waterfall not far from the cottage. A little water-wheel pumped water into a big stone cistern, and there was a pipe that led into the house.

The garden was full of ornaments. They were rather sad, cheap ones – bunny rabbits with mad grins, pottery deer with big eyes, gnomes with pointy red hats and expressions that suggested they were on bad medication.

Things hung from the apple trees or were tied to posts all around the place. There were some dreamcatchers and curse-nets, which she sometimes saw hanging up outside cottages at home. Other things looked like big shambles, spinning and tinkling gently. Some . . . well, one looked like a bird made out of old brushes, but most looked like piles of junk. Odd junk, though. It seemed to Tiffany that some of it moved slightly as she went past.

When she went back into the cottage, Miss Level was sitting at the kitchen table.

So was Miss Level. There were, in fact, two of her.

'Sorry,' said the Miss Level on the right. 'I thought it was best to get it over with right now.'

The two women were exactly alike. 'Oh, I see,' said Tiffany. 'You're twins.'

'No,' said the Miss Level on the left, 'I'm not. This might be a little difficult –'

'– for you to understand,' said the other Miss Level. 'Let me see, now. You know –'

'– how twins are sometimes said to be able to share thoughts and feelings?' said the first Miss Level.

Tiffany nodded.

'Well,' said the second Miss Level, 'I'm a bit more complicated than that, I suppose, because –'

'– I'm one person with two bodies,' said the first Miss Level, and now they spoke like players in a tennis match, slamming the words back and forth.

'I wanted to break this to you –'

'– gently, because some people get upset by the –'

'– idea and find it creepy or –'

'– just plain –'

'– weird.'

The two bodies stopped.

'Sorry about that last sentence,' said the Miss Level on the left. 'I only do that when I'm really nervous.'

'Er, do you mean that you both—' Tiffany began, but the Miss Level on the right said quickly, 'There is no both. There's just me, do you understand? I know it's hard. But I have a right right hand and a right left hand and a left right hand and a left left hand. It's all me. I can go shopping and stay home at the same time, Tiffany. If it helps, think of me as one –'

'– person with four arms and –'

'– four legs and –'

'– four eyes.'

All four of those eyes now watched Tiffany nervously.

'And two noses,' said Tiffany.

'That's right. You've got it. My right body is slightly clumsier than my left body, but I have better eyesight in my right pair of eyes. I'm human, just like you, except that there's more of me.'

'But one of you – that is, one half of you – came all the way to Twoshirts for me,' said Tiffany.

'Oh yes, I can split up like that,' said Miss Level. 'I'm quite good at it. But if there's a gap of more than twenty miles or so, I get rather clumsy. And now a cup of tea would do us both good, I think.'

Before Tiffany could move both the Miss Levels stood up and crossed the kitchen.

Tiffany watched one person make a cup of tea using four arms.

There are quite a few things that need to be done to make a cup of tea and Miss Level did them all at once. The bodies stood side by side, passing things from hand to hand to hand, moving kettle and cups and spoon in a sort of ballet.

'When I was child they thought I was twins,' she said over one of her shoulders. 'And then . . . they thought I was evil,' she said over another shoulder.

'Are you?' said Tiffany.

Both of Miss Level turned round, looking shocked.

'What kind of question is that to ask anyone?' she said.

'Um . . . the obvious one?' said Tiffany. 'I mean, if they said "Yes I am! Mwahahaha!", that would save a lot of trouble, wouldn't it?'

Four eyes narrowed.

'Mistress Weatherwax was right,' said Miss Level. 'She said you were a witch to your boots.'

Inside, Tiffany beamed with pride.

'Well, the thing about the obvious,' said Miss Level, 'is that it so often isn't . . . Did Mistress Weatherwax *really* take off her hat to you?'

'Yes.'

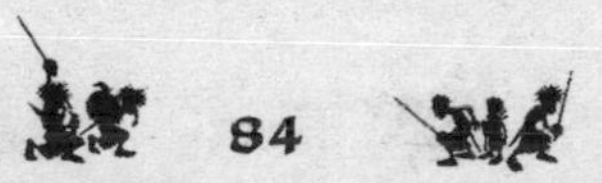

'One day perhaps you'll know how much honour she did you,' said Miss Level. 'Anyway . . . no, I'm not evil. But I nearly became evil, I think. Mother died not long after I was born, my father was at sea and never came back—'

'Worse things happen at sea,' said Tiffany. It was something Granny Aching had told her.

'Yes, right, and probably they did, or possibly he never wanted to come back in any case,' said Miss Level dryly. 'And I was put in a charity home, bad food, horrible teachers, blah, blah, and I fell into the worst company possible, which was my own. It's *amazing* the tricks you can get up to when you've got two bodies. Of course, everyone thought I was twins. In the end I ran away to join the circus. Me! Can you imagine that?'

'Topsy and Tipsy, The Astounding Mind-Reading Act?' said Tiffany.

Miss Level stood stock still, her mouth open.

'It was on the posters over the stairs,' Tiffany added.

Now Miss Level relaxed.

'Oh, yes. Of course. Very . . . quick of you, Tiffany. Yes. You do notice things, don't you . . .'

'I know I wouldn't pay money to see the egress,' said Tiffany. 'It just means "the way out".'*

'Clever!' said Miss Level. 'Monty put that on a sign

*Knowing the dictionary all the way through does have *some* uses.

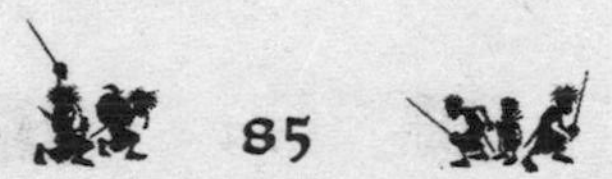

to keep people moving though the Believe-It-or-Not tent. *"This way to the Egress!"* Of course, people thought it was a female eagle or something, so Monty had a big man with a dictionary outside to show them they got exactly what they paid for! Have you ever been to a circus?'

Once, Tiffany admitted. It hadn't been much fun. Things that try too hard to be funny often aren't. There had been a moth-eaten lion with practically no teeth, a tight-rope walker who was never more than a few feet above the ground, and a knife-thrower who threw a lot of knives at an elderly woman in pink tights on a big spinning wooden disc and completely failed to hit her every time. The only real amusement was afterwards, when a cart ran over the clown.

'My circus was a lot bigger,' said Miss Level when Tiffany mentioned this. 'Although as I recall our knife-thrower was also very bad at aiming. We had elephants and camels and a lion so fierce it bit a man's arm nearly off.'

Tiffany had to admit that this sounded a lot more entertaining.

'And what did *you* do?' she said.

'Well, I just bandaged him up while I shoo'd the lion off him—'

'Yes, Miss Level, but I meant in the circus. Just reading your own mind?'

Miss Level beamed at Tiffany. 'That, yes, and nearly everything else, too,' she said. 'With different wigs on I was the Stupendous Bohunkus Sisters. I juggled plates, you know, and wore costumes covered in sequins. And I helped with the high wire act. Not walking the wire, of course, but generally smiling and glittering at the audience. Everyone assumed I was twins, and circus people don't ask too many personal questions in any case. And then what with one thing and another, this and that . . . I came up here and became a witch.'

Both of Miss Level watched Tiffany carefully.

'That was quite a long sentence, that last sentence,' said Tiffany.

'Yes, it was, wasn't it,' said Miss Level. 'I can't tell you *everything*. Do you still want to stay? The last three girls didn't. Some people find me slightly . . . odd.'

'Um . . . I'll stay,' said Tiffany, slowly. 'The thing that moves things about is a bit strange, though.'

Miss Level looked surprised, and then said, 'Oh, do you mean Oswald?'

'There's an invisible man called Oswald who can get into my *bedroom*?' said Tiffany, horrified.

'Oh, no. That's just a name. Oswald isn't a man, he's an *ondageist*. Have you heard of poltergeists?'

'Er . . . invisible spirits that throw things around?'

'Good,' said Miss Level. 'Well, an ondageist is the opposite. They're obsessive about tidiness. He's quite handy around the house but he's absolutely dreadful if he's in the kitchen when I'm cooking. He keeps putting things away. I think it makes him happy. Sorry, I should have warned you, but he normally hides if anyone comes to the cottage. He's shy.'

'And he's a man? I mean, a male spirit?'

'How would you tell? He's got no body and he doesn't speak. I just called him Oswald because I always picture him as a worried little man with a dustpan and brush.' The left Miss Level giggled when the right Miss Level said this. The effect was odd and, if you thought that way, also creepy.

'Well, we *are* getting on well,' said the right Miss Level nervously. 'Is there anything more you want to know, Tiffany?'

'Yes, please,' said Tiffany. 'What do you want me to do? What do *you* do?'

And mostly, it turned out, what Miss Level did was chores. Endless chores. You could look in vain for much broomstick tuition, spelling lessons or pointy-hat management. They were, mostly, the kind of chores that are just . . . chores.

There was a small flock of goats, technically led by Stinky Sam who had a shed of his own and was kept on a chain, but really led by Black Meg, the senior nanny, who patiently allowed Tiffany to milk her and then, carefully and deliberately, put a hoof in the milk bucket. That's a goat's idea of getting to know you. A goat is a worrying thing if you're used to sheep, because a goat is a sheep with *brains*. But Tiffany had met goats before, because a few people in the village kept them for their milk, which was very nourishing. And she knew that with goats you had to use persykology.* If you got excited, and shouted, and hit them (hurting your hand, because it's like slapping a sack full of coat hangers) then they had Won and sniggered at you in goat language, which is almost all sniggering anyway.

By day two, Tiffany learned that the thing to do was reach out and grab Black Meg's hind leg just as she lifted it up to kick the bucket, *and lift it up further*. That made her unbalanced and nervous and the other goats sniggered at *her* and Tiffany had Won.

Next there were the bees. Miss Level kept a dozen hives, for the wax as much as the honey, in a little clearing that was loud with buzzing. She made Tiffany wear a veil and gloves before she opened a hive. She wore some, too.

'Of course,' she observed, 'if you are careful and sober and well centred in your life the bees won't sting. Unfortunately, not all the bees have heard about this theory. Good morning, Hive Three, this is Tiffany, she will be staying with us for a while . . .'

Tiffany half expected the whole hive to pipe up, in some horrible high-pitched buzz, *'Good morning, Tiffany!'* It didn't.

'Why did you tell them that?' she asked.

'Oh, you have to talk to your bees,' said Miss Level. 'It's very bad luck not to. I generally have a little chat with them most evenings. News and

*Tiffany knew what psychology was, but it hadn't been a *pronunciation* dictionary.

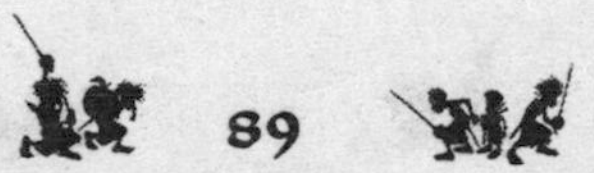

gossip, that sort of thing. Every beekeeper knows about "Telling the Bees".'

'And who do the bees tell?' asked Tiffany.

Both of Miss Level smiled at her.

'Other bees, I suppose,' she said.

'So . . . if you knew how to *listen* to the bees, you'd know everything that was going on, yes?' Tiffany persisted.

'You know, it's funny you should say that,' said Miss Level. 'There have been a few rumours . . . But you'd have to learn to think like a swarm of bees. One mind with *thousands* of little bodies. Much too hard to do, even for me.' She exchanged a thoughtful glance with herself. 'Maybe not *impossible*, though.'

Then there were the herbs. The cottage had a big herb garden, although it contained very little that you'd stuff a turkey with, and at this time of year there was still a lot of work to be done collecting and drying, especially the ones with important roots. Tiffany quite enjoyed that. Miss Level was big on herbs.

There is something called the Doctrine of Signatures. It works like this: when the Creator of the Universe made helpful plants for the use of people, he (or in some versions, she) put little clues on them to give people hints. A plant useful for toothache would look like teeth, one to cure earache would look like an ear, one good for nose problems would drip green goo and so on. Many people believed this.

You had to use a certain amount of imagination to be good at it (but not much in the case of Nose Dropwort) and in Tiffany's world the Creator had got a little more . . . creative. Some plants had writing on them, if you knew where to look. It was often hard to find and usually difficult to read, because plants can't spell. Most people didn't even know about it and just used the traditional method of finding out whether plants were poisonous or useful by testing them on some elderly aunt they didn't need, but Miss Level was pioneering new techniques that she hoped would mean life would be better for everyone (and, in the case of the aunts, often longer, too).

'This one is False Gentian,' she told Tiffany when they were in the long, cool workroom behind the cottage. She was holding up a weed triumphantly. 'Everyone thinks it's another toothache cure, but just look at the cut root by stored moonlight, using my blue magnifying glass . . .'

Tiffany tried it, and read: **'GoOD F4r Colds May cors drowsniss Do nOt opratc heavE mashinry.'**

'Terrible spelling, but not bad for a daisy,' said Miss Level.

'You mean plants *really* tell you how to use them?' said Tiffany.

'Well, not all of them, and you have to know where to look,' said Miss Level. 'Look at this, for example, on the common walnut. You have to use the green magnifying glass by the light of a taper made from red cotton, thus . . .'

Tiffany squinted. The letters were small and hard to read.

'"May contain Nut"?' she ventured. 'But it's a nutshell. Of *course* it'll contain a nut. Er . . . won't it?'

'Not necessarily,' said Miss Level. 'It may, for example, contain an exquisite miniature scene wrought from gold and many coloured precious stones depicting a strange and interesting temple set in a far-off land. Well, it *might*,' she added, catching Tiffany's expression. 'There's no actual law against it. As such. The world is full of surprises.'

That night Tiffany had a lot more to put in her diary. She kept it on top of her chest of drawers with a large stone on it. Oswald seemed to get the message about this, but he had started to polish the stone.

And pull back, and rise above the cottage, and fly the eye across the night-time . . .

Miles away, pass invisibly across something that is itself invisible, but which buzzes like a swarm of flies as it drags itself over the ground . . .

Continue, the roads and towns and trees rushing behind you with *zip-zip* noises, until you come to the big city and, near the centre of the city, the high old tower, and beneath the tower the ancient magical university, and in the university the library, and in the library the bookshelves, and . . . the journey has hardly begun.

Bookshelves stream past. The books are on chains. Some snap at you as you pass.

And here is the section of the more dangerous books, the ones that are kept locked in cages or in vats of iced water or simply clamped between lead plates.

But here is a book, faintly transparent and glowing with thaumic radiation, under a glass dome. Young wizards about to engage in research are *encouraged* to go and read it.

The title is *Hivers: A Dissertation Upon a Device of Amazing Cunning* by Sensibility Bustle, D.M. Phil., B.El L., Patricius Professor of Magic. Most of the hand-written book is about how to construct a large and powerful magical apparatus to capture a hiver without harm to the user, but on the very last page Dr Bustle writes, or wrote:

According to the ancient and famous volume *Res Centum et Una Quas Magus Facere Potest*,* hivers are a type of demon (indeed, Professor Poledread classifies them as such in ***I Spy Demons***, and Cuvee gives them a section under 'wandering spirits' in ***LIBER IMMANIS MONSTRORUM***.† However, ancient texts discovered in the Cave of Jars by the ill-fated First Expedition to the Loko Region give quite a

*'One Hundred and One Things a Wizard Can Do'
†The Monster Book of Monsters

different story, which bears out my own not inconsiderable research.

Hivers were formed in the first seconds of Creation. They are not alive but they have, as it were, the *shape* of life. They have no body, brain or thoughts of their own and a naked hiver is a sluggish thing indeed, tumbling gently through the endless night between the worlds. According to Poledread, most end up at the bottom of deep seas, or in the bellies of volcanoes, or drifting through the hearts of stars. Poledread was a very inferior thinker compared to myself, but in this case he is right.

Yet a hiver does have the ability to fear and to crave. We cannot guess what frightens a hiver, but they seem to take refuge in bodies that have power of some sort - great strength, great intellect, great prowess with magic. In this sense they are like the common hermit elephant of Howondaland, *Elephantus Solitarius*, that will always seek the strongest mud hut as its shell.

There is no doubt in my mind that hivers have advanced the cause of life. Why did fish crawl out of the sea? Why did humanity grasp such a dangerous thing as fire? Hivers, I believe, have been behind this, firing *outstanding* creatures of various species with the flame of necessary ambition which drove them onwards and upwards! What is it that a hiver seeks? What is it that drives them forward? What is it they want? This I shall find out!

Oh, lesser wizards warn us that a hiver distorts the mind of its host, curdling it and inevitably causing an early death through brain fever. I say, Poppycock! People have always been afraid of what they do not understand!

But *I* have *understanding*!!

This morning, at two o'clock, I captured a hiver with my device! And now it is locked inside my head. I can sense its memories, the memories of every creature it has inhabited. Yet, because of my superior intellect, I control the hiver. It does not control me. I do not feel that it has changed me in any way. My mind is as extraordinarily powerful as it always has been!!

At this point the writing is smudgy, apparently because Bustle was beginning to dribble.

Oh, how they have held me back over the years, those worms and cravens that have through sheer luck been allowed to call themselves my superiors! They laughed at me! BUT THEY ARE NOT LAUGHING NOW!!! Even those who *called* themselves my friends, OH YES, they did nothing but hinder me. What about the warnings? they said. Why did the jar you found the plans in have the words 'Do Not Open in Any

Circumstances!' engraved in fifteen ancient languages on the lid? they said. Cowards! So-called 'chums'! Creatures inhabited by a hiver become paranoid and insane, they said! Hivers cannot be controlled, they squeaked!! **DO ANY OF US BELIEVE THIS FOR ONE MINUTE???** Oh, what glories AWAIT!!! Now I have cleansed my life of such worthlessness!!! And as for those even now having the DISRESPECT YES DISRESPECT to hammer on my door because of what I did to the so-called Archchancellor and the College Council ... HOW DARE THEY JUDGE ME!!!!! Like all insects they have NO CONCEPT OF GREATNESS!!!!! I WILL SHOW THEM!!!!! But ... I insoleps ... blit!!!!! hammeringggg dfgujf blort ...

... And there the writing ends. On a little card beside the book some wizard of former times has written: *All that could be found of Professor Bustle was buried in a jar in the old Rose Garden. We advise all research students to spend some time there, and reflect upon the manner of his death.*

The moon was on the way to being full. A gibbous moon, it's called. It's one of the duller phases of the moon and seldom gets illustrated. The full moon and the crescent moon get all the publicity.

Rob Anybody sat alone on the mound, just outside the fake rabbit hole, staring at the distant mountains where the snow on the peaks gleamed in the moonlight.

A hand touched him lightly on the shoulder.

''Tis not like ye to let someone creep up on ye, Rob Anybody,' said Jeannie, sitting down beside him.

Rob Anybody sighed.

'Daft Wullie was telling me ye havenae been eatin' your meals,' said Jeannie, carefully.

Rob Anybody sighed.

'And Big Yan said when ye wuz out huntin' today ye let a fox go past wi'out gieing it a good kickin'?'

Rob sighed again.

There was a faint *pop* followed by a glugging noise. Jeannie held out a tiny wooden cup. In her other hand was a small leather bottle.

Fumes from the cup wavered in the air.

'This is the last o' the Special Sheep Liniment your big wee hag gave us at our wedding,' said Jeannie. 'I put it safely by for emergencies.'

'She's no' *my* big wee hag, Jeannie,' said Rob, without looking at the cup. 'She's *oor* big wee hag. An' I'll tell ye, Jeannie, she has it in her tae be the hag o' hags. There's power in her she doesnae dream of. But the hiver smells it.'

'Aye, well, a drink's a drink whomsoever ye call her,' said Jeannie, soothingly. She waved the cup under Rob's nose.

He sighed, and looked away.

Jeannie stood up quickly. 'Wullie! Big Yan! Come

quick!' she yelled. 'He willnae tak' a drink! I think he's *deid*!'

'Ach, this is no' the time for strong licker,' said Rob Anybody. 'My heart is heavy, wumman.'

'Quickly now!' Jeannie shouted down the hole . . . '*He's deid and still talkin'!*'

'She's the hag o' these hills,' said Rob, ignoring her. 'Just like her granny. She tells the hills what they are, every day. She has them in her bones. She holds 'em in her heart. Wi'out her, I dinnae like tae think o' the future.'

The other Feegles had come scurrying out of the hole and were looking uncertainly at Jeannie.

'Is somethin' wrong?' said Daft Wullie.

'Aye!' snapped the kelda. 'Rob willnae tak' a drink o' Special Sheep Liniment!'

Wullie's little face screwed up in instant grief.

'Ach, the Big Man's *deid*!' he sobbed. 'Oh waily waily waily—'

'Will ye hush yer gob, ye big mudlin!' shouted Rob Anybody, standing up. 'I am no' deid! I'm trying to have a moment o' existential dreed here, right? Crivens, it's a puir lookout if a man cannae feel the chilly winds o' Fate lashing aroound his nethers wi'out folks telling him he's deid, eh?'

'Ach, and I see ye've been talking to the toad again, Rob,' said Big Yan. 'He's the only one arroond here that used them lang words that tak' all day to walk the length of . . .' He turned to Jeannie. 'It's a bad case o' the thinkin' he's caught, missus. When a man starts messin' wi' the readin' and the writin' then he'll come doon with a dose o' the thinkin' soon enough. I'll fetch some o' the lads and we'll hold his heid under water until he stops doin' it, 'tis the only cure. It can kill a man, the thinkin'.'

'I'll wallop ye and ten like ye!' yelled Rob Anybody in Big Yan's face, raising his fists. 'I'm the Big Man in this clan and—'

'And I am the Kelda,' said their kelda, and one of the hiddlins of keldaring is to use your voice like that: hard, cold, sharp, cutting the air like a dagger of ice. 'And I tell you men to go back doon the hole and dinnae show you faces back up here until I say. *Not you, Rob Anybody Feegle!* You stay here until I tell ye!'

'Oh waily waily—' Daft Wullie began, but Big Yan clapped a hand over his mouth and dragged him away quickly.

When they were alone, and scraps of cloud were beginning to mass around the moon, Rob Anybody hung his head.

'I willnae go, Jeannie, if you say,' he said.

'Ach, Rob, *Rob*,' said Jeannie, beginning to cry. 'Ye dinnae *understand*. I want no harm to come to the big wee girl, truly I don't. But I cannae face thinkin' o' you out there fightin' this monster that cannae be killed! It's you I'm worried aboot, can ye no' *see*?'

Rob put his arm around her. 'Aye, I see,' he said.

'I'm your wife, Rob, askin' ye not to go!'

'Aye, aye. I'll stay,' said Rob.

Jeannie looked up to him. Tears shone in the moonlight. 'Ye mean it?'

'I never braked my word yet,' said Rob. 'Except to polis'men and other o' that kidney, ye ken, and they dinnae count.'

'Ye'll stay? Ye'll abide by my word?' said Jeannie, sniffing.

Rob sighed. 'Aye. I will.'

Jeannie was quiet for a while, and then said, in the sharp cold voice of a kelda: 'Rob Anybody Feegle, I'm tellin' ye now to go and save the big wee hag.'

'Whut?' said Rob Anybody, amazed. 'Jus' noo ye said I was tae stay—'

'That was as your wife, Rob. Now I'm telling you as your kelda.' Jeannie stood up, chin out and looking determined. 'If ye dinnae heed the word o' yer kelda, Rob Anybody Feegle, ye can be banished fra' the clan. Ye ken that. So you'll listen t' me guid. Tak' what men you need afore it's too late, and go to the mountains, and see that the big wee girl comes tae nae harm. And come back safe yoursel'. That is an order! Nay, 'tis more'n an order. 'Tis a geas I'm laying on ye! That cannae be brake!'

'But I—' Rob began, completely bewildered.

'I'm the *kelda*, Rob,' said Jeannie. 'I cannae run a clan with the Big Man pinin'. And the hills of our children need their hag. Everyone knows the land needs someone tae tell it whut it is.'

There was something about the way Jeannie had

said 'children'. Rob Anybody was not the fastest of thinkers, but he always got there in the end.

'Aye, Rob,' said Jeannie, seeing his expression. 'Soon I'll be birthing seven sons.'

'Oh,' said Rob Anybody. He didn't ask how she knew the number. Keldas just knew.

'That's *great*!' he said.

'And one daughter, Rob.'

Rob blinked. 'A daughter? This soon?'

'Aye,' said Jeannie.

'That's wonderful good luck for a clan!' said Rob.

'Aye. So you've got something to come back safe to me for, Rob Anybody. An' I beg ye to use your heid for somethin' other than nuttin' folk.'

'I thank ye, Kelda,' said Rob Anybody. 'I'll do as ye bid. I'll tak' some lads and find the big wee hag, for the good o' the hills. It cannae be a good life for the puir wee big wee thing, all alone and far fra' home, among strangers.'

'Aye,' said Jeannie, turning her face away. 'I ken that, too.'

Chapter 4

The PLN

At dawn Rob Anybody, watched with awe by his many brothers, wrote the word:

PLN

. . . on a scrap of paper bag. Then he held it up.

'Plan, ye ken,' he said to the assembled Feegles. 'Now we have a Plan, all we got tae do is work out what tae *do*. Yes, Wullie?'

'Whut was that about this geese Jeannie hit ye with?' said Daft Wullie, lowering his hand.

'Not geese, geas,' said Rob Anybody. He sighed. 'I *told* yez. That means it's serious. It means I got tae bring back the big wee hag, an' no excuses, otherwise my soul gaes slam-bang intae the big cludgie in the sky. It's like a magical order. 'Tis a heavy thing, tae be under a geas.'

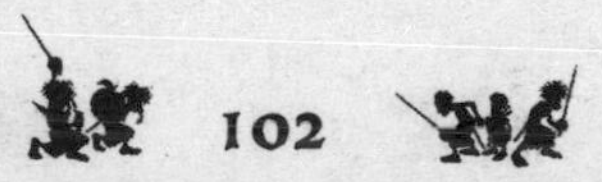

'Well, they're big birds,' said Daft Wullie.

'Wullie,' said Rob, patiently, 'ye ken I said I would tell ye when there wuz times you should've kept your big gob shut?'

'Aye, Rob.'

'Weel, that wuz one o' them times.' He raised his voice. 'Now, lads, ye ken all aboot hivers. They cannae be killed! But 'tis oor duty to save the big wee hag, so this is, like, a sooey-side mission and ye'll probably all end up back in the land o' the living doin' a borin' wee job. So . . . I'm askin' for volunteers!'

Every Feegle over the age of four automatically put his hand up.

'Oh, come *on*,' said Rob. 'You cannae *all* come! Look, I'll tak' . . . Daft Wullie, Big Yan and . . . you, Awf'ly Wee Billy Bigchin. An' I'm takin' no weans, so if yez under three inches high ye're not comin'! Except for ye, o'course, Awf'ly Wee Billy. As for the rest of youse, we'll settle this the traditional Feegle way. I'll tak' the last fifty men still standing!'

He beckoned the chosen three to a place in the corner of the mound while the rest of the crowd squared up cheerfully. A Feegle liked to face enormous odds all by himself, because it meant you didn't have to look where you were hitting.

'She's more'n a hundret miles awa',' said Rob as the big fight started. 'We cannae run it, 'tis too far. Any of youse scunners got any ideas?'

'Hamish can get there on his buzzard,' said Big

Yan, stepping aside as a cluster of punching, kicking Feegles rolled past.

'Aye, and he'll come wi' us, but he cannae tak' more'n one passenger,' shouted Rob over the din.

'Can we swim it?' said Daft Wullie, ducking as a stunned Feegle hurtled over his head.

The others looked at him. 'Swim it? How can we swim there fra' here, yer daftie?' said Rob Anybody.

'It's just worth consid'ring, that's all,' said Wullie, looking hurt. 'I wuz just tryin' to make a contribution, ye ken? Just wanted to show willin'.'

'The big wee hag left in a cart,' said Big Yan.

'Aye, so what?' said Rob.

'Weel, mebbe we could?'

'Ach, no!' said Rob. 'Showin' oursels tae hags is one thing, but not to other folks! You remember what happened a few years back when Daft Wullie got spotted by that lady who wuz painting the pretty pictures doon in the valley? I dinnae want to have them Folklore Society bigjobs pokin' aroound again!'

'I have an idea, Mister Rob. It's me, Awf'ly Wee Billy Bigchin Mac Feegle. We could disguise oursels.'

Awf'ly Wee Billy Bigchin Mac Feegle always announced himself in full. He seemed to feel that if he didn't tell people who he was, they'd forget about him and he'd disappear. When you're half the size of most grown pictsies you're *really* short; much shorter and you'd be a hole in the ground.

He was the new gonnagle. A gonnagle is the clan's

bard and battle poet, but they don't spend all their lives in the same clan. In fact, they're a sort of clan all by themselves. Gonnagles move around among the other clans, making sure the songs and stories get spread around all the Feegles. Awf'ly Wee Billy had come with Jeannie from the Long Lake clan, which often happens. He was very young for a gonnagle, but as Jeannie had said, there was no age limit to gonnagling. If the talent was in you, you gonnagled. And Awf'ly Wee Billy knew all the songs and could play the mousepipes so sadly that outside it would start to rain.

'Aye, lad?' said Rob Anybody kindly. 'Speak up, then.'

'Can we get hold o' some human clothes?' said Awf'ly Wee Billy. 'Because there's an old story about the big feud between the Three Peaks clan and the Windy River clan and the Windy River boys escaped by making a tattie-bogle walk, and the men o' Three Peaks thought it was a bigjob and kept oot o' its way.'

The others looked puzzled, and Awf'ly Wee Billy remembered that they were men of the Chalk and had probably never seen a tattie-bogle.

'A scarecrow?' he said. 'It's like a bigjob made o' sticks, wi' clothes on, for to frighten away the birdies fra' the crops? Now, the song says the Windy River's kelda used magic to make it walk, but I reckon it was done by cunnin' and strength.'

He sang about it. They listened.

He explained how to make a human that would

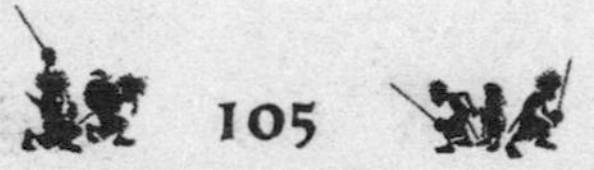

walk. They looked at one another. It was a mad, desperate plan, which was very dangerous and risky and would require tremendous strength and bravery to make it work.

Put like that, they agreed to it instantly.

Tiffany found that there was more than chores and the research, though. There was what Miss Level called 'filling what's empty and emptying what's full'.

Usually only one of Miss Level's bodies went out at a time. People thought Miss Level was twins, and she made sure they continued to do so, but she found it a little bit safer all round to keep the bodies apart. Tiffany could see why. You only had to watch both of Miss Level when she was eating. The bodies would pass plates to one another without saying a word, sometimes they'd eat off one another's forks, and it was rather strange to see one person burp and the other one say 'Oops, pardon me'.

'Filling what's empty and emptying what's full' meant wandering round the local villages and the isolated farms and, mostly, doing medicine. There were always bandages to change or expectant mothers to talk to. Witches did a lot of midwifery, which is a kind of 'emptying what's full', but Miss Level, wearing her pointy hat, had only to turn up at a cottage for other people to suddenly come visiting, by sheer accident. And there was an awful lot of gossip and tea-drinking. Miss Level moved in a twitching, living world of gossip, although Tiffany noticed that she picked up a lot more than she passed on.

It seemed to be a world made up entirely of women, but occasionally, out in the lanes, a man would strike up a conversation about the weather and somehow, by some sort of code, an ointment or a potion would get handed over.

Tiffany couldn't quite work out how Miss Level got paid. Certainly the basket she carried filled up more than it emptied. They'd walk past a cottage and a woman would come scurrying out with a fresh-baked loaf or a jar of pickles, even though Miss Level hadn't stopped there. But they'd spend an hour somewhere else, stitching up the leg of a farmer who'd been careless with an axe, and get a cup of tea and a stale biscuit. It didn't seem fair.

'Oh, it evens out,' said Miss Level, as they walked on through the woods. 'You do what you can. People give what they can, when they can. Old Slapwick there, with the leg, he's as mean as a cat, but there'll be a big cut of beef on my doorstep before the week's end, you can bet on it. His wife will see to it. And pretty soon people will be killing their pigs for the winter, and I'll get more brawn, ham, bacon and sausages turning up than a family could eat in a year.'

'You do? What do you do with all that food?'

'Store it,' said Miss Level.

'But you—'

'I store it in other people. It's amazing what you

can store in other people.' Miss Level laughed at Tiffany's expression. 'I mean, I take what I don't need round to those who don't have a pig, or who're going through a bad patch, or who don't have anyone to remember them.'

'But that means they'll owe *you* a favour!'

'Right! And so it just keeps on going round. It all works out.'

'I bet some people are too mean to pay—'

'Not *pay*,' said Miss Level, severely. 'A witch never expects payment and never asks for it and just hopes she never needs to. But, sadly, you are right.'

'And then what happens?'

'What do you mean?'

'You stop helping them, do you?'

'Oh, no,' said Miss Level, genuinely shocked. 'You can't not help people just because they're stupid or forgetful or unpleasant. Everyone's poor round here. If I don't help them, who will?'

'Granny Aching . . . that is, my grandmother said someone has to speak up for them as has no voices,' Tiffany volunteered after a moment.

'Was she a witch?'

'I'm not sure,' said Tiffany. 'I think so, but she didn't know she was. She mostly lived by herself in an old shepherding hut up on the downs.'

'She wasn't a cackler, was she?' said Miss Level, and when she saw Tiffany's expression she said hurriedly, 'Sorry, sorry. But it can happen, when you're a witch who doesn't know it. You're like a ship with no rudder. But obviously she wasn't like that, I can tell.'

'She lived on the hills and talked to them and she knew more about sheep than anybody!' said Tiffany hotly.

'I'm sure she did, I'm sure she did—'

'She *never* cackled!'

'Good, good,' said Miss Level soothingly. 'Was she clever at medicine?'

Tiffany hesitated. 'Um . . . only with sheep,' she said, calming down. 'But she was very good. Especially if it involved turpentine. Mostly if it involved turpentine, actually. But always she . . . was . . . just . . . there. Even when she wasn't *actually* there . . .'

'Yes,' said Miss Level.

'You know what I mean?' said Tiffany.

'Oh, yes,' said Miss Level. 'Your Granny Aching lived down on the uplands—'

'No, up on the downland,' Tiffany corrected her.

'Sorry, up on the downland, with the sheep, but people would look up sometimes, look up at the hills, knowing she was there somewhere, and say to themselves "What would Granny Aching do?" or "What would Granny Aching say if she found out?" or "Is this the sort of thing Granny Aching would be angry about?"' said Miss Level. 'Yes?'

Tiffany narrowed her eyes. It was true. She remembered when Granny Aching had hit a pedlar who'd overloaded his donkey and was beating it.

Granny usually used only words, and not many of them. The man had been so frightened by her sudden rage that he'd stood there and taken it.

It had frightened Tiffany, too. Granny, who seldom said anything without thinking about it for ten minutes beforehand, had struck the wretched man twice across the face in a brief blur of movement. And then news had got around, all along the Chalk. For a while, at least, people were a little more gentle with their animals . . . For months after that moment with the pedlar, carters and drovers and farmers all across the downs would hesitate before raising a whip or a stick, and think: *Suppose Granny Aching is watching?*

But—

'How did you *know* that?' she said.

'Oh, I guessed. She sounds like a witch to me, whatever she thought she was. A good one, too.'

Tiffany inflated with inherited pride.

'Did she help people?' Miss Level added.

The pride deflated a bit. The instant answer 'yes' jumped onto her tongue, and yet . . . Granny Aching hardly ever came down off the hills, except for Hogswatch and the early lambing. You seldom saw her in the village unless the pedlar who sold Jolly Sailor tobacco was late on his rounds, in which case she'd be down in a hurry and a flurry of greasy black skirts to cadge a pipeful off one of the old men.

But there wasn't a person on the Chalk, from the Baron down, who didn't owe something to Granny. And what they owed to her, she made them pay to others. She always knew who was short of a favour or two.

'She made them help one another,' she said. 'She made them help themselves.'

In the silence that followed, Tiffany heard the birds singing by the road. You got a lot of birds here, but she missed the high scream of the buzzards.

Miss Level sighed. 'Not many of us are *that* good,' she said. 'If *I* was that good, we wouldn't be going to visit old Mr Weavall again.'

Tiffany said 'Oh dear' inside.

Most days included a visit to Mr Weavall. Tiffany dreaded them.

Mr Weavall's skin was paper-thin and yellowish. He was always in the same old armchair, in a tiny room in a small cottage that smelled of old potatoes and was surrounded by a more or less overgrown garden. He'd be sitting bolt upright, his hands on two walking sticks, wearing a suit that was shiny with age, staring at the door.

'I make sure he has something hot every day, although he eats like a bird,' Miss Level had said. 'And old Widow Tussy down the lane does his laundry, such as it is. He's ninety-one, you know.'

Mr Weavall had very bright eyes and chatted away to and at them as they tidied up the room. The first time Tiffany had met him he'd called her Mary. Sometimes he still did. And he'd grabbed her wrist with surprising force as she walked past . . . It had been a real shock, that claw of a hand suddenly gripping her. You could see blue veins under the skin.

'I shan't be a burden on anyone,' he'd said urgently. 'I got money put by for when I go. My boy Toby won't have nothin' to worry about. I can pay my way! I want the proper funeral show, right? With the black horses and the plumes and the mutes and a knife-and-fork tea for everyone afterwards. I've written it all down, fair and square. Check in my box to make sure, will you? That witch woman's always hanging around here!'

Tiffany had given Miss Level a despairing look. She'd nodded, and pointed to an old wooden box tucked under Mr Weavall's chair.

It had turned out to be full of coins, mostly copper, but there were quite a few silver ones. It looked like a fortune, and for a moment she'd wished she had as much money.

'There's a lot of coins in here, Mr Weavall,' she'd said.

Mr Weavall relaxed. 'Ah, that's right,' he'd said. 'Then I won't be a burden.'

Today Mr Weavall was asleep when they called on him, snoring with his mouth open and his yellow-brown teeth showing. But he awoke in an instant, stared at them and then said, 'My boy Toby's coming to see I Sat'day.'

'That's nice, Mr Weavall,' said Miss Level, plumping up his cushions. 'We'll get the place nice and tidy.'

'He's done very well for hisself, you know,' said Mr

Weavall, proudly. 'Got a job indoors with no heavy lifting. He said he'll see I all right in my old age, but I told him, I *told* him I'd pay my way when I go – the whole thing, the salt and earth and tuppence for the ferryman, too!'

Today, Miss Level gave him a shave. His hands shook too much for him to do it himself. (Yesterday she'd cut his toenails, because he couldn't reach them; it was not a safe spectator sport, especially when one smashed a windowpane.)

'It's all in a box under my chair,' he said as Tiffany nervously wiped the last bits of foam off him. 'Just check for me, will you, Mary?'

Oh, yes. That was the ceremony, every day.

There was the box, and there was the money. He asked every time. There was always the same amount of money.

'Tuppence for the ferryman?' said Tiffany, as they walked home.

'Mr Weavall remembers all the old funeral traditions,' said Miss Level. 'Some people believe that when you die you cross the River of Death and have to pay the ferryman. People don't seem to worry about that these days. Perhaps there's a bridge now.'

'He's always talking about . . . his funeral.'

'Well, it's important to him. Sometimes old people are like that. They'd hate people to think that they were too poor to pay for their own funeral. Mr Weavall'd die of shame if he couldn't pay for his own funeral.'

'It's very sad, him being all alone like that. Something should be done for him,' said Tiffany.

'Yes. We're doing it,' said Miss Level. 'And Mrs Tussy keeps a friendly eye on him.'

'Yes, but it shouldn't have to be us, should it?'

'Who should it *have* to be?' said Miss Level.

'Well, what about this son he's always talking about?' said Tiffany.

'Young Toby? He's been dead for fifteen years. And Mary was the old man's daughter, she died quite young. Mr Weavall is very short-sighted, but he sees better in the past.'

Tiffany didn't know what to reply except: 'It shouldn't be like this.'

'There isn't a way things *should* be. There's just what happens, and what we do.'

'Well, couldn't you help him by magic?'

'I see to it that he's in no pain, yes,' said Miss Level.

'But that's just herbs.'

'It's still magic. Knowing things is magical, if other people don't know them.'

'Yes, but *you* know what I mean,' said Tiffany, who felt she was losing this argument.

'Oh, you mean make him young again?' said Miss Level. 'Fill his house with gold? That's not what witches do.'

'We see to it that lonely old men get a cooked dinner and cut their toenails?' said Tiffany, just a little sarcastically.

'Well, yes,' said Miss Level. 'We do what can be done. Mistress Weatherwax said you've got to learn that witchcraft is mostly about doing quite ordinary things.'

'And you have do what she says?' said Tiffany.

'I listen to her advice,' said Miss Level, coldly.

'Mistress Weatherwax is the head witch, then, is she?'

'Oh no!' said Miss Level, looking shocked. 'Witches are all equal. We don't have things like head witches. That's *quite* against the spirit of witchcraft.'

'Oh, I see,' said Tiffany.

'Besides,' Miss Level added, 'Mistress Weatherwax would never allow that sort of thing.'

Suddenly, things were going missing from the households around the Chalk. This wasn't the occasional egg or chicken. Clothes were vanishing off washing lines. A pair of boots mysteriously disappeared from under the bed of Nosey Hinds, the oldest man in the village – 'And they was damn good boots, they could walk home from the pub all by themselves if I but pointed they in the right direction,' he complained to anyone who would listen. 'And they marched off wi' my old hat, too. And I'd got he just as I wanted he, all soft and floppy!'

A pair of trousers and a long coat vanished from a hook belonging to Abiding Swindell, the ferret-keeper, and the coat still had ferrets living in the inside pockets. And who, *who* climbed through the bedroom window of Clem Doins and shaved off his beard, which had been so long that he could tuck it into his belt? Not a hair was left. He had to go around with a scarf over his face, in case the sight of his poor pink chin frightened the ladies . . .

It was probably witches, people agreed, and made a few more curse-nets to hang in their windows.

However . . .

On the far side of the Chalk, where the long green slopes came down to the flat fields of the plain, there were big thickets of bramble and hawthorn. Usually, these were alive with birdsong, but this particular one, the one just here, was alive with cussing.

'Ach, crivens! Will ye no' mind where ye're puttin' yer foot, ye spavie!'

'I cannae help it! It's nae easy, bein' a knee!'

'Ye think ye got troubles? Ye wannae be doon here in the boots! That old man Swindell couldnae ha' washed his feet in years! It's fair reekin' doon here!'

'Reekin', izzit? Well, you try bein' in this pocket! Them ferrets ne'er got oot to gae to the lavie, if you get my meanin'!'

'Crivens! Will ye dafties no' shut up?'

'Oh, aye? Hark at him! Just 'cuz ye're up in the heid, you think you know everythin'? Fra' doon here ye're nothing but dead weight, pal!'

'Aye, right! I'm wi' the elbows on this one! Where'd you be if it wuzn't for us carryin' ye aroound? Who's ye think ye are?'

'I'm Rob Anybody Feegle, as you ken well enough, an' I've had enough o' the lot o' yez!'

'OK, Rob, but it's real stuffy in here!'

'Ach, an' I'm fed up wi' the stomach complainin', too!'

'Gentlemen.' This was the voice of the toad; no one else would dream of calling the Nac Mac Feegle gentlemen. 'Gentlemen, time is of the essence. The cart will be here soon! You must *not* miss it!'

'We need more time to practise, Toad! We're walkin' like a feller wi' nae bones and a serious case o' the trots!' said a voice a little higher up than the rest.

'At least you *are* walking. That's good enough. I wish you luck, gentlemen.'

There was a cry from further along the thickets, where a lookout had been watching the road.

'The cart's comin' doon the hill!'

'OK, lads!' shouted Rob Anybody. 'Toad, you look after Jeannie, y'hear? She'll need a thinkin' laddie to rely on while I'm no' here! Right, ye scunners! It's do or die! Ye ken what to do! Ye lads on the ropes, pull us up noo!' The bushes shook. 'Right! Pelvis, are ye ready?'

'Aye, Rob!'

'Knees? Knees? I said, *knees?'*

'Aye, Rob, but—'

'Feets?'

'Aye, Rob!'

The bushes shook again.

'Right! Remember: right, left, right, left! Pelvis,

knee, foot on the groond! Keep a spring in the step, feets! Are you ready? Altogether, boys . . . walk!'

It was a big surprise for Mr Crabber the carter. He'd been staring vaguely at nothing, thinking only of going home, when *something* stepped out of the bushes and into the road. It looked human or, rather, looked slightly more human than it looked like anything else. But it seemed to be having trouble with its knees, and walked as though they'd been tied together.

However, the carter didn't spend too much time thinking about that because, clutched in one gloved hand that was waving vaguely in the air, was something gold.

This *immediately* identified the stranger, as far as the carter was concerned. He was not, as first sight might suggest, some old tramp to be left by the roadside, but an obvious gentleman down on his luck, and it was practically the carter's *duty* to help him. He slowed the horse to a standstill.

The stranger didn't really have a face. There was nothing much to see between the droopy hat brim and the turned-up collar of the coat except a lot of beard. But from somewhere within the beard a voice said:

'. . . *Shudupshudup . . . will ye all shudup while I'm talkin'* . . . Ahem. Good day ta' ye, carter fellow my ol' fellowy fellow! If ye'll gie us – me a lift as far as ye are goin', we – I'll gie ye this fine shiny golden coin!'

The figure lurched forward and thrust its hand in front of Mr Crabber's face.

It was quite a large coin. And it was certainly gold. It had come from the treasure of the old dead king who was buried in the main part of the Feegles' mound. Oddly enough, the Feegles weren't hugely interested in gold once they'd stolen it, because you couldn't drink it and it was difficult to eat. In the mound, they mostly used the old coins and plates to reflect candlelight and give the place a nice glow. It was no hardship to give some away.

The carter stared at it. It was more money than he had ever seen in his life.

'If . . . sir . . . would like to . . . hop on the back of the cart, sir,' he said, carefully taking it.

'Ach, right you are, then,' said the bearded mystery man after a pause. 'Just a moment, this needs a wee bitty organizin' . . . OK, youse hands, you just grab the side o' the cart, and' you leftie leg, ye gotta kinda sidle along . . . ach, crivens! Ye gotta bend! Bend! C'mon, get it right!' The hairy face turned to the carter. 'Sorry aboot this,' it said. 'I talk to my knees, but they dinnae listen to me.'

'Is that right?' said the carter weakly. 'I have trouble with my knees in the wet weather. Goose grease works.'

'Ah, weel, these knees is gonna get more'n a greasin' if I ha' to get doon there an' sort them oot!' snarled the hairy man.

The carter heard various bangs and grunts behind

him as the man hauled himself onto the tail of the cart.

'OK, let's gae,' said a voice. 'We' havenae got all day. And youse knees, you're sacked! Crivens, I'm walkin' like I got a big touch of the stoppies! You gae up to the stomach and send doon a couple of good knee men!'

The carter bit the coin thoughtfully as he urged the horse into a walk. It was such pure gold that he left toothmarks. That meant his passenger was very, very rich. That was becoming very important at this point.

'Can ye no' go a wee bitty faster, my good man, my good man?' said the voice behind him, after they had gone a little way.

'Ah, well, sir,' said the carter, 'see them boxes and crates? I've got a load of eggs, and those apples mustn't be bruised, sir, and then there's those jugs of—'

There were some bangs and crashes behind him, including the *sploosh* that a large crate of eggs makes when it hits a road.

'Ye can gae faster noo, eh?' said the voice.

'Hey, that was my—' Mr Crabber began.

'I've got another one o' they big wee gold coins for ye!' And a heavy and smelly arm landed on the carter's shoulder. Dangling from the glove on the end of it was, indeed, another coin. It was ten times what the load had been worth.

'Oh, well . . .' said the carter, carefully taking the coin. 'Accidents do happen, eh, sir?'

'Aye, especially if I dinnae think I'm goin' fast enough,' said the voice behind him. 'We – I mean I'm in a big hurry tae get tae yon mountains, ye ken!'

'But I'm not a stagecoach, sir,' said the carter reproachfully as he urged his old horse into a trot.

'Stagecoach, eh? What's one o' them things?'

'That's what you'll need to catch to take you up into the mountains, sir. You can catch one in Twoshirts, sir. I never go any further than Twoshirts, sir. But you won't be able to get the stage today, sir.'

'Why not?'

'I've got to make stops at the other villages, sir, and it's a long way, and on Wednesdays it runs early, sir, and this cart can only go so fast, sir, and—'

'If we – I dinnae catch yon coach today I'll gi'e ye the hidin' o' yer life,' growled the passenger. 'But if I *do* catch yon coach today, I'll gie ye five o' them gold coins.'

Mr Crabber took a deep breath, and yelled:

'Hi! Hyah! Giddyup, Henry!'

All in all, it seemed to Tiffany, most of what witches did really *was* very similar to work. Dull work. Miss Level didn't even use her broomstick very much.

That was a bit depressing. It was all a bit . . . well, goody-goody. Obviously that was better than being baddy-baddy, but a little more . . . excitement would be nice. Tiffany wouldn't like anyone to think she'd expected to be issued with a magic wand on Day One but, well, the way Miss Level talked about magic, the whole *point* of witchcraft lay in not using any.

Mind you, Tiffany thought she would be depressingly good at not using any. It was doing the simplest magic that was hard.

Miss Level patiently showed her how to make a shamble, which could more or less be made of anything that seemed a good idea at the time provided it also contained something alive, like a beetle or a fresh egg.

Tiffany couldn't even get the hang of it. That was . . . annoying. Didn't she have the virtual hat? Didn't she have First Sight and Second Thoughts? Miss Tick and Miss Level could throw a shamble together in seconds, but Tiffany just got a tangle, dripping with egg. Over and over again.

'I know I'm doing it right but it just twists up!' Tiffany complained. 'What can I do?'

'We could make an omelette?' said Miss Level cheerfully.

'Oh, please, Miss Level!' Tiffany wailed.

Miss Level patted her on the back. 'It'll happen. Perhaps you're trying too hard. One day it'll come. The power does come, you know. You just have to put yourself in its path—'

'Couldn't you make one that I could use for a while, to get the hang of it?'

'I'm afraid I can't,' said Miss Level. 'A shamble is a very tricky thing. You can't even carry one around, except as an ornament. You have to make it for yourself, there and then, right where and when you want to use it.'

'Why?' said Tiffany.

'To catch the moment,' said the other part of Miss Level, coming in. 'The way you tie the knots, the way the string runs –'

'– the freshness of the egg, perhaps, and the moisture in the air –' said the first Miss Level.

'– the tension of the twigs and the kind of things that you just happen to have in your pocket at that moment –'

'– even the way the wind is blowing,' the first Miss Level concluded. 'All these things make a kind of . . . of picture of the here-and-now when you move them right. And I can't even tell you how to move them, because I don't know.'

'But you *do* move them,' said Tiffany, getting lost. 'I saw you—'

'I do it but I don't know *how* I do,' said Miss Level, picking up a couple of twigs and taking a length of thread. Miss Level sat down at the table opposite Miss Level, and all four hands started to put a shamble together.

'This reminds me of when I was in the circus,' she said. 'I was –'

'– walking out for a while with Marco and Falco, the Flying Pastrami Brothers,' the other part of Miss Level went on. 'They would do –'

'– triple somersaults fifty feet up with no safety net. What lads they were! As alike as two –'

'– peas, and Marco could catch Falco blindfolded. Why, for a moment I wondered if they were just like me –'

She stopped, went a bit red on both faces and coughed. *'Anyway,'* she went on, 'one day I asked them how they managed to stay on the high wire and Falco said, "Never ask the tight-rope walker how he keeps his balance. If he stops to think about it, he falls off." Although actually –'

'– he said it like this, "Nev-ah aska tightaroper walkerer . . ." because the lads pretended they were from Brindisi, you see, because that sounds foreign and impressive and they thought no one would want to watch acrobats called The Flying Sidney and Frank Cartwright. Good advice, though, wherever it came from.'

The hands worked. This was not a lone Miss Level, a bit flustered, but the full Miss Level, all twenty fingers working together.

'Of course,' she said, 'it can be helpful to have the right sort of things in your pocket. I always carry a few sequins –'

'– for the happy memories they bring back,' said Miss Level from the other side of the table, blushing again.

She held up the shamble. There were sequins, and a fresh egg in a little bag made of thread, and a chicken bone and many other things hanging or spinning in the threads.

Each part of Miss Level put both its hands into the threads and *pulled* . . .

The threads took up a pattern. Did the sequins jump from one thread to another? It looked like it. Did the chicken bone pass *through* the egg? So it seemed.

Miss Level peered into it.

She said: 'Something's coming . . .'

The stagecoach left Twoshirts half full and was well out over the plains when one of the passengers sitting on the rooftop tapped the driver on the shoulder.

'Excuse me, did you know there's something trying to catch us up?' he said.

'Bless you, sir,' said the driver, because he hoped for a good tip at the end of the run, 'there's nothing that can catch *us* up.'

Then he heard the screaming in the distance, getting louder.

'Er, I think he means to,' said the passenger as the carter's wagon overtook them.

'Stop! Stop, for pity's sake *stop*!' yelled the carter as he sailed past.

But there was no stopping Henry. He'd spent years pulling the carrier's cart around the villages, very slowly, and he'd always had this idea in his big horse head that he was cut out for faster things. He'd plodded along, being overtaken by coaches and carts and three-legged dogs, and now he was having the time of his life.

Besides, the cart was a lot lighter than usual, and

the road was slightly downhill here. All he was really having to do was gallop fast enough to stay in front. And, finally, he'd actually overtaken the stagecoach. Him, Henry!

He only stopped because the stagecoach driver stopped first. Besides, the blood was pumping through Henry now, and there were a couple of mares in the team of horses pulling the coach who he felt he'd really like to get to know – find out when was their day off, what kind of hay they liked, that kind of thing.

The carter, white in the face, got down carefully and then lay on the ground and held on tight to the dirt.

His one passenger, who looked to the coach driver like some sort of scarecrow, climbed unsteadily down from the back and lurched towards the coach.

'I'm sorry, we're full up,' the driver lied. They weren't full, but there was certainly no room for a thing that looked like that.

'Ach, and there wuz me willin' to pay wi' gold,' said the creature. 'Gold such as this here,' it added, waving a ragged glove in the air.

Suddenly there was plenty of space for an eccentric millionaire. Within a few seconds he was seated inside and, to the annoyance of Henry, the coach set off again.

Outside Miss Level's cottage, a broomstick was

heading through the trees. A young witch – or, at least, someone dressed as a witch: it never paid to jump to conclusions – was sitting on it side-saddle.

She wasn't flying it very well. It jerked sometimes and it was clear the girl was no good at making it turn corners because sometimes she stopped, jumped off and pointed the stick in a new direction by hand. When she reached the garden gate she got off again quickly and tethered the stick to it with string.

'Nicely done, Petulia!' said Miss Level, clapping with all four hands. 'You're getting quite good!'

'Um, thank you, Miss Level,' said the girl, bowing. She stayed bowed, and said, 'Um, oh dear . . .'

Half of Miss Level stepped forward.

'Oh, I can see the problem,' she said, peering down. 'Your amulet with the little owls on it is tangled up with your necklace of silver bats and they've both got caught around a button. Just hold still, will you?'

'Um, I've come to see if your new girl would like come to the sabbat tonight,' said the bent Petulia, her voice a bit muffled.

Tiffany couldn't help noticing that Petulia had jewellery everywhere; later she found that it was hard to be around Petulia for any length of time without having to unhook a bangle from a necklace or, once, an earring from an ankle bracelet (nobody ever found out how that one happened). Petulia couldn't resist occult jewellery. Most of the stuff was to magically protect her from things, but she hadn't found anything to protect her from looking a bit silly.

She was short and plump and permanently red-faced and slightly worried.

'Sabbat? Oh, one of your meetings,' said Miss Level. 'That would be nice, wouldn't it, Tiffany?'

'Yes?' said Tiffany, not quite sure yet.

'Some of the girls meet up in the woods in the evenings,' said Miss Level. 'For some reason the craft is getting popular again. That's very welcome, of course.'

She said it as if she wasn't quite sure. Then she added: 'Petulia here works for Old Mother Blackcap, over in Sidling Without. Specializes in animals. Very good woman with pig diseases. I mean, with pigs that've got diseases, I don't mean she *has* pig diseases. It'll be nice for you to have friends here. Why don't you go? There, everything's unhooked.'

Petulia stood up and gave Tiffany a worried smile.

'Um, Petulia Gristle,' she said, holding out a hand.

'Tiffany Aching,' said Tiffany, shaking it gingerly in case the sound of all the bangles and bracelets jangling together deafened everyone.

'Um, you can ride with me on the broomstick, if you like,' said Petulia.

'I'd rather not,' said Tiffany.

Petulia looked relieved, but said: 'Um, do you want to get dressed?'

Tiffany looked down at her green dress. 'I am.'

'Um, don't you have any gems or beads or amulets or anything?'

'No, sorry,' said Tiffany.

'Um, you must at least have a shamble, surely?'

'Um, can't get the hang of them,' said Tiffany. She hadn't meant the 'um', but around Petulia it was catching.

'Um . . . a black dress, perhaps?'

'I don't really like black. I prefer blue or green,' said Tiffany. 'Um . . .'

'Um. Oh well, you're just starting,' said Petulia generously. 'I've been Crafty for three years.'

Tiffany looked desperately at the nearest half of Miss Level.

'In the craft,' said Miss Level helpfully. 'Witchcraft.'

'Oh.' Tiffany knew she was being very unfriendly, and Petulia with her pink face was clearly a nice person, but she felt awkward in front of her and she couldn't work out why. It was stupid, she knew. She could do with a friend. Miss Level was nice enough, and she managed to get along with Oswald, but it would be good to have someone around her own age to talk to.

'Well, I'd love to come,' she said. 'I know I've got a lot to learn.'

The passengers inside the stagecoach had paid good money to be inside on the soft seats and out of the wind and the dust and, therefore, it was odd that so many got out at the next stop and went and sat on the roof.

The few who didn't want to ride up there or

couldn't manage the climb sat huddled together on the seat opposite, watching the new traveller like a group of rabbits watching a fox and trying not to breathe.

The problem wasn't that he smelled of ferrets. Well, that *was* a problem, but compared to the *big* problem it wasn't much of one. He talked to himself. That is, bits of him talked to other bits of him. *All the time.*

'Ah, it's fair boggin' doon here. Ah'm tellin ye! Ah'm sure it's my turn to be up inna heid!'

'Hah, at least youse people are all cushy in the stomach, it's us in the legs that has tae do all the work!'

At which the right hand said: *'Legs? Youse dinnae know the meanin' of the word "work"! Ye ought tae try being stuck in a glove! Ach, blow this forra game o' sojers! Ah'm gonna stretch ma legs!'*

In horrified silence the other passengers watched one of the man's gloved hands drop off and walk around on the seat.

'Aye, weel, it's nae picnic doon here inna troosers, neither. A'm gonna let some fresh air in right noo!'

'Daft Wullie, don't you dare do that—'

The passengers, squeezing even closer together, watched the trousers with terrible fascination. There was some movement, some swearing-under-the-breath in a place where nothing should be breathing, and then a couple of buttons popped and a very small red-headed blue man stuck his head out, blinking in the light.

He froze when he saw the people.

He stared.

They stared.

Then his face widened into a mad smile.

'Youse folks all right?' he said, desperately. 'That's greaaat! Dinnae worry aboout me, I'm one o' they opper-tickle aloosyon's, ye ken?'

He disappeared back into the trousers, and they heard him whisper: 'I'm thinkin' I fooled 'em easily, no problemo!'

A few minutes later, the coach stopped to change horses. When it set off again, it was minus the inside passengers. They got off, and asked for their luggage to be taken off, too. No thank you, they did not want to continue their ride. They'd catch the coach tomorrow, thank you. No, there was no problem in waiting here in this delightful little, er, town of Dangerous Corner. Thank you. Goodbye.

The coach set off again, somewhat lighter and faster. It didn't stop that night. It should have done, and the rooftop passengers were still eating their dinner in the last inn when they heard it set off without them. The reason probably had something to do with the big heap of coins now in the driver's pocket.

Chapter 5

The Circle

Tiffany walked through the woods while Petulia flew unsteadily alongside in a series of straight lines. Tiffany learned that Petulia *was* nice, had three brothers, wanted to be a midwife for humans as well as pigs when she grew up, and was afraid of pins. She also learned that Petulia hated to disagree about *anything*.

So parts of the conversation went like this:

Tiffany said, 'I live down on the Chalk.'

And Petulia said, 'Oh, where they keep all those sheep? I don't like sheep much, they're so kind of . . . baggy.'

Tiffany said, 'Actually, we're very proud of our sheep.'

And then you could stand back as Petulia reversed her opinions like someone trying to turn a cart round in a very narrow space: 'Oh, I didn't really mean I *hate* them. I expect some sheep are all right. We've got to *have* sheep, obviously. They're better than goats, and woollier. I mean, I actually like sheep, really. Sheep are nice.'

Petulia spent a lot of time trying to find out what other people thought so that she could think the same way. It would be impossible to have an argument with her. Tiffany had to stop herself from saying 'The sky is green' just to see how long it would take for Petulia to agree. But she liked her. You couldn't *not* like her. She was restful company. Besides, you couldn't help liking someone who couldn't make a broomstick turn corners.

It was a long walk through the woods. Tiffany had always wanted to see a forest so big that you couldn't see daylight through the other side, but now she'd lived in one for a couple of weeks it got on her nerves. It was quite open woodland here, at least around the villages, and not hard to walk though. She'd had to learn what maples and birches were, and she'd never before seen the spruces and firs that grew higher up the slopes. But she wasn't happy in the company of trees. She missed the horizons. She missed the sky. Everything was too close.

Petulia chattered nervously. Old Mother Blackcap was a pig-borer, cow-shouter and all-round veterinary witch. Petulia liked animals, especially pigs because they had wobbly noses. Tiffany quite liked animals too, but no one except other animals liked animals as much as Petulia.

'So . . . what's this meeting about?' she said, to change the subject.

'Um? Oh, it's just to keep in touch,' said Petulia. 'Annagramma says it's important to make contacts.'

'Annagramma's the leader, then, is she?' said Tiffany.

'Um, no. Witches don't have leaders, Annagramma says.'

'Hmm,' said Tiffany.

They arrived at last at a clearing in the woods, just as the sun was setting. There were the remains of an old cottage there, now covered mostly in brambles. You might miss it completely if you didn't spot the rampant growth of lilac and the gooseberry bushes, now a forest of thorns. Someone had lived here once, and had a garden.

Someone else, now, had lit a fire. Badly. And they had found that lying down flat to blow on a fire because you hadn't started it with enough paper and dry twigs was not a good idea, because it would then cause your pointy hat, which you had forgotten to take off, to fall into the smoking mess and then, because it was dry, catch fire.

A young witch was now flailing desperately at her burning hat, watched by several interested spectators.

Another one, sitting on a log, said: 'Dimity Hubbub, that is literally the most stupid thing anyone has ever done anywhere in the whole world, ever.' It was a sharp, not very nice voice, the sort most people used for being sarcastic with.

'Sorry, Annagramma!' said Miss Hubbub, pulling off the hat and stamping on the point.

'I mean, just look at you, will you? You really are letting everyone down.'

'Sorry, Annagramma!'

'Um,' said Petulia.

Everyone turned to look at the new arrivals.

'You're *late*, Petulia Gristle!' snapped Annagramma. 'And who's this?'

'Um, you *did* ask me to call in at Miss Level's to bring the new girl, Annagramma,' said Petulia, as if she'd been caught doing something wrong.

Annagramma stood up. She was at least a head taller than Tiffany and had a face that seemed to be built backwards from her nose, which she held slightly in the air. To be looked at by Annagramma was to know that you'd already taken up too much of her valuable time.

'Is this her?'

'Um, yes, Annagramma.'

'Let's have a look at you, new girl.'

Tiffany stepped forward. It was amazing. She hadn't really meant to. But Annagramma had the kind of voice that you obeyed.

'What is your name?'

'Tiffany Aching?' said Tiffany, and found herself saying her name as if she was asking permission to have it.

'Tiffany? That's a funny name,' said the tall girl. '*My* name is Annagramma Hawkin.'

'Um, Annagramma works for—' Petulia began.

'– works *with*,' said Annagramma sharply, still

looking Tiffany up and down.

'Um, sorry, works *with* Mrs Earwig,' said Petulia. 'But she—'

'I intend to leave next year,' said Annagramma. 'Apparently, I'm doing *extremely* well. So you're the girl who's joined Miss Level, are you? She's weird, you know. The last three girls all left very quickly. They said it was just too strange trying to keep track of which one of her was which.'

'Which witch was which,' said one of the girls cheerfully.

'Anyone can do that pun, Lucy Warbeck,' said Annagramma without looking round. 'It's not funny, and it's not clever.'

She turned her attention back to Tiffany, who felt that she was being examined as critically and thoroughly as Granny Aching would check a ewe she might be thinking of buying. She wondered if Annagramma would actually try to open her mouth and make sure she had all her teeth.

'They say you can't breed good witches on chalk,' said Annagramma.

All the other girls looked from Annagramma to Tiffany, who thought: Ha!, so witches don't have leaders, do they? But she was in no mood to make enemies.

'Perhaps they do,' she said quietly. This did not seem to be what Annagramma wanted to hear.

'You haven't even dressed the part,' said Annagramma.

'Sorry,' said Tiffany.

'Um, Annagramma says that if you want people to treat you like a witch you should look like one,' Petulia said.

'Hmm,' said Annagramma, staring at Tiffany as if she'd failed a simple test. Then she nodded her head. 'Well, we all had to start somewhere.' She stood back. 'Ladies, this is Tiffany. Tiffany, you know Petulia. She crashes into trees. Dimity Hubbub is the one with the smoke coming out of her hat, so that she looks like a chimney. That's Gertruder Tiring, that's the hilariously funny Lucy Warbeck, that's Harrieta Bilk, who can't seem to do anything about the squint, and then that's Lulu Darling, who can't seem to do anything about the name. You can sit in for this evening . . . Tiffany, wasn't it? I'm sorry you've been taken on by Miss Level. She's rather sad. Complete amateur. Hasn't really got a clue. Just bustles about and hopes. Oh, well, it's too late now. Gertruder, Summon the World's Four Corners and Open the Circle, please.'

'Er . . .' said Gertruder, nervously. It was amazing how many people around Annagramma became nervous.

'Do I have to do everything around here?' said Annagramma. '*Try* to remember, please! We must have been through this *literally* a million times!'

'I've never heard of the world's four corners,' said Tiffany.

'Really? There's a surprise,' said Annagramma.

'Well, they're the directions of power, Tiffany, and I *would* advise you to do something about that name, too, please.'

'But the world's round, like a plate,' said Tiffany.

'Um, you have to imagine them,' Petulia whispered.

Tiffany wrinkled her forehead. 'Why?' she said.

Annagramma rolled her eyes. 'Because that's the way to do things properly.'

'Oh.'

'You *have* done *some* kind of magic, haven't you?' Annagramma demanded.

Tiffany was a bit confused. She wasn't used to people like Annagramma. 'Yes,' she said. All the other girls were staring at her, and Tiffany couldn't help thinking about sheep. When a dog attacks a sheep, the other sheep run away to a safe distance and then turn and watch. They don't gang up on the dog. They're just happy it's not them.

'What are you best at then?' snapped Annagramma.

Tiffany, her mind still full of sheep, spoke without thinking. 'Soft Nellies,' she said. 'It's a sheep cheese. It's quite hard to make . . .'

She looked around at the circle of blank faces and felt embarrassment rise inside her like hot jelly.

'Um, Annagramma meant what magic can you do best,' said Petulia kindly.

'Although Soft Nellies is good,' said Annagramma

with a cruel little smile. One or two of the girls gave that little snort that meant they were trying not to laugh out loud but didn't mind showing that they were trying.

Tiffany looked down at her boots again. 'I don't know,' she mumbled, 'but I did throw the Queen of the Fairies out of my country.'

'Really?' said Annagramma. 'The Queen of the Fairies, eh? How did you do that?'

'I'm . . . not sure. I just got angry with her.' And it was hard to remember exactly what had happened that night. Tiffany recalled the anger, terrible anger, and the world . . . changing. She'd seen it clearer than a hawk sees, heard it better than a dog hears, felt its age beneath her feet, felt the hills still living. And she remembered thinking that no one could do this for long and still be human.

'Well, you've got the right boots for stamping your foot,' said Annagramma. There were a few more half-concealed giggles. 'A Queen of the Fairies,' she added. 'I'm *sure* you did. Well, it helps to dream.'

'I don't tell lies,' mumbled Tiffany, but no one was listening.

Sullen and upset, she watched the girls Open the Corners and Summon the Circle, unless she'd got that the wrong way round. This went on for some time. It would have gone better if they'd all been sure what to do, but it was probably hard to *know* what to do when Annagramma was around, since she kept correcting everyone. She was standing with a big book open in her arms.

'. . . now you, Gertruder, go widdershins, *no, that's the other way, I must have told you literally a thousand times*, and Lulu – where's Lulu? Well, you shouldn't have been there! Get the shriven chalice – not that one, no, the one without handles . . . yes. Harrieta, hold the Wand of the Air a bit higher, I mean, it must *be* in the air, d'you understand? And for goodness' sake, Petulia, *please* try to look a little more stately, will you? I appreciate that it doesn't come naturally to you, but you might at least show you're making an effort. By the way, I've been meaning to tell you, no invocation ever written starts with "um", unless I'm very much mistaken. Harrieta, is that the Cauldron of the Sea? Does it even *look* like a Cauldron of the Sea? I don't think so, do you? *What was that noise?*'

The girls looked down. Then someone mumbled: 'Dimity trod on the Circlet of Infinity, Annagramma.'

'Not the one with the genuine seed-pearls on it?' said Annagramma in a tight little voice.

'Um, yes,' said Petulia. 'But I'm sure she's very sorry. Um . . . shall I make a cup of tea?'

The book slammed shut.

'What is the point?' said Annagramma to the world in general. 'What. Is. The. *Point?* Do you want to spend the rest of your lives as village witches, curing boils and warts for a cup of tea and a biscuit? Well? Do you?'

There was a shuffling among the huddled witches, and a general murmur of 'No, Annagramma.'

'You did all *read* Mrs Earwig's book, didn't you?' she demanded. 'Well, did you?'

Petulia raised a hand nervously. 'Um—' she began.

'Petulia, I've told you literally a million times not to start. Every. Single. Sentence. With "Um" – haven't I?'

'Um—' said Petulia, trembling with nervousness.

'Just speak up, for goodness' sake! Don't hesitate all the time!'

'Um—'

'Petulia!'

'Um—'

Really, you might make an *effort*. Honestly, I don't know what's the matter with all of you!'

I do, Tiffany thought. You're like a dog worrying sheep all the time. You don't give them time to obey you and you don't let them know when they've done things right. You just keep barking.

Petulia had lapsed into tongue-tied silence.

Annagramma put the book down on the log. 'Well, we've *completely* lost the moment,' she said. 'We may as well have that cup of tea, Petulia. Do hurry up.'

Petulia, relieved, grabbed the kettle. People relaxed a little.

Tiffany looked at the cover of the book. It read:

The Higher MagiK

by Letice Earwig, Witch

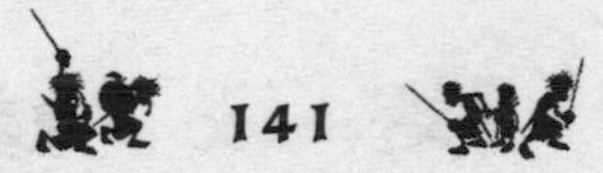

'Magic with a K?' she said aloud. 'Magik*kkk*?'

'That's deliberate,' said Annagramma coldly. 'Mrs Earwig says that if we are to make any progress at all we *must* distinguish the higher MagiK from the everyday sort.'

'The *everyday* sort of magic?' said Tiffany.

'Exactly. None of that mumbling in hedgerows for *us*. Proper sacred circles, spells written down. A proper hierarchy, not everyone running around doing whatever they feel like. Real wands, not bits of grubby stick. Professionalism, with respect. Absolutely no warts. That's the only way forward.'

'Well, I think—' Tiffany began.

'I don't really care what you think because you don't know enough yet,' said Annagramma sharply. She turned to the group in general. 'Do we all at least have something for the Trials this year?' she asked. There were general murmurs and nods in the theme of 'yes'.

'What about you, Petulia?' said Annagramma.

'I'm going to do the pig trick, Annagramma,' said Petulia meekly.

'Good. You're nearly good at that,' said Annagramma, and pointed around the circle, from one girl to another, nodding at their answers, until she came to Tiffany.

'Soft Nellies?' she said, to sniggering amusement.

'What are Witch Trials?' said Tiffany. 'Miss Tick mentioned them, but I don't know what they are.'

Annagramma gave one of her noisy sighs.

'You tell her, Petulia,' she said. '*You* brought her, after all.'

Hesitantly, with lots of 'um's and glances at Annagramma, Petulia explained about the Witch Trials. Um, it was a time when witches from all over the mountains could meet up, and um see old friends and um pick up the latest news and gossip. Ordinary people could come along too, and there was a fair and um sideshows.

It was quite an um big event. And in the afternoon all the witches that um wanted to could show off a spell or um something they'd been working on, which was very um popular.

To Tiffany, they sounded like sheepdog trials, without the dogs or the sheep. They were in Sheercliff this year, which was quite close.

'And is there a prize?' she asked.

'Um, oh no,' said Petulia. 'It's all done in spirit of fun and good fellow— um, good sistership.'

'Hah!' said Annagramma. 'Not even she will believe that! It's all a fix, anyway. They'll all applaud Mistress Weatherwax. She always wins, whatever she does. She just messes up people's minds. She just fools them into thinking she's good. She wouldn't last five minutes against a wizard. They do *real* magic. And she dresses like a scarecrow, too! It's ignorant old women like her who keep witchcraft rooted in the past, as Mrs Earwig points out in chapter one!'

One or two girls looked uncertain. Petulia even looked over her shoulder.

'Um, people do say she's done amazing things, Annagramma,' she said. 'And, um, they say she can spy on people miles away—'

'Yes, they *say* that,' said Annagramma. 'That's because they're all frightened of her! She's such a bully! That's all she does, bully people and mess up their heads! That's *old* witchcraft, that is. Just one step away from cackling, in *my* opinion. She's half cracked now, they say.'

'She didn't seem cracked to me.'

'*Who said that?*' snapped Annagramma.

Everyone looked at Tiffany, who wished she hadn't spoken. But now there was nothing for it but to go on.

'She was just a bit old and stern,' she said. 'But she was quite . . . polite. She didn't cackle.'

'You've met her?'

'Yes.'

'*She* spoke to *you*, did she?' snarled Annagramma. 'Was that before or after you kicked out the Fairy Queen?'

'Just after,' said Tiffany, who was not used to this sort of thing. 'She turned up on a broomstick,' she added. 'I *am* telling the truth.'

'Of course you are,' said Annagramma, smiling grimly. 'And she congratulated you, I expect.'

'Not really,' said Tiffany. 'She seemed pleased, but it was hard to tell.'

And then Tiffany said something really, really stupid. Long afterwards, and long after all sorts of things had happened, she'd go 'la la la!' to blot out the memory whenever something reminded her of that evening.

She said: 'She did give me this hat.'

And they said, all of them, with one voice: *'What hat?'*

Petulia took her back to the cottage. She did her best, and assured Tiffany that *she* believed her, but Tiffany knew she was just being nice. Miss Level tried to talk to her as she ran upstairs, but she bolted her door, kicked off her boots and lay down on the bed with the pillow over her head to drown out the laughter echoing inside.

Downstairs, there was some muffled conversation between Petulia and Miss Level and then the sound of the door closing as Petulia left.

After a while there was a scraping noise as Tiffany's boots were dragged across the floor and arranged neatly under the bed. Oswald was never off duty.

After another while the laughter died down, although she was sure it'd never go completely.

Tiffany could feel the hat. At least, she *had* been able to feel it. The virtual hat, on her real head. But no one could see it, and Petulia had even waved a hand back and forth over Tiffany's head and encountered a complete absence of hat.

The worst part – and it was hard to find the worst part, so humiliatingly bad had it been – was hearing

Annagramma say, 'No, don't laugh at her. That's too cruel. She's just foolish, that's all. I told you the old woman messes with people's heads!'

Tiffany's First Thoughts were running around in circles. Her Second Thoughts were caught up in the storm. Only her Third Thoughts, which were very weak, came up with: *Even though your world is completely and utterly ruined and can never be made better, no matter what, and you're completely inconsolable, it would be nice if you heard someone bringing some soup upstairs* . . .

The Third Thoughts got Tiffany off the bed and over to the door, where they guided her hand to slide the bolt back. Then they let her fling herself on the bed again.

A few minutes later there was a creak of footsteps on the landing. It's nice to be right.

Miss Level knocked, then came in after a decent pause. Tiffany heard the tray go down on the table, then felt the bed move as a body sat down on it.

'Petulia is a capable girl, I've always thought,' said Miss Level, after a while. 'She'll make some village a very serviceable witch one day.'

Tiffany stayed silent.

'She told me all about it,' said Miss Level. 'Miss Tick never mentioned the hat, but if I was you I wouldn't have told her about it anyway. It sounds the sort of thing Mistress Weatherwax would do. You know, sometimes it helps to talk about these things.'

More silence from Tiffany . . .

'Actually, that's not true,' Miss Level added. 'But as

a witch I am incredibly inquisitive and would love to know more.'

That had no effect either. Miss Level sighed and stood up. 'I'll leave the soup, but if you let it get too cold Oswald will try to take it away.'

She went downstairs.

Nothing stirred in the room for about five minutes, then there was faintest of tinkles as the soup began to move.

Tiffany's hand shot out and gripped the tray firmly. That's the job of Third Thoughts: First and Second Thoughts might understand your current tragedy, but *something* has to remember that you haven't eaten since lunch time.

Afterwards, and after Oswald had speedily taken the empty bowl away, Tiffany lay in the dark, staring at nothing.

The novelty of this new country had taken all her attention in the past few days, but now that had drained away in the storm of laughter, and homesickness rushed to fill in the empty spaces.

She missed the sounds and the sheep and the silences of the Chalk. She missed seeing the blackness of the hills from her bedroom window, outlined against the stars. She missed . . . part of herself . . .

But they'd laughed at her. They'd said, 'What hat?' and they'd laughed even more when she'd raised her hand to touch the invisible brim and hadn't found it . . .

She'd touched it every day for eighteen months, and now it had gone. And she couldn't make a shamble. And she just had a green dress, while all the other girls wore black ones. Annagramma had a lot of jewellery, too, in black and silver. *All* the other girls had shambles, too, beautiful ones. Who cared if they were just for show?

Perhaps she wasn't a witch at all. Oh, she'd defeated the Queen, with the help of the little men and the memory of Granny Aching, but she hadn't used magic. She wasn't sure, now, what she *had* used. She'd felt something go down through the soles of the boots, down through the hills and through the years, and come back loud and roaring in a rage that shook the sky:

. . . *how dare you invade* my *world,* my *land,* my *life* . . .

But what had the virtual hat done for her? Perhaps the old woman had tricked her, had just made her *think* there was a hat there. Perhaps she was a bit cracked, like Annagramma had said, and had just got things wrong. Perhaps Tiffany should go home and make Soft Nellies for the rest of her life.

Tiffany turned round and crawled down the bed and opened her suitcase. She pulled out the rough box, opened it in the dark and closed a hand around the lucky stone.

She'd hoped that there'd be some kind of spark, some kind of friendliness in it. There was none. There was just the roughness of the outside of the stone, the smoothness on the face where it had split, and the sharpness between the two. And the piece of sheep's wool did nothing but make her fingers smell of sheep, and this made her long for home and feel even more upset. The silver horse was cold.

Only someone quite close would have heard the sob. It was quite faint, but it was carried on the dark red wings of misery. She wanted, *longed for* the hiss of wind in the turf and the feel of centuries under her feet. She wanted that sense, which had never left her before, of being where Achings had lived for thousands of years. She needed blue butterflies and the sounds of sheep and the big empty skies.

Back home, when she'd felt upset, she'd gone up to the remains of the old shepherding hut and sat there for a while. That had always worked.

It was a long way away now. Too far. Now, she was full of a horrible, heavy dead feeling, and there was nowhere to leave it. And it wasn't how things were supposed to go.

Where was the *magic*? Oh, she understood that you had learn about the basic, everyday *craft*, but when did the 'witch' part turn up? She'd been trying to learn, she really had, and she was turning into . . . well, a good worker, a handy girl with potions and a reliable person. Dependable, like Miss Level.

She'd expected – well, what? Well . . . to be doing serious witch stuff, you know, broomsticks, magic, guarding the world against evil forces in a noble yet modest way, and then *also* doing good for poor people *because she was a really nice person*. And the people she'd seen in the picture had rather less messy ailments and their children didn't have such runny noses. Mr Weavall's flying toenails weren't in it *anywhere*. Some of them *boomeranged*.

She got *sick* on broomsticks. *Every time*. She couldn't even make a shamble. She was going to spend her days running around after people who, to be honest, could sometimes be doing a bit more for themselves. No magic, no flying, no secrets . . . just toenails and bogeys.

She belonged to the Chalk. Every day, she'd told the hills what they were. Every day, they'd told her who she was. But now she couldn't hear them.

Outside it began to rain, quite hard, and in the distance Tiffany heard the mutter of thunder.

What would Granny Aching have done? But even folded in the wings of despair she knew the answer to that.

Granny Aching never gave up. She'd search all night for a lost lamb . . .

She lay looking at nothing for a while, and then lit the candle by the bed and swivelled her legs onto the floor. This couldn't wait until morning.

Tiffany had a little trick for seeing the hat. If you moved your hand behind it quickly, there was a slight, brief blurriness to what you saw, as though the light coming through the invisible hat took a little more time.

It *had* to be there . . .

Well, the candle should give enough light to be sure. If the hat was there, everything would be fine and it wouldn't matter what other people thought . . .

She stood in the middle of the carpet, while lightning danced across the mountains outside, and closed her eyes.

Down in the garden the apple-tree branches flayed in the wind, the dreamcatchers and curse-nets clashing and jangling . . .

'See me,' she said.

The world went quiet, totally silent. It hadn't done that before. But Tiffany tiptoed around until she knew she was opposite herself, and opened her eyes again . . .

And there she was, and so was the hat, as clear as it had ever been—

And the image of Tiffany below, a young girl in a green dress, opened its eyes and smiled at her and said:

'We see you. Now we are you.'

Tiffany tried to shout 'See me not!' But there was no mouth to shout . . .

Lightning struck somewhere nearby. The window blew in. The candle flame flew out in a streamer of fire, and died.

And then there was only darkness, and the hiss of the rain.

Chapter 6

The Hiver

Thunder rolled across the Chalk.

Jeannie carefully opened the package that her mother had given her on the day she left the Long Lake mound. It was a traditional gift, one that every young kelda got when she went away, never to return. Keldas could never go home. Keldas *were* home.

The gift was this: memory.

Inside the bag was a triangle of tanned sheepskin, three wooden stakes, a length of string twisted out of nettle fibres, a tiny leather bottle and a hammer.

She knew what to do, because she'd seen her mother do it many times. The hammer was used to bang in the stakes around the smouldering fire. The string was used to tie the three corners of the leather triangle to the stakes so that it sagged in the centre, just enough to hold a small bucket of water which

Jeannie had drawn herself from the deep well.

She knelt down and waited until the water very slowly began to seep through the leather, then built up the fire.

She was aware of all the eyes of the Feegles in the shadowy galleries around and above her. None of them would come near her while she was boiling the cauldron. They'd rather chop their own leg off. This was *pure* hiddlins.

And this was what a cauldron really was, back in the days before humans had worked copper or poured iron. It looked like magic. It was supposed to. But if you knew the trick, you could see how the cauldron would boil dry before the leather burned.

When the water in the skin was steaming, she damped down the fire and added to the water the contents of the little leather bottle, which contained some of the water from her mother's cauldron. That's how it had always gone, from mother to daughter, since the very beginning.

Jeannie waited until the cauldron had cooled some more, then took up a cup, filled it and drank. There was a sigh from the shadowy Feegles.

She lay back and closed her eyes, waiting. Nothing happened except that the thunder rattled the land and the lightning turned the world black and white.

And then, so gently that it had already happened before she realized that it was starting to happen, the past caught up with her. There, around her, were all the old keldas, starting with her mother, her grandmothers, their mothers . . . back until there was no one to remember . . . one big memory, carried for a while by many, worn and hazy in parts but old as a mountain.

But all the Feegles knew about that. Only the kelda knew about the real hiddlin, which was this: the river of memory wasn't a river, it was a sea.

Keldas yet to be born would remember, one day. On nights yet to come, they'd lie by their cauldron and become, for a few minutes, part of the eternal sea. By listening to unborn keldas remembering their past, you remember your future . . .

You needed skill to find those faint voices, and Jeannie did not have all of it yet, but *something* was there.

As lightning turned the world to black and white again she sat bolt upright.

'It's found her,' she whispered . . . 'Oh, the puir wee thing!'

Rain had soaked into the rug when Tiffany woke up. Damp daylight spilled into the room.

She got up and closed the window. A few leaves had blown in.

O-K.

It hadn't been a dream. She was certain of that. Something . . . strange had happened. The tips of her fingers were tingling. She felt . . . different. But not, now she took stock, in a bad way. No. Last night she'd felt awful, but now, *now* she felt . . . full of life.

Actually, she felt happy. She was going to take charge. She was going to take control of *her* life. Get-up-and-go had got up and come.

The green dress was rumpled and really it needed a wash. She'd got her old blue one in the chest of drawers but, somehow, it didn't seem right to wear it now. She'd have to make do with the green until she could get another one.

She went to put on her boots, then stopped and stared at them.

They just wouldn't do, not now. She got the new shiny ones out of her case and wore them instead.

She found both of Miss Level was out in the wet garden in her nighties, sadly picking up bits of dreamcatcher and fallen apples. Even some of the garden ornaments had been smashed, although the madly grinning gnomes had unfortunately escaped destruction.

Miss Level brushed her hair out of one pair of her eyes and said: 'Very, very strange. All the curse-nets seem to have exploded. Even the boredom stones are discharged! Did you notice anything?'

'No, Miss Level,' said Tiffany meekly.

'And all the old shambles in the workroom are in pieces! I mean, I know they are really only ornamental and have next to no power left, but something really *strange* must have happened.'

Both of her gave Tiffany a look that Miss Level probably thought was very sly and cunning, but it made her look slightly ill.

'The storm seemed a touch magical to me. I suppose you girls weren't doing anything . . . odd last night, were you, dear?' she said.

'No, Miss Level. I thought they were a bit silly.'

'Because, you see, Oswald seems to have gone,' said Miss Level. 'He's very sensitive to atmospheres . . .'

It took Tiffany a moment to understand what she was talking about. Then she said: 'But he's always here!'

'Yes, ever since I can remember!' said Miss Level.

'Have you tried putting a spoon in the knife drawer?'

'Yes, of course! Not so much as a rattle!'

'Dropped an apple core? He always—'

'That was the first thing I tried!'

'How about the salt and sugar trick?'

Miss Level hesitated. 'Well, no . . .' She brightened up. 'He does love that one, so he's *bound* to turn up, yes?'

Tiffany found the big bag of salt and another of sugar, and poured both of them into a bowl. Then she stirred up the fine white crystals with her hand.

She'd found this was the ideal away of keeping Oswald occupied while they did the cooking. Sorting the salt and sugar grains back into the right bags could take him an entire happy afternoon. But now the mixture just lay there, Oswaldless.

'Oh, well . . . I'll search the house,' said Miss Level, as if that was a good way of finding an invisible person. 'Go and see to the goats, will you, dear? And then we'll have to try to remember how to do the washing up!'

Tiffany let the goats out of the shed. Usually, Black Meg immediately went and stood on the milking platform and gave her an expectant look as if to say: I've thought up a *new* trick.

But not today. When Tiffany looked inside the shed the goats were huddled in the dark at the far end. They panicked, nostrils flaring, and scampered around as she went towards them, but she managed to grab Black Meg by her collar. The goat twisted and fought her as she dragged it out towards the milking stand. It climbed up because it was either that or having its head pulled off, then stood there snorting and bleating.

Tiffany stared at the goat. Her bones felt as though they were itching. She wanted to . . . do things, climb the highest mountain, leap into the sky, run around the world. And she thought: This is *silly*, I start every day with a battle of wits with an *animal*!

Well, let's show this creature who is in charge . . .

She picked up the broom that was used for sweeping out the milking parlour. Black Meg's slot eyes widened in fear, and *wham!* went the broom.

It hit the milking stand. Tiffany hadn't intended to miss like that. She'd wanted to give Meg the wallop the creature richly deserved but, somehow, the stick had twisted in her hand. She raised it again, but the look in her eye and the whack on the wood had achieved the right effect. Meg cowered.

'No more games!' hissed Tiffany, lowering the stick.

The goat stood as still as a log. Tiffany milked her out, took the pail back into the dairy, weighed it, chalked up the amount on the slate by the door, and tipped the milk into a big bowl.

The rest of the goats were nearly as bad, but a herd learns fast.

Altogether they gave three gallons, which was pretty pitiful for ten goats. Tiffany chalked this up without enthusiasm and stood staring at it, fiddling with the chalk. What was the point of this? Yesterday she'd been full of plans for experimental cheeses, but now cheese was *dull*.

Why was she here, doing silly chores, helping people too stupid to help themselves? She could be doing . . . *anything!*

She looked down at the scrubbed wooden table.

Someone had written on the wood in chalk. And the piece of chalk was still in her hand—

'Petulia's come to see you, dear,' said Miss Level, behind her.

Tiffany quickly shifted a milking bucket over the words and turned round guiltily.

'What?' she said. 'Why?'

'Just to see if you're all right, I think,' said Miss Level, watching Tiffany carefully.

The dumpy girl stood very nervously on the doorstep, her pointy hat in her hands.

'Um, I just thought I ought to see how you, um, are . . .' she muttered, looking Tiffany squarely in the boots. 'Um, I don't think anyone really wanted to be unkind . . .'

'You're not very clever and you're too fat,' said Tiffany. She stared at the round pink face for a moment and *knew* things. 'And you still have a teddy bear help me and you believe in fairies.'

She slammed the door, went back to the dairy and stared at the bowls of milk and curds as if she were seeing them for the first time.

Good with Cheese. That was one of the things everyone remembered about her: Tiffany Aching, brown hair, Good with Cheese. But now the dairy looked all wrong and unfamiliar.

She gritted her teeth. Good with Cheese. Was that *really* what she wanted to be? Of all the things people could be in the world, did she want to be known just as a dependable person to have around rotted milk? Did she *really* want to spend all day scrubbing slabs and washing pails and plates and . . . and . . . and that weird wire thing just there, that—

. . . cheese-cutter . . .

– that cheese-cutter? Did she want her whole life to—

Hold on . . .

'Who's there?' said Tiffany. 'Did someone just say "cheese-cutter"?'

She peered around the room, as if someone could be hiding behind the bundles of dried herbs. It couldn't have been Oswald. He'd gone, and he never spoke in any case.

Tiffany grabbed the pail, spat on her hand and rubbed out the chalked

– *tried* to rub it out. But her hand gripped the edge of the table and held it firmly, no matter how much she pulled. She flailed with her left hand, managing to knock over a pail of milk, which washed across the letters . . . and her right hand let go suddenly

The door was pushed open. Both of Miss Level was there. When she pulled herself together like that, standing side by side, it was because she felt she had something important to say.

'I have to say, Tiffany, that I think –'

'– you were very nasty to Petulia just –'

'– now. She went off crying.'

She stared at Tiffany's face. 'Are you all right, child?'

Tiffany shuddered. 'Er . . . yes. Fine. Feel a bit odd. Heard a voice in my head. Gone now.'

Miss Level looked at her with her heads on one side, right and left in different directions.

'If you're sure, then. I'll get changed. We'd better leave soon. There's a lot to do today.'

'A lot to do,' said Tiffany weakly.

'Well, yes. There's Slapwick's leg, and I've got to see to the sick Grimly baby, and it's been a week since I've visited Surleigh Bottom, and, let's see, Mr Plover's got Gnats again, and I'd better just find a moment to have a word with Mistress Slopes . . . then there's Mr Weavall's lunch to cook, I think I'll have to do that here and run down with it for him, and of course Mrs Fanlight is near her time and,' she sighed, 'so is Miss Hobblow, *again* . . . It's going to be a full day. It's really hard to fit it all in, really it is.'

Tiffany thought: You stupid woman, standing there looking worried because you just haven't got time to give people everything they demand! Do you think you could ever give them *enough* help? Greedy, lazy, dumb people, always *wanting* all the time! The Grimly baby? Mrs Grimly's got eleven children! Who'd miss one?

Mr Weavall's dead already! He just won't go! You think they're grateful, but all they are doing is making sure you come round again! That's not gratitude, that's just insurance!

The thought horrified part of her, but it had turned up and it flamed there in her head, just itching to escape from her mouth.

'Things need tidying up here,' she muttered.

'Oh, I can do that while we're gone,' said Miss Level cheerfully. 'Come on, let's have a smile! There's lots to do!'

There was *always* lots to do, Tiffany growled in her head as she trailed after Miss Level to the first village. Lots and lots. And it never made any difference. There was no end to the *wanting*.

They went from one grubby, smelly cottage to another, ministering to people too stupid to use soap, drinking tea from cracked cups, gossiping with old women with fewer teeth than toes. It made her feel ill.

It was a bright day, but it seemed dark as they walked on. The feeling was like a thunderstorm inside her head.

Then the daydreams began. She was helping to splint the arm of some dull child who'd broken it when she glanced up and saw her reflection in the glass of the cottage window.

She was a tiger, with huge fangs.

She yelped, and stood up.

'Oh, do be careful,' said Miss Level, and then saw her face. 'Is there something wrong?' she said.

'I . . . I . . . something bit me!' lied Tiffany. That was a safe bet in these places. The fleas bit the rats and the rats bit the children.

She managed to get out into the daylight, her head spinning. Miss Level came out a few minutes later and found her leaning against the wall, shaking.

'You look *dreadful,*' she said.

'Ferns!' said Tiffany. 'Everywhere! Big ferns! And big things, like cows made out of lizards!' She turned a wide, mirthless smile onto Miss Level, who took a step back. 'You can *eat* them!' She blinked. 'What's happening?' she whispered.

'I don't know but I'm coming right down here this minute to fetch you,' said Miss Level. 'I'm on the broomstick right now!'

'They laughed at me when I said I could trap one. Well, who's laughing now, tell me that, eh?'

Miss Level's expression of concern turned into something close to panic.

'That didn't sound like your voice. That sounded like a man! Do you *feel* all right?'

'Feel . . . crowded,' murmured Tiffany.

'Crowded?' said Miss Level.

'Strange . . . memories . . . help me . . .'

Tiffany looked at her arm. It had scales on. Now it had hair on it. Now it was smooth and brown, and holding—

'A scorpion sandwich?' she said.

'Can you hear me?' said Miss Level, her voice a long way away. 'You're delirious. Are you sure you girls haven't been playing with potions or anything like that?'

The broomstick dropped out of the sky and the other part of Miss Level nearly fell off. Without speaking, both of Miss Level got Tiffany onto the stick and part of Miss Level got on behind her.

It didn't take long to fly back to the cottage. Tiffany spent the flight with her mind full of hot cotton-wool and wasn't at all certain where she was, although her body did know and threw up again.

Miss Level helped her off the stick and sat her on the garden seat just outside the cottage door.

'Now just you wait there,' said Miss Level, who dealt with emergencies by talking incessantly and using the word 'just' too often because it's a calming word, 'and I'll just get you a drink and then we'll just see what the matter is . . .' There was a pause and then the stream of words came out of the house again, dragging Miss Level after them '. . . and I'll just check on . . . things. Just drink this, please!'

Tiffany drank the water and, out of the corner of her eye, saw Miss Level weaving string around an egg. She was trying to make a shamble without Tiffany noticing.

Strange images were floating around Tiffany's mind. There were scraps of voices, fragments of memories . . . and one little voice that was her own, small and defiant and getting fainter:

You're not me. You just think you are! Someone help me!

'Now, then,' said Miss Level, 'let's just see what we can see—'

The shamble exploded, not just into pieces but into fire and smoke.

'Oh, Tiffany,' said Miss Level, frantically waving smoke away. 'Are you all right?'

Tiffany stood up slowly. It seemed to Miss Level that she was slightly taller than she remembered.

'Yes, I think I am,' said Tiffany. 'I think I've been all wrong, but *now* I'm all right. And I've been wasting my time, Miss Level.'

'What—?' Miss Level began.

Tiffany pointed a finger at her. 'I *know* why you had to leave the circus, Miss Level,' she said. 'It was to do with the clown Floppo, the trick ladder and . . . some *custard* . . .'

Miss Level went pale. 'How could you possibly know that?'

'Just by looking at you!' said Tiffany, pushing past her into the dairy. 'Watch this, Miss Level!'

She pointed a finger. A wooden spoon rose an inch from the table. Then it began to spin, faster and faster until, with a cracking sound, it broke into splinters. They whirled away across the room.

'And I can do *this*!' Tiffany shouted. She grabbed a bowl of curds, tipped them out on the table and waved a hand at them. They turned into a cheese.

'Now *that's* what cheesemaking should be!' she said. 'To think that I spent stupid *years* learning the hard way! That's how a *real* witch does it! Why do we crawl in the dirt, Miss Level? Why do we amble around with herbs and bandage smelly old men's legs? Why do we get paid with eggs and stale cakes? Annagramma is as stupid as a hen but even she can see it's wrong. Why don't we *use* magic? Why are you so *afraid*?'

Miss Level tried to smile. 'Tiffany, dear, we all go through this,' she said, and her voice was shaking. 'Though not as . . . explosively as you, I have to say. And the answer is . . . well, it's dangerous.'

'Yes, but that's what people always say to scare children,' said Tiffany. 'We get told stories to frighten us, to keep us scared! Don't go into the big bad wood help me because it's full of scary things, that's what we're told. But really, the big bad wood should be scared of *us*! I'm going out!'

'I think that would be a good idea,' said Miss Level weakly. 'Until you behave.'

'I *don't* have to do things your way,' snarled Tiffany, slamming the door behind her.

Miss Level's broomstick was leaning against the wall a little way away. Tiffany stopped and stared at it, her mind on fire.

She'd tried to keep away from it. Miss Level had wheedled her into a trial flight with Tiffany clinging on tightly with arms and legs while both of Miss Level ran alongside her, holding onto ropes and making encouraging noises. They had stopped when Tiffany threw up for the fourth time.

Well, that was then!

She grabbed the stick, swung a leg over it – and found that her other foot stuck to the ground as though nailed there. The broomstick twisted around wildly as she tried to pull it up and, when the boot was finally tugged off the ground, turned over so that Tiffany was upside down. This is not the best position in which to make a grand exit.

She said, quietly, 'I am not going to learn you, *you* are going to learn *me*. Or the next lesson will involve an axe!'

The broomstick turned upright, then gently rose.

'Right,' said Tiffany. There was no fear this time. There was just impatience. The ground dropping away below her didn't worry her at all. If it didn't have the sense to stay away from her, she'd *hit* it . . .

As the stick drifted away, there was whispering in the long grass of the garden.

'Ach, we're too late, Rob. That wuz the hiver, that wuz.'

'Aye, but did ye see that foot? It's nae won yet – oor hag's in there somewhere! She's fighting it! It cannae win until it's taken the last scrap o' her! Wullie, will ye stop tryin' to grab them apples!'

'It's sorry I am tae say this, Rob, but no one can fight a hiver. 'Tis like fightin' yoursel. The more you fight, the more it'll tak' o' ye. And when it has all o' ye—'

'Wash oot yer mouth wi' hedgehog pee, Big Yan! That isnae gonna happen—'

'Crivens! Here comes the big hag!'

Half of Miss Level stepped out into the ruined garden.

She stared up at the departing broomstick, shaking her head.

Daft Wullie was stuck out in the open where he'd been trying to snag a fallen apple. He turned to flee and would have got clean away if he hadn't run straight into a pottery garden gnome. He bounced off, stunned, and staggered wildly, trying to focus on the big, fat, chubby-cheeked figure in front of him. He was far too angry to hear the click of the garden gate and soft tread of approaching footsteps.

When it comes to choosing between running and fighting, a Feegle doesn't think twice. He doesn't think at all.

'What're ye grinnin' at, pal?' he demanded. 'Oh aye, you reckon you're the big man, eh, jus' 'cos yez got a fishin' rod?' He grabbed a pink pointy ear in each hand and aimed his head at what turned out be quite a hard pottery nose. It smashed anyway, as things tend to in these circumstances, but it did slow the little man down and cause him to stagger in circles.

Too late, he saw Miss Level bearing down on him from the doorway. He turned to flee, right into the hands of *also* Miss Level.

Her fingers closed around him.

'I'm a witch, you know,' she said. 'And if you don't stop struggling this minute I will subject you to the most dreadful torture. Do you know what that is?'

Daft Wullie shook his head in terror. Long years of juggling had given Miss Level a grip like steel. Down in the long grass, the rest of the Feegles listened so hard it hurt.

Miss Level brought him a little closer to her mouth. 'I'll let you go right now *without* giving you a taste of the twenty-year-old MacAbre single malt I have in my cupboard,' she said.

Rob Anybody leaped up. 'Ach, crivens, mistress, what a thing to taunt a body wi'! D'ye no' have a drop of mercy in you?' he shouted. 'Ye're a cruel hag indeed tae—' He stopped. Miss Level was smiling. Rob Anybody looked around, flung his sword on the ground and said: 'Ach, *crivens*!'

The Nac Mac Feegle respected witches, even if they did call them hags. And this one had brought out a big loaf and a whole bottle of whisky on the table for the taking. You had to respect someone like that.

'Of course, I'd *heard* of you, and Miss Tick mentioned you,' she said, watching them eat, which is not something to be done lightly. 'But I always thought you were just a myth.'

'Aye, weel, we'll stay that way if ye dinnae mind,' said Rob Anybody, and belched. ' 'Tis bad enough wi' them arky-olly-gee men wantin' to dig up oour mounds wi'oot them folklore ladies wantin' to tak' pichoors o' us an' that.'

'And you watch over Tiffany's farm, Mr Anybody?'

'Aye, we do that, an' we dinnae ask for any

reward,' said Rob Anybody stoutly.

'Aye, we just tak' a few wee eiggs an' fruits an' old clothes and—' Daft Wullie began.

Rob gave him a look.

'Er . . . wuz that one o' those times when I shouldna' open my big fat mouth?' said Wullie.

'Aye. It wuz,' said Rob. He turned back to both of Miss Level. 'Mebbe we tak' the odd bitty thing lyin' aboot—'

'– in locked cupboards an' such—' added Daft Wullie happily.

'– but it's no' missed, an' we keeps an eye on the ships in payment,' said Rob, glaring at his brother.

'You can see the sea from down there?' said Miss Level, entering that state of general bewilderment that most people fell into when talking to the Feegles.

'Rob Anybody means the sheep,' said Awf'ly Wee Billy. Gonnagles know a bit more about language.

'Aye, I said so, ships,' said Rob Anybody. 'Anywa' . . . aye, we watch her farm. She's the hag o' oor hills, like her granny.' He added proudly, 'It's through her the hills knows they are alive.'

'And a hiver is . . . ?'

Rob hesitated. 'Dunno the proper haggin' way o' talking aboot it,' he said. 'Awf'ly Wee Billy, you know them lang words.'

Billy swallowed. 'There's old poems, mistress. It's like a – a mind wi'oot a body, except it disnae think. Some say it's nothing but a fear, and never dies. And what it does . . .' His tiny face wrinkled. 'It's like them things you get on sheep,' he decided.

The Feegles who weren't eating and drinking came to his aid.

'Horns?'

'Wools?'

'Tails?'

'Legs?'

'Chairs?' This was Daft Wullie.

'Sheep ticks,' said Billy, thoughtfully.

'A parasite, you mean?' said Miss Level.

'Aye, that could be the word,' said Billy. 'It creeps in, ye ken. It looks for folks wi' power and strength. Kings, ye ken, magicians, leaders. They say that way back in time, afore there *wuz* people, it live in beasts. The strongest beasts, ye ken, the one wi' big, big teeths. An' when it finds ye, it waits for a chance tae creep intae your head and it *becomes* ye.'

The Feegles fell silent, watching Miss Level.

'Becomes you?' she said.

'Aye. Wi' your memories an' all. Only . . . it changes ye. It gives ye a lot o' power, but it takes ye over, makes ye its own. An' the last wee bit of ye that still is ye . . . well, that'll fight and fight, mebbe, but it will dwindle and dwindle until it's a' gone an' ye're just a memory . . .'

The Feegles watched both of Miss Level. You never knew what a hag would do at a time like this.

'Wizards used to summon demons,' she said. 'They may still do so, although I think that's considered so fifteen centuries ago these days. But that takes a lot of magic. And you could talk to demons, I believe. And there were rules.'

'Never heard o' a hiver talkin',' said Billy. 'Or obeyin' rules.'

'But why would it want Tiffany?' said Miss Level. 'She's not powerful!'

'She has the power o' the land in her,' said Rob Anybody stoutly. ''Tis a power that comes at need, not for doin' wee conjurin' tricks. We seen it, mistress!'

'But Tiffany doesn't do *any* magic,' said Miss Level, helplessly. 'She's very bright but she can't even make a shamble. You must be wrong about that.'

'Any o' youse lads *seen* the hag do any hagglin' lately?' Rob Anybody demanded. There were a lot of shaken heads, and a shower of beads, beetles, feathers and miscellaneous head items.

'Do you spy— I mean, do you watch over her *all* the time?' said Miss Level, slightly horrified.

'Oh, aye,' said Rob, airily. 'No' in the privy, o'course. An' it's getting harder in her bedroom 'cuz she's blocked up a lot o' the cracks, for some reason.'

'I can't imagine why,' said Miss Level carefully.

'No' us, neither,' said Ron. 'We reckon it was 'cuz o' the draughts.'

'Yes, I expect that's why it was,' said Miss Level.

'So mostly we get in through a mousehole and hides out in her old dolly house until she guz tae sleep,' said Rob. 'Dinnae look at me like that, mistress, all the lads is perrrfect gentlemen an' keeps their eyes tight shut when she's gettin' intae her nightie. Then there's one guarding her window and another at the door.'

'Guarding her from what?'

'Everything.'

For a moment Miss Level had a picture in her mind of a silent, moonlit bedroom with a sleeping child. She saw, by the window, lit by the moon, one small figure on guard, and another in the shadows by the door. What were they guarding her from? *Everything* . . .

But now something, this *thing*, has taken her over and she's locked inside somewhere. But she never used to do magic! I could understand it if it was one of the other girls, messing around, but . . . Tiffany?

One of the Feegles was slowly raising a hand.

'Yes?' she said.

'It's me, mistress, Big Yan. I dinnae know if it wuz proper hagglin', mistress,' he said nervously, 'but me an' Nearly Big Angus saw her doin' something odd a few times, eh, Nearly Big Angus?' The Feegle next to him nodded and the speaker went on. 'It was when she got her new dress and her new hat . . .'

'And verra bonny she looked, too,' said Nearly Big Angus.

'Aye, she did that. But she'd put 'em on, and then standing in the middle o' the floor and said – whut wuz it she said, Nearly Big Angus?'

' "See me",' Nearly Big Angus volunteered.

Miss Level looked blank. The speaker, now looking a bit sorry that he'd raised this, went on: 'Then after a wee while we'd hear her voice say "See me not" and then she'd adjust the hat, ye know, mebbe to a more fetchin' angle.'

'Oh, you mean she was looking at herself in what we call a *mirror,*' said Miss Level. 'That's a kind of—'

'We ken well what them things are, mistress,' said Nearly Big Angus. 'She's got a tiny one, all cracked and dirty. But it's nae good for a body as wants tae see herself properly.'

'Verra good for the stealin', mirrors,' said Rob Anybody. 'We got oor Jeannie a silver one wi' garnets in the frame.'

'And she'd say "See me"?' said Miss Level.

'Aye, an' then "See me not",' said Big Yan. 'An' betweentimes she'd stand verra still, like a stachoo.'

'Sounds like she was trying to invent some kind of invisibility spell,' Miss Level mused. 'They don't work like that, of course.'

'We reckoned she was just tryin' to throw her voice,' said Nearly Big Angus. 'So it sounds like it's comin' fra' somewhere else, ye ken? Wee Iain can do that a treat when we're huntin'.'

'Throw her voice?' said Miss Level, her brow wrinkling. 'Why did you think that?'

''Cuz when she said "See me not", it sounded like it wuz no' comin fra' her and her lips didnae move.'

Miss Level stared at the Feegles. When she spoke next, her voice was a little strange.

'Tell me,' she said, 'when she was just standing there, was she moving at *all*?'

'Just breathin' verra slow, mistress,' said Big Yan.

'Were her eyes shut?'

'Aye!'

Miss Level started to breathe very fast.

'She walked out of her own body! There's not one –'

'– witch in a hundred who can do that!' she said. 'That's Borrowing, that is! It's better than any circus trick! It's putting –'

'– your mind somewhere else! You have to –'

'– learn how to protect yourself before you ever *try* it! And *she* just invented it because she didn't have a mirror? The little fool, why didn't she –'

'– *say*? She walked out of her own body and left it there for anything to take over! I wonder what –'

'– she *thought* she was –'

'– doing?'

After a while Rob Anybody gave a polite cough.

'We're better at questions about fightin', drinkin' and stealin',' he mumbled. 'We dinna have the knowin' o' the hagglin'.'

Chapter 7

The Matter of Brian

Something that called itself Tiffany flew across the treetops.

It thought it was Tiffany. It could remember everything – nearly everything – about being Tiffany. It looked like Tiffany. It even thought like Tiffany, more or less. It had everything it needed to be Tiffany . . .

. . . except Tiffany. Except the tiny part of her that was . . . me.

It peered from her own eyes, tried to hear with her own ears, think with her own brain.

A hiver took over its victim not by force, exactly, but simply by moving into any space, like the hermit elephant. It just*

*The hermit elephant of Howondaland has a very thin hide, except on its head, and young ones will often move into a small mud hut while the owners are out. It is far too shy to harm anyone, but most people quit their huts pretty soon after an elephant moves in. For one thing, it lifts the hut off the ground and carries it away on its back across the veldt, settling it down over any patch of nice grass that it finds. This makes housework very unpredictable. Nevertheless, an entire village of hermit elephants moving across the plains is one of the finest sights on the continent.

took you over because that was what it did, until it was in all the places and there was no room left . . .

Except –

– it was having trouble. It had flowed through her like a dark tide but there was a place, tight and sealed, that was still closed. If it had the brains of a tree, it would have been puzzled.

If it had the brains of a human, it would have been frightened . . .

Tiffany brought the broomstick in low over the trees, and landed it neatly in Mrs Earwig's garden. There really was nothing to it, she decided. You just had to *want* it to fly.

Then she was sick again or, at least, tried to be, but since she'd thrown up twice in the air there wasn't much left to be sick with. It was ridiculous! She wasn't frightened of flying any more, but her stupid stomach was!

She wiped her mouth carefully and looked around.

She'd landed on a lawn. She'd heard of them, but had never seen a real one before. There was grass all round Miss Level's cottage, but that was just, well, the grass of the clearing. Every other garden she'd seen was used for growing vegetables, with perhaps just a little space for flowers if the wife had got tough about it. A lawn meant you were posh enough to afford to give up valuable potato space.

This lawn had stripes.

Tiffany turned to the stick and said, 'Stay!' and then marched across the lawn to the house. It was a lot grander than Miss Level's cottage but, from what Tiffany had heard, Mrs Earwig was a more senior witch. She'd also married a wizard, although he didn't do any wizarding these days. It was a funny thing, Miss Level said, but you didn't often meet a poor wizard.

She knocked at the door and waited.

There was a curse-net hanging in the porch. You'd have thought that a witch wouldn't need such a thing, but Tiffany supposed they used them as decoration. There was also a broomstick leaning against the wall, and a five-pointed silver star on the door. Mrs Earwig *advertised*.

Tiffany knocked on the door again, much harder.

It was instantly opened by a tall, thin woman, all in black. But it was a very decorative rich, deep black, all lacy and ruffled, and set off with more silver jewellery than Tiffany imagined could exist. She didn't just have rings on her fingers. Some fingers had sort of silver finger gloves, designed to look like claws. She gleamed like the night sky.

And she was wearing her pointy hat, which Miss Level never did at home. It was taller than any hat that Tiffany had ever seen. It had stars on it, and silver hatpins glittered.

All of this should have added up to something pretty impressive. It didn't. Partly it was because there was just too much of *everything*, but mostly it was because of Mrs Earwig. She had a long sharp face and looked very much as though she was about to complain about the cat from next door widdling on her lawn. And she looked like that all the time. Before she spoke, she very pointedly looked at the door to see if the heavy knocking had made a mark.

'Well?' she said, haughtily, or what she probably thought was haughtily. It sounded a bit strangled.

'Bless all in this house,' said Tiffany.

'What? Oh, yes. Favourable runes shine on this our meeting,' said Mrs Earwig hurriedly. 'Well?'

'I've come to see Annagramma,' said Tiffany. There really *was* too much silver.

'Oh, are you one of her girls?' said Miss Earwig.

'Not . . . exactly,' said Tiffany. 'I work with Miss Level.'

'Oh, *her*,' said Mrs Earwig, looking her up and down. 'Green is a very dangerous colour. What is your name, child?'

'Tiffany.'

'Hmm,' said Mrs Earwig, not approving at all. 'Well, you had better come in.' She glanced up and made a *tch!* sound. 'Oh, will you look at that? I bought that at the craft fair over in Slice, too. It was *very* expensive!'

The curse-net was hanging in tatters.

'You didn't do that, did you?' Mrs Earwig demanded.

'It's too high, Mrs Earwig,' said Tiffany.

'It's pronounced Ah-wij,' said Mrs Earwig coldly.

'Sorry, Mrs Earwig.'

'Come.'

It was a strange house. You couldn't doubt that a witch lived in it, and not just because every doorframe had a tall pointy bit cut out of the top of it to allow Mrs Earwig's hat to pass through. Miss Level had nothing on her walls except circus posters, but Mrs Earwig had proper big paintings everywhere and they were all . . . witchy. There were lots of crescent moons and young women with quite frankly not enough clothes on, and big men with horns and, ooh, not just horns. There were suns and moon on the tiles of the floor, and the ceiling of the room Tiffany was led into was high, blue and painted with stars. Mrs Earwig (pronounced *Ah-wij*) pointed to a chair with gryphon's feet and crescent-shaped cushions.

'Sit there,' she said. 'I will tell Annagramma you are here. Do not kick the chairlegs, please.'

She went out via another door.

Tiffany looked around –

– the hiver looked around –

– and thought: I've got to be the strongest. When I am strongest, I shall be safe. *That* one is weak. She thinks you can buy magic.

'Oh, it really *is* you,' said a sharp voice behind her. 'The cheese girl.'

Tiffany stood up.

– the hiver had been many things, including a number of wizards, because wizards sought power all the time and

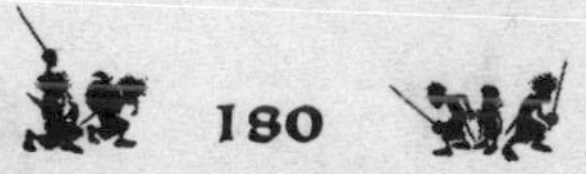

sometimes found, in their treacherous circles, not some demon who was so stupid that it could be tricked with threats and riddles, but the hiver, which was so stupid that it could not be tricked at all. And the hiver remembered—

Annagramma was drinking a glass of milk. Once you'd seen Mrs Earwig, you understood something about Annagramma. There was an air about her that she was taking notes about the world in order to draw up a list of suggestions for improvements.

'Hello,' said Tiffany.

'I suppose you came along to beg to be allowed to join after all, have you? I suppose you might be fun.'

'No, not really. But I might let you join *me*,' said Tiffany. 'Are you enjoying that milk?'

The glass of milk turned into a bunch of thistles and grass. Annagramma dropped it hurriedly. When it hit the floor, it became a glass of milk again, and shattered and splashed.

Tiffany pointed at the ceiling. The painted stars flared, filling the room with light. But Annagramma stared at the spilled milk. 'You know they say the power comes?' said Tiffany, walking around her. 'Well, it's come to *me*. Do you want to be my friend? Or do you want to be . . . in my way? I should clean up that milk, if I was you.'

She concentrated. She didn't know where this was coming from, but it seemed to know exactly what to do.

Annagramma rose a few inches off the floor. She

struggled and tried to run, but that only made her spin. To Tiffany's dreadful delight, the girl started to cry.

'*You* said we ought to use our power,' said Tiffany, walking around her as Annagramma tried to break free. '*You* said if we had the gift, people ought to know about it. You're a girl with her head screwed on right.' Tiffany bent down a bit to look her in the eye. 'Wouldn't it be *awful* if it got screwed on wrong?'

She waved a hand and her prisoner dropped to the ground. But while Annagramma was unpleasant she wasn't a coward, and she rose up with her mouth open to yell and a hand upraised—

'Careful,' said Tiffany. 'I can do it again.'

Annagramma wasn't stupid either. She lowered her hand and shrugged.

'Well, you *have* been lucky,' she said grudgingly.

'But I still need your help,' said Tiffany.

'Why would you need my help?' said Annagramma sulkily.

– *We need allies,* the hiver thought with Tiffany's mind. *They can help protect us. If necessary, we can sacrifice them. Other creatures will always want to be friends with the powerful, and this one loves power* –

'To start with,' said Tiffany, 'where can I get a dress like yours?'

Annagramma's eyes lit up. 'Oh, you want Zakzak Stronginthearm, over in Sallett Without,' she said. 'He sells *everything* for the modern witch.'

'Then I want everything,' said Tiffany.

'*He'll* want paying,' Annagramma went on. 'He's a dwarf. They know real gold from illusion gold. Everyone tries it out on him, of course. He just laughs. If you try it twice, he'll make a complaint to your mistress.'

'Miss Tick said a witch should have just enough money,' said Tiffany.

'That's right,' said Annagramma. 'Just enough to buy everything she wants! Mrs Earwig says that just because we're witches we don't have to live like peasants. But Miss Level is old-fashioned, isn't she? Probably hasn't got any money in the house.'

And Tiffany said, 'Oh, I know where I can get some money. I'll meet you please help me! here this afternoon and you can show me where his place is.'

'What was that?' said Annagramma sharply.

'I just said I'd stop me! meet you here this—' Tiffany began.

'There it was again! There was a sort of . . . odd echo in your voice,' said Annagramma. 'Like two people trying to talk at once.'

'Oh, that,' said the hiver. 'That's nothing. It'll stop soon.'

It was an interesting mind and the hiver enjoyed using it – but always there was that one place, that little place that was closed; it was annoying, like an itch that wouldn't go away . . .

It did not think. The mind of the hiver was just

what remained of all the other minds it had once lived in. They were like echoes after the music is taken away. But even echoes, bouncing off one another, can produce new harmonies.

They clanged now. They rang out things like: *Fit in. Not strong enough yet to make enemies. Have friends . . .*

Zakzak's low-ceilinged, dark shop had plenty to spend your money on. Zakzak was indeed a dwarf, and they're not traditionally interested in using magic, but he certainly knew how to display merchandise, which is what they are very good at.

There were wands, mostly of metal, some of rare woods. Some had shiny crystals stuck on them, which of course made them more expensive. There were bottles of coloured glass in the 'potions' section and, oddly enough, the smaller the bottle, the more expensive it was.

'That's because there's often very rare ingredients, like the tears of some rare snake or something,' said Annagramma.

'I didn't know snakes cried,' said Tiffany.

'Don't they? Oh, well, I expect that's why it's expensive.'

There was plenty of other stuff. Shambles hung from the ceiling, much prettier and more interesting than the working ones that Tiffany had seen. Since they were made up complete, then surely they were dead, just like the ones Miss Level kept for ornamentation. But they looked good – and looking good was important.

There were even stones for looking *into*.

'Crystal balls,' said Annagramma as Tiffany picked one up. 'Careful! They're *very* expensive!' She pointed to a sign, which had been placed thoughtfully amongst the glittering globes. It said:

Lovely to look at
Nice to hold
If you drop it
You get torn apart by wild horses

Tiffany held the biggest one in her hand and saw how Zakzak moved slightly away from his counter, ready to rush forward with a bill if she dropped it.

'Miss Tick uses a saucer of water with a bit of ink poured into it,' she said. 'And she usually borrows the water and cadges the ink, at that.'

'Oh, a *fundamentalist,*' said Annagramma. 'Letice – that's Mrs Earwig – says they let us down terribly. Do we really want people to think witches are just a bunch of mad old women who look like crows? That's *so* gingerbread-cottagey! We really ought to be professional about these things.'

'Hmm,' said Tiffany, throwing the crystal ball up into the air and catching it again with one hand. 'People should be made to *fear* witches.'

'Well, er, certainly they should respect us,' said Annagramma. 'Um . . . I should be careful with that, if I was you . . .'

'Why?' said Tiffany, tossing the ball over her shoulder.

'That was finest quartz!' shouted Zakzak, rushing around his counter.

'Oh, *Tiffany,*' said Annagramma, shocked but trying not to giggle.

Zakzak rushed past them to where the shattered ball lay in hundreds of very expensive fragmen—

– did *not* lie in very expensive fragments.

Both he and Annagramma turned to Tiffany.

She was spinning the crystal globe on the tip of her finger.

'Quickness of the hand deceives the eye,' she said.

'But I heard it smash!' said Zakzak.

'Deceives the ear, too,' said Tiffany, putting the ball back on its stand. 'I don't want this, *but*' – and she pointed a finger – 'I'll take that necklace and that one and the one with the cats and that ring and a set of *those* and two, no, three of those and – what are these?'

'Um, that's a Book of Night,' said Annagramma nervously. 'It's a sort of magical diary. You write down what you've been working on . . .'

Tiffany picked up the leather-bound book. It had an eye set in heavier leather on the cover. The eye rolled to look at her. This was a real witch's diary, and much more impressive than some shamefully cheap old book bought off a pedlar.

'Whose eye was it?' said Tiffany. 'Anyone interesting?'

'Er, I get the books from the wizards at Unseen University,' said Zakzak, still shaken. 'They're not real eyes, but they're clever enough to swivel around until they see another eye.'

'It just blinked,' said Tiffany.

'Very clever people, wizards,' said the dwarf, who knew a sale when he saw one. 'Shall I wrap it up for you?'

'Yes,' said Tiffany. 'Wrap everything up. And now can anyone hear me? show me the clothes department . . .'

. . . where there were hats. There are fashions in witchery, just like everything else. Some years the slightly concertina'd look is in, and you'll even see the point twisting around so much it's nearly pointing at the ground. There are varieties even in the most traditional hat (Upright Cone, Black), such as 'the Countrywoman' (inside pockets, waterproof), 'the Cloudbuster' (low drag coefficient for broomstick use), and, quite importantly, 'the Safety' (guaranteed to survive 80% of falling farmhouses).

Tiffany chose the tallest upright cone. It was more than two feet high and had big stars sewn on it.

'Ah, the Sky Scraper. Very much your Look,' said Zakzak, bustling around and opening drawers. 'It's for the witch on the way up, who knows what she wants and doesn't care how many frogs it takes, aha. Incidentally, many ladies like a cloak with that. Now, we have the Midnight, pure wool, fine knit, very warm, but' – he gave Tiffany a knowing look – 'we currently have *very* limited supplies of the Zephyr

Billow, just in, very rare, black as coal and thin as a shadow. Completely useless for keeping you warm or dry but it looks *fabulous* in even the slightest breeze. Observe—'

He held up the cloak and blew gently. It billowed out almost horizontally, flapping and twisting like a sheet in a gale.

'Oh, *yes,*' breathed Annagramma.

'I'll take it,' said Tiffany. 'I shall wear it to the Witch Trials on Saturday.'

'Well, if you win, be sure to tell everyone you bought it here,' said Zakzak.

'*When* I win I shall tell them I got it at a considerable discount,' said Tiffany.

'Oh, I don't do discounts,' said Zakzak, as loftily as a dwarf can manage.

Tiffany stared at him, then picked up one of the most expensive wands from the display. It glittered.

'That's a Number Six,' whispered Annagramma. 'Mrs Earwig has one of those!'

'I see it's got runes on it,' said Tiffany, and something about the way she said it made Zakzak go pale.

'Well, of *course,*' said Annagramma. 'You've got to have *runes.*'

'These are in Oggham,' said Tiffany, smiling nastily at Zakzak. 'It's a very ancient language of the dwarfs. Shall I tell you what they *say*? They say "Oh What A Wally Is Waving This".'

'Don't you take that nasty lying tone with me, young lady!' said the dwarf. 'Who's your mistress? I know your type! Learn one spell and you think you're Mistress Weatherwax! I'm not standing for this kind of behaviour! *Brian!*'

There was a rustling from the bead curtains that led to the back of the shop and a wizard appeared.

You could tell he was a wizard. Wizards never wanted you to have to guess. He had long flowing robes, with stars and magical symbols on them; there were even some sequins. His beard would have been long and flowing if indeed he'd been the kind of young man who could really grow a beard. Instead, it was ragged and wispy and not very clean. And the general effect was also spoiled by the fact that he was smoking a cigarette, had a mug of tea in his hand and a face that looked a bit like something that lives under damp logs.

The mug was chipped and on it were the jolly words 'You Don't Have to Be Magic to Work Here But It Helps!!!!!'

'Yeah?' he said, adding reproachfully, 'I *was* on my tea break, you know.'

'This young . . . lady is being awkward,' said Zakzak. 'Throwing magic about. Talking back and being smart at me. The usual stuff.'

Brian looked at Tiffany. She smiled.

'Brian's been to Unseen University,' said Zakzak with a 'so there' smirk. 'Got a *degree*. What he doesn't know about magic could fill a book! These ladies need showing the way out, Brian.'

'Now then, ladies,' said Brian nervously, putting

down his mug. 'Do what Mr Stronginthearm says and push off, right? We don't want trouble, do we? Go on, there's good kids.'

'Why do you need a wizard to protect you, with all these magical amulets around the place, Mr Stronginthearm?' said Tiffany sweetly.

Zakzak turned to Brian. 'What're you standing there for?' he demanded. 'She's doing it again! I pay you, don't I? Put a 'fluence on 'em, or something!'

'Well, er . . . that one could be a bit of an awkward customer . . .' Brian said, nodding towards Tiffany.

'If you studied wizardry, Brian, then you know about conservation of mass, don't you?' she said. 'I mean, you know what *really* happens when you try to turn someone into a frog?'

'Well, er . . .' the wizard began.

'Ha! That's just a figure of speech!' snapped Zakzak. 'I'd like to see *you* turn someone into a frog!'

'Wish granted,' said Tiffany, and waved the wand.

Brian started to say, 'Look, when I said I'd been to Unseen University I meant—'

But he ended up saying, '*Erk.*'

Take the eye away from Tiffany, up through the shop, high, high about the village until the landscape spreads out in a patchwork of field, woods and mountains.

The magic spreads out like the ripples made when a stone is dropped in water. Within a few miles of the place it makes shambles spin and breaks the threads of curse-nets. As the ripples widen the magic gets fainter, although it never dies, and still can be felt by things far more sensitive than any shamble . . .

Let the eye move and fall now on *this* wood, *this* clearing, *this* cottage . . .

There is nothing on the walls but whitewash, nothing on the floor but cold stone. The huge fireplace doesn't even have a cooking stove. A black tea kettle hangs on a black hook over what can hardly be called a fire at all; it's just a few little sticks huddling together.

This is the house of a life peeled to the core.

Upstairs, an old woman, all in faded black, is lying on a narrow bed. But you wouldn't think she was dead, because there is a big card on a string around her neck which reads:

. . . and you have to believe it when it's written down like that.

Her eyes are shut, her hands are crossed on her chest, her mouth is open.

And bees crawl into her mouth, and over her ears, and all over her pillow. They fill the room, flying in and out of the open window, where someone has put a row of saucers filled with sugary water on the sill.

None of the saucers match, of course. A witch never has matching crockery. But the bees work on, coming and going . . . busy as bees.

When the ripple of magic passes through, the buzz rises to a roar. Bees pour in though the window urgently, as though driven by a gale. They land on the still old woman until her head and shoulders are a boiling mass of tiny brown bodies.

And then, as one insect, they rise in a storm and pour away into the outside air, which is full of whirling seeds from the sycamore trees outside.

Mistress Weatherwax sat bolt upright and said: 'Bzzzt!' Then she stuck a finger into her mouth, rootled around a bit and pulled out a struggling bee. She blew on it and shooed it out of the window.

For a moment her eyes seemed to have many facets, just like a bee.

'So,' she said. 'She's learned how to Borrow, has she? Or she's been Borrowed!'

Annagramma fainted. Zakzak stared, too *afraid* to faint.

'You see,' said Tiffany, while something in the air went *gloop, gloop* above them, 'a frog weighs only a few ounces but Brian weighs, oh, about a hundred and twenty pounds, yes? *So*, to turn someone big into a frog you've got to find something to do with all the bits you can't fit into a frog, right?'

She bent down and lifted up the pointy wizard's hat on the floor.

'Happy, Brian?' she said.

A small frog, squatting on a heap of clothes, looked up and said, '*Erk!*'

Zakzak didn't look at the frog. He was looking at the thing that went *gloop, gloop*. It was like a large pink balloon full of water, quite pretty really, wobbling gently against the ceiling.

'You've killed him!' he mumbled.

'What? Oh, no. That's just the stuff he doesn't need right now. It's sort of . . . *spare* Brian.'

'Erk,' said Brian. *Gloop* went the rest of him.

'About this discount—' Zakzak began hurriedly. 'Ten per cent would be—'

Tiffany waved the wand. Behind her, the whole display of crystals rose in the air and began to orbit one another in a glittering and above all *fragile* way.

'That wand shouldn't do that!' he said.

'Of course it can't. It's rubbish. But *I* can,' said Tiffany. 'Ninety per cent discount, did I hear you say? Think quickly, I'm getting tired. And the spare Brian is getting . . . heavy.'

'You can keep it all!' Zakzak screamed. 'For free! Just don't let him splash! Please!'

'No, no, I'd like you to stay in business,' said Tiffany. 'A ninety per cent discount would be fine. I'd like you to think of me as . . . a friend . . .'

'Yes! Yes! I *am* your friend! I'm a very friendly person! Now please put him baaack! Please!' Zakzak dropped to his knees, which wasn't very far. *'Please!* He's not really a wizard! He just did evening classes there in fretwork! They hire out classrooms, that sort of thing. He thinks I don't know! But he read a few of the magic books on the quiet and he pinched the robes and he can talk wizard lingo so's you'd hardly know the difference! Please! I'd never get a *real* wizard for the money I pay him! Don't hurt him, *please*!'

Tiffany waved a hand. There was a moment even more unpleasant than the one which had ended up with the spare Brian bumping against the ceiling, and then the whole Brian stood there, blinking.

'Thank you! Thank you! Thank you!' gasped Zakzak.

Brian blinked. 'What just happened?' he said.

Zakzak, beside himself with horror and relief, patted him frantically. 'You're all there?' he said. 'You're not a balloon?'

'Here, get off!' said Brian, pushing him away.

There was a groan from Annagramma. She opened her eyes, saw Tiffany and tried to scramble to her feet *and* back away, which meant that she went backwards like a spider.

'Please don't do that to me! Please don't!' she shouted.

Tiffany ran after her and pulled her to her feet. 'I wouldn't do anything to *you*, Annagramma,' she said happily. 'You're my friend! We're *all* friends! Isn't that *nice* please please stop me . . .'

You had to remember that pictsies weren't brownies. In theory, brownies would do the housework for you if you left them a saucer of milk.

The Nac Mac Feegle . . . wouldn't.

Oh, they'd try, if they liked you and you didn't

insult them with *milk* in the saucer. They *were* helpful. They just weren't good at it. For example, you shouldn't try to remove a stubborn stain from a plate by repeatedly hitting it with your head.

And you didn't want to see a sink full of them and your best china. Or a precious pot rolling backwards and forwards across the floor while the Feegles inside simultaneously fought the ground-in dirt *and* each other.

But Miss Level, once she'd got the better china out of the way, found she rather liked the Feegles. There was something unsquashable about them. And they were entirely unamazed by a woman with two bodies, too.

'Ach, that's nothin',' Rob Anybody had said. 'When we wuz raidin' for the Quin, we once found a world where there wuz people wi' five bodies each. All sizes, ye ken, for doin' a' kinds of jobs.'

'Really?' said both of Miss Level.

'Aye, and the biggest body had a huge left hand, just for openin' pickle jars.'

'Those lids can get very tight, it's true,' Miss Level had agreed.

'Oh, we saw some muckle eldritch places when we wuz raiding for the Quin,' said Rob Anybody. 'But we gave that up for she wuz a schemin', greedy, ill-fared carlin, that she was!'

'Aye, and it wuz no' because she threw us oot o' Fairyland for being completely pished at two in the afternoon, whatever any scunner might mphf mphf . . .' said Daft Wullie.

'Pished?' said Miss Level.

'Aye . . . oh, aye, it means . . . tired. Aye. Tired. That's whut it means,' said Rob Anybody, holding his hands firmly over his brother's mouth. 'An' ye dinnae ken how to talk in front o' a lady, yah shammerin' wee scunner!'

'Er . . . thank you for doing the washing up,' said Miss Level. 'You really didn't need to . . .'

'Ach, it wasnae any trouble,' said Rob Anybody cheerfully, letting Daft Wullie go. 'An' I'm sure all them plates an' stuff will mend fine wi' a bit o' glue.'

Miss Level looked up at the clock with no hands. 'It's getting late,' she said. 'What exactly is it you propose to do, Mr Anybody?'

'Whut?'

'Do you have a plan?'

'Oh, aye!'

Rob Anybody rummaged around in his spog, which is a leather bag most Feegles have hanging from their belt. The contents are usually a mystery, but sometimes include interesting teeth.

He flourished a much-folded piece of paper.

Miss Level carefully unfolded it.

' "PLN"?' she said.

'Aye,' said Rob proudly. 'We came prepared! Look, it's *written doon*. Pee El Ner. Plan.'

'Er . . . how can I put this . . . ?' Miss Level mused. 'Ah, yes. You came rushing all this way to save Tiffany from a creature that can't be seen, touched, smelled or killed. What did you intend to do when you found it?'

Rob Anybody scratched his head, to a general shower of objects.

'I think mebbe you've put yer finger on the one weak spot, mistress,' he admitted.

'Do you mean you charge in regardless?'

'Oh, aye. That's the plan, sure enough,' said Rob Anybody, brightening up.

'And then what happens?'

'Weel, gen'raly people are tryin' tae wallop us by then, so we just mak' it up as we gae along.'

'Yes, Robert, but the creature is inside her head!'

Rob Anybody gave Billy a questioning look.

'Robert is a heich-heidit way o' sayin' Rob,' said the gonnagle, and to save time he said to Miss Level: 'That means kinda posh.'

'Ach, we can get inside her heid, if we have to,' said Rob. 'I'd hoped tae get here afore the thing got to her, but we can chase it.'

Miss Level's face was a picture. Two pictures.

'*Inside* her *head*?' she said.

'Oh, aye,' said Rob, as if that sort of thing happened every day. 'No problemo. We can get in or oot o' anywhere. Except maybe pubs, which for some reason we ha' trouble leavin'. A heid? Easy.'

'Sorry, we're talking about a real head here, are we?' said Miss Level, horrified. 'What do you do, go in through the ears?'

Once again, Rob stared at Billy, who looked puzzled.

'No, mistress. They'd be too small,' he said,

patiently. 'But we can move between worlds, ye ken. We're fairy folk.'

Miss Level nodded both heads. It was true, but it was hard to look at the assembled ranks of the Nac Mac Feegle and remember that they were, technically, fairies. It was like watching penguins swimming underwater and having to remember that they were birds.

'And?' she said.

'We can get intae dreams, ye see . . . And what's a mind but another world o' dreamin'?'

'No, I must forbid that!' said Miss Level. 'I can't have you running around inside a young girl's head! I mean, look at you! You're fully-grow . . . well, you're men! It'd be like, like . . . well, it'd be like you looking at her diary!'

Rob Anybody looked puzzled. 'Oh, aye?' he said. 'We looked at her diary loads o' times. Nae harm done.'

'You *looked* at her *diary*?' said Miss Level, horrified. 'Why?'

Really, she thought later, she should have expected the answer.

''Cuz it wuz locked,' said Daft Wullie. 'If she didnae want anyone tae look at it, why'd she keep it at the back o' her sock drawer? Anyway, all there wuz wuz a load o' words we couldnae unnerstan' an' wee drawings o' hearts and flowers an' that.'

'Hearts? Tiffany?' said Miss Level. *'Really?'* She shook herself. 'But you shouldn't have done that! And going into someone's mind is even worse!'

'The hiver is in there, mistress,' said Awf'ly Wee Billy meekly.

'But you said you can't do anything about it!'

'*She* might. If we can track her doon,' said the gonnagle. 'If we can find the wee bitty bit o' her that's still *her*. She's a bonny fighter when she's roused. Ye see, mistress, a mind's like a world itself. She'll be hidin' in it somewhere, lookin' oot through her own eyes, listenin' wi' her own ears, tryin' to make people hear, tryin' no' to let yon beast find her . . . and it'll be hunting her all the time, trying tae break her doon . . .'

Miss Level began to look hunted herself. Fifty small faces, full of worry and hope and broken noses, looked up at her. And she knew she didn't have a better plan. Or even a PLN.

'All right,' she said. 'But at least you ought to have a bath. I know that's silly, but it will make me feel better about the whole thing.'

There was a general groan.

'A bath? But we a' had one no' a year ago,' said Rob Anybody. 'Up at the big dew pond for the ships!'

'Ach, crivens!' said Big Yan. 'Ye cannae ask a man tae take a bath again this soon, mistress! There'll be nothin' left o' us!'

'With hot water and soap!' said Miss Level. 'I mean it! I'll run the water and I . . . I'll put some rope over the edge so you can climb in and out, but you *will* get clean. I'm a wi— a hag, and you'd better do what I say!'

'Oh, all reet!' said Rob. 'We'll do it for the big wee hag. But ye're no' tae peek, OK?'

'Peek?' said Miss Level. She pointed a trembling finger. 'Get into that bathroom now!'

Miss Level did, however, listen at the door. It's the sort of thing a witch does.

There was nothing to hear at first but the gentle splash of water, and then:

'This is no' as bad as I thought!'

'Aye, very pleasin'.'

'Hey, there's a big yellow duck here. Who're ye pointin' that beak at, yer scunner—'

There was a wet quack and some bubbling noises as the rubber duck sank.

'Rob, we oughtae get one o' these put in back in the mound. Verra warmin' in the winter time.'

'Aye, it's no' that good for the ship, havin' tae drink oot o' that pond after we've been bathin'. It's terrible, hearin' a ship try tae spit.'

'Ach, it'll make us softies! It's nae a guid wash if ye dinnae ha' the ice formin' on yer heid!'

'Who're you callin' a softie?'

There followed a lot more splashing and water started to seep under the door.

Miss Level knocked. 'Come on out now, and dry yourselves off!' she commanded. 'She could be back at any minute!'

In fact it wasn't for another two hours, by which time Miss Level had got so nervous that her necklaces jingled all the time.

She'd come to witching later than most, being naturally qualified by reason of the two bodies, but she'd never been very happy about magic. In truth, most witches could get through their whole life without having to do serious, undeniable magic (making shambles and curse-nets and dreamcatchers didn't really count, being rather more like arts-and-crafts, and most of the rest of it was practical medicine, common sense and the ability to look stern in a pointy hat). But being a witch and wearing the big black hat was like being a policeman. People saw the uniform, not you. When the mad axeman was running down the street you weren't allowed to back away muttering, 'Could you find someone else? Actually, I mostly just do, you know, stray dogs and road safety . . .' You were there, you had the hat, you did the job. That was a basic rule of witchery: *It's up to you*.

She was two bags of nerves when Tiffany arrived back, and stood side by side holding hands with herself to give herself confidence.

'Where have you been, dear?'

'Out,' said Tiffany.

'And what have you been doing?'

'Nothing.'

'I see you've been shopping.'

'Yes.'

'Who with?'

'Nobody.'

'Ah, yes,' Miss Level trilled, completely adrift. 'I remember when I used to go out and do nothing. Sometimes you can be your own worst company. Believe me, I know—'

But Tiffany had already swept upstairs.

Without anyone actually seeming to move, Feegles started to appear everywhere in the room.

'Well, that could ha' gone better,' said Rob Anybody.

'She looked so different!' Miss Level burst out. 'She moved differently! I just didn't know what to do! And those clothes!'

'Aye. Sparklin' like a young raven,' said Rob.

'Did you see all those bags? Where could she have got the money? *I* certainly don't have that kind of—'

She stopped, and both of Miss Level spoke at once.

'Oh, no –'

'– surely not! She wouldn't –'

'– have, would she?'

'I dinnae ken whut ye're talkin' aboot,' said Awf'ly Wee Billy, 'but whut *she* would dae isnae the point. That's the hiver doin' the thinkin'!'

Miss Level clasped all four hands together in distress. 'Oh dear . . . I *must* go down to the village and check!'

One of her ran towards the door.

'Well, at least she's brought the broomstick back,' muttered the Miss Level who stayed. She started to wear the slightly unfocused expression she got when both her bodies weren't in the same place.

They could hear noises from upstairs.

'I vote we just tap her gently on the heid,' said Big Yan. 'It cannae give us any trouble if it's gone sleepies, aye?'

Miss Level clenched and unclenched her fists nervously. 'No,' she said. 'I'll go up there and have a *serious* talk with her!'

'I told yez, mistress, it's not her,' said Awf'ly Wee Billy, wearily.

'Well, at least I'll wait until I've visited Mr Weavall,' said Miss Level, standing in her kitchen. 'I'm nearly there . . . ah . . . he's asleep. I'll just *eease* the box out quietly . . . if she's taken his money I'm going to be *so* angry—'

It was a *good* hat, Tiffany thought. It was at least as tall as Mrs Earwig's hat, and it shone darkly. The stars gleamed.

The other packages covered the floor and the bed. She pulled out another one of the black dresses, the one covered in lace, and the cloak, which spread out in the air. She really liked the cloak. In anything but a complete dead calm, it floated and billowed as if whipped by a gale. If you were going to be a witch, you had to start by looking like one.

She twirled in it once or twice, and then said something without thinking, so that the hiver part of her was caught unawares.

'See me.'

The hiver was suddenly thrust outside her body, Tiffany was free. She hadn't expected it . . .

She felt herself to the tips of her fingers. She dived towards the bed, grabbed one of Zakzak's best wands and waved it desperately in front of her like a weapon.

'You stay out!' she said. 'Stay away! It's my body, not yours! You've made it do dreadful things! You *stole* Mr Weavall's money! Look at these stupid clothes! And don't you know about eating and drinking? You stay away! You're not coming back! Don't you dare! I've got power, you know!'

So have we, said her own voice, in her own head. *Yours.*

They fought. A watcher would have seen only a girl in a black dress, spinning around the room and flailing her arms as if she'd been stung, but Tiffany fought for every toe, every finger. She bounced off a wall, banged against the chest of drawers, slammed into another wall –

– and the door was flung open.

One of Miss Level was there, no longer nervous, but trembling with rage. She pointed a shaking finger.

'Listen to me, whoever you are! Did you steal Mr Weav—?' she began.

The hiver turned.

The hiver struck.

The hiver . . . killed.

Chapter 8

The Secret Land

It's bad enough being dead. Waking up and seeing a Nac Mac Feegle standing on your chest and peering intently at you from an inch away only makes things worse.

Miss Level groaned. It felt as though she was lying on the floor.

'Ach, this one's alive, right enough,' said the Feegle. 'Told yez! That's a weasel skull ye owe me!'

Miss Level blinked one set of eyes, and then froze in horror.

'What happened to me?' she whispered.

The Feegle in front of her was replaced by the face of Rob Anybody. It was not an improvement.

'How many fingers am I holdin' up?' he said.

'Five,' whispered Miss Level.

'Am I? Ah, well, ye could be right, ye'd have the knowin' o' the countin',' said Rob, lowering his

hand. 'Ye've had a wee bittie accident, ye ken. You're a wee bittie dead.'

Miss Level's head slumped back. Through the mist of something that wasn't exactly pain, she heard Rob Anybody say to someone she couldn't see:

'Hey, I *wuz* breakin' it tae her gently! I did say "wee bittie" twice, right?'

'It's as though part of me is . . . a long way off,' murmured Miss Level.

'Aye, you're aboot right there,' said Rob, champion of the bedside manner.

Some memories bobbed to the surface of the thick soup in Miss Level's mind.

'Tiffany killed me, didn't she,' she said. 'I remember seeing that black figure turn round and her expression was horrible—'

'That wuz the hiver,' said Rob Anybody. 'That was no' Tiffany! She was fightin' it! She still is, inside! But it didnae remember you ha' *two* bodies! We got tae help her, mistress!'

Miss Level pushed herself upright. It *wasn't* pain she felt, but it was the . . . ghost of pain.

'How did I die?' she said, weakly.

'There was, like, an explosion, an' smoke an' that,' said Rob. 'Not messy, really.'

'Oh, well, that's a small mercy, anyway,' said Miss Level, sagging back.

'Aye, there was just this, like, big purple cloud o', like, dust,' said Daft Wullie.

'Where's my . . . I can't feel . . . where's my other body?'

'Aye, that was what got blown up in that big cloud, right enough,' said Rob. 'Good job ye has a spare, eh?'

'She's all mithered in her heid,' whispered Awf'ly Wee Billy. 'Take it gently, eh?'

'How do you manage, only seeing one side of things?' said Miss Level dreamily to the world in general. 'How will I get everything done with only one pair of hands and feet? Being in just one place all the time . . . how do people manage? It's impossible . . .'

She shut her eyes.

'Mistress Level, we *need* ye!' shouted Rob Anybody into her ear.

'Need, need, need,' murmured Miss Level. 'Everyone needs a witch. No one cares if a witch *needs*. *Giving* and *giving* always . . . a fairy godmother never gets a wish, let me tell you . . .'

'Mistress Level!' Rob screamed. 'Ye cannae pass oot on us noo!'

'I'm weary,' whispered Miss Level. 'I'm very, very pished.'

'Mistress Level!' Rob Anybody yelled. 'The big wee hag is lying on the floor like a dead person, but she's cold as ice and sweatin' like a horse! She's fightin' the beast inside her, mistress! An' she's losin'!' Rob peered into Miss Level's face, and shook his head. 'Auchtahelweit! She's swooned! C'mon, lads, let's move her!'

Like many small creatures, Feegles are immensely strong for their size. It still took ten of them to carry Miss Level up the narrow stairs without banging her head more than necessary, although they did use her feet to push open the door to Tiffany's room.

Tiffany lay on the floor. Sometimes a muscle twitched.

Miss Level was propped up like a doll.

'How're we gonna bring the big hag rooound?' said Big Yan.

'I heard where ye has to put someone's heid between their legs,' said Rob, doubtfully.

Daft Wullie sighed, and drew his sword. 'Sounds a wee bit drastic tae me,' he said, 'but if someone will help me hold her steady—'

Miss Level opened her eyes, which was just as well. She focused unsteadily on the Feegles and smiled a strange, happy little smile.

'Ooo, fairies!' she mumbled.

'Ach, noo she's ramblin',' said Rob Anybody.

'No, she means fairies like bigjobs *think* they are,' said Awf'ly Wee Billy. 'Tiny wee tinkly creatures that live in flowers an' fly aroound cuddlin' butterflies an' that.'

'What? Have they no' *seen* real fairies? They're worse'n wasps!' said Big Yan.

'We havnae got *time* for this!' snapped Rob Anybody. He jumped onto Miss Level's knee.

'Aye, ma'am, we's fairies from the land o'—' He stopped and looked imploringly at Billy.

'Tinkle?' Billy suggested.

'Aye, the land o' Tinkle, ye ken, and we found this puir wee –'

'– princess,' said Billy.

'Aye, princess, who's been attacked by a bunch o' scunners—'

'– wicked goblins,' said Billy.

'– yeah, wicked goblins, right, an' she's in a bad way, so we wuz wonderin' if ye could kinda tell us how tae look after her –'

'– until the handsome prince turns up on a big white horse wi' curtains rooound it an' wakes her with a magical kiss,' said Billy.

Rob gave him a desperate look, and turned back to the bemused Miss Level.

'Aye, what ma friend Fairy Billy just said,' he managed.

Miss Level tried to focus. 'You're very *ugly* for fairies,' she said.

'Aye, well, the ones you gen'rally see are for the *pretty* flowers, ye ken,' said Rob Anybody, inventing desperately. 'We're more for the stingin' nettles and bindweed an' Old Man's Troosers an' thistles, OK? It wouldna be fair for only the bonny flowers tae have fairies noo, would it? It'd prob'ly be against the law, eh? Noo, can ye *please* help us wi' this princess here before them scunners—'

'– wicked goblins—' said Billy.

'Aye, before they come back,' said Rob.

Panting, he watched Miss Level's face. There

seemed to be a certain amount of thinking going on.

'Is her pulse rapid?' murmured Miss Level. 'You say her skin is cold but she's sweating? Is she breathing rapidly? It sounds like shock. Keep her warm. Raise her legs. Watch her carefully. Try to remove . . . the cause . . .' Her head slumped.

Rob turned to Awf'ly Wee Billy. 'A horse wi' *curtains* roond it?' he said. 'Where did ye get all that blethers?'

'There's a big hoose near the Long Lake an' they read stories tae their wee bairn an' I go along an' listen fra' a mousehole,' said Awf'ly Wee Billy. 'One day I snuck in and looked at the pichurs, and there was bigjobs called k'nits wi' shields and armour and horses wi' curtains—'

'Weel, it worked, blethers though it be,' said Rob Anybody. He looked at Tiffany. She was lying down, so he was about as high as her chin. It was like walking around a small hill. 'Crivens, it does me nae guid at all ta see the puir wee thing like this,' he said, shaking his head. 'C'mon, lads, get that cover off the bed and put that cushion under her feet.'

'Er, Rob?' said Daft Wullie.

'Aye?' Rob was staring up at the unconscious Tiffany.

'How are we goin' taw get *inta* her heid? There's got tae be somethin' tae guide us in.'

'Aye, Wullie, an' I ken whut it's gonna be, 'cuz I've been usin' mah heid for thinkin'!' said Rob. 'Ye've seen the big wee hag often enough, right? Well, see this necklet?'

He reached up. The silver horse had slipped around Tiffany's neck as she lay on the floor. It hung there, amid the amulets and dark glitter.

'Aye?' said Wullie.

'It was a present from that son o' the Baron,' said Rob. 'An' she's kept it. She's tried tae turn hersel' intae some kind of creature o' the night, but somethin' made her keep this. It'll be in her heid, too. 'Tis important tae her. All we need tae do is frannit a wheelstone on it and it'll tak' us right where she is.'*

Daft Wullie scratched his head. 'But I thought *she* thought he was just a big pile of jobbies?' he said. 'I seen her oot walkin', an' when he comes ridin' past she sticks her nose in th' air and looks the other wa'. In fact, sometimes I seen her wait aroond a full five-and-twenty minutes for him tae come past, just so's she can do that.'

'Ah, weel, no man kens the workin's o' the female mind,' said Rob Anybody loftily. 'We'll follow the horse.'

From 'Fairies and How to Avoid Them' by Miss Perspicacia Tick:

No one knows exactly *how* the Nac Mac Feegle step from one world to another. Those who have seen Feegles actually travel this way say that they apparently throw back their shoulders and

*If anyone knew what this meant, they'd know a lot more about the Nac Mac Feegles' way of travelling.

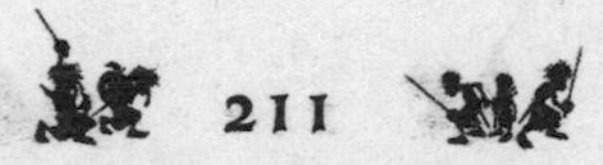

thrust out one leg straight ahead of them. Then they wiggle their foot and are gone. This is known as 'the crawstep', and the only comment on the subject by a Feegle is 'It's all in the ankle movement, ye ken.' They appear to be able to travel magically between worlds of all kinds but not *within* a world. For *this* purpose, they assure people, they have 'feets'.

The sky was black, even though the sun was high. It hung at just past noon, lighting the landscape as brilliantly as a hot summer day, but the sky was midnight black, shorn of stars.

This was the landscape of Tiffany Aching's mind.

The Feegles looked around them. There seemed to be downland underfoot, rolling and green.

'She tells the land what it is. The land tells her who she is,' whispered Awf'ly Wee Billy. 'She really *does* hold the soul o' the land in her *heid* . . .'

'Aye, so 'tis,' muttered Rob Anybody. 'But there's nae creatures, ye ken. Nae ships. Nae burdies.'

'Mebbe . . . mebbe somethin's scared them awa'?' said Daft Wullie.

There was, indeed, no life. Stillness and silence ruled here. In fact Tiffany, who cared a lot about getting words right, would have said it was a hush, which is not the same as silence. A hush is what you get in cathedrals at midnight.

'OK, lads,' Rob Anybody whispered. 'We dinnae ken what we're goin' tae find, so ye tread as light as e'er foot can fall, unnerstan'? Let's find the big wee hag.'

They nodded, and stepped forward like ghosts.

The land rose slightly ahead of them, to some kind of earthworks. They advanced on it carefully, wary of ambush, but nothing stopped them as they climbed two long mounds in the turf which made a sort of cross.

'Man-made,' said Big Yan, when they reached the top. 'Just like in the old days, Rob.' The silence sucked his speech away.

'This is deep inside o' the big wee hag's head,' said Rob Anybody, looking around warily. 'We dinnae know *whut* made 'em.'

'I dinnae like this, Rob,' said a Feegle. 'It's too quiet.'

'Aye, Slightly Sane Georgie, it is that—'

'*You are my sunshine, my only su—*'

'Daft Wullie!' snapped Rob, without taking his eyes off the strange landscape.

The singing stopped. 'Aye, Rob?' said Daft Wullie from behind him.

'Ye ken I said I'd tell ye when ye wuz guilty o' stupid and inna-pro-pre-ate behaviour?'

'Aye, Rob,' said Daft Wullie. 'That wuz another one o' those times, wuz it?'

'Aye.'

They moved on again, staring around them. And still there was the hush. It was the pause before an orchestra plays, the quietness before thunder. It was as if all the small sounds of the hills had shut down to make room for one big sound to happen.

And then they found the Horse.

They'd seen it, back on the Chalk. But here it was, not carved into the hillside but spread out before them. They stared at it.

'Awf'ly Wee Billy?' said Rob, beckoning the young gonnagle towards him. 'You're a gonnagle, ye ken aboot poetry and dreams. What's this? Why's it up here? It shouldnae be on the *top* o' the hills!'

'Serious hiddlins, Mr Rob,' said Billy. 'This is *serious* hiddlins. I cannae work it out yet.'

'She knows the Chalk. Why'd she get this wrong?'

'I'm thinkin' aboot it, Mr Rob.'

'You wouldnae care tae think a bit faster, would ye?'

'Rob?' said Big Yan, hurrying up. He'd been scouting ahead.

'Aye?' said Rob gloomily.

'Ye'd better come and see this . . .'

On top of a round hill was a four-wheeled shepherding hut, with a curved roof and a chimney for the pot-bellied stove. Inside, the walls were covered with the yellow and blue wrappers from hundreds of packets of Jolly Sailor tobacco. There were old sacks hanging up there, and the back of the door was covered with chalk marks where Granny Aching had counted sheep and days. And there was a narrow iron bedstead, made comfortable with old fleeces and feed sacks.

'D'ye have the unnerstandin' of this, Awf'ly Wee Billy?' said Rob. 'Can ye tell us where the big wee hag is?'

The young gonnagle looked worried. 'Er, Mister Rob, ye ken I've only just been made a gonnagle? I mean, I know the songs an' a', but I'm no' verra experienced at this . . .'

'Aye?' said Rob Anybody. 'An' just how many gonnagles afore ye ha' walked through the dreams o' a hag?'

'Er . . . none I've ever heard of, Mister Rob,' Billy confessed.

'Aye. So you already know more aboot it than any o' them big men,' said Rob. He gave the boy a smile. 'Do yer best, laddie. I dinnae expect any more of you than that.'

Billy looked out of the shed door, and took a deep breath: 'Then I'll tell ye I think she's hidin' somewhere close like a hunted creature, Mr Rob. This is a wee bit o' her memory, the place o' her granny, the place where she's always felt safe. I'll tell ye I think that we're in the soul and centre o' her. The bit o' her that *is* her. And I'm frightened for her. Frightened to mah boots.'

'Why?'

'Because I've been watchin' the shadows, Mr Rob,' said Billy. 'The sun is movin'. It's slippin' doon the sky.'

'Aye, weel, that's whut the sun does—' Rob began.

Billy shook his head. '*Nay*, Mr Rob. Ye dinnae understand! I'm tellin' ye that's no' the sun o' the big wide world. That's the sun o' the soul o' her.'

The Feegles looked at the sun, and at the shadows,

then back at Billy. He'd stuck his chin out bravely but he was trembling.

'She'll die when night comes?' Rob said.

'There's worser things than death, Mr Rob. The hiver will have her, head tae toe—'

'That is *nae* gonna happen!' shouted Rob Anybody, so suddenly that Billy backed away. 'She's a strong big wee lass! She fought the Quin wi' no more than a fryin' pan!'

Awf'ly Wee Billy swallowed. There were a lot of things he'd rather do than face Rob Anybody now. But he pressed on.

'Sorry, Mr Rob, but I'm telling ye she had iron then, an' she wuz on her ain turf. She's a lang, lang way fra' hame here. An' it'll squeeze this place when it finds it, leave no more room for it, and the night will come, an'—'

''Scuse me, Rob. I ha' an idea.'

It was Daft Wullie, twisting his hands nervously. Everyone turned to look at him.

'*Ye* ha' an idea?' said Rob.

'Aye, an' if I tell youse, I dinnae want you ta' say it's inna-pro-pre-ate, OK, Rob?'

Rob Anybody sighed. 'OK, Wullie, ye ha' my word on it.'

'Weel,' said Wullie, his fingers knotting and unknotting. 'What is *this* place if it's not truly her ain place? What is it if not her ain turf? If she cannae fight the creature here, she cannae fight it anywhere!'

'But it willnae come here,' said Billy. 'It doesnae need to. As she grows weaker, this place will fade away.'

'Oh, crivens,' mumbled Daft Wullie. 'Weel, it was a good idea, right? Even if it doesnae work?'

Rob Anybody wasn't paying any attention. He stared around the shepherding hut. My man's got to use his heid for something other than nuttin' folk, Jeannie had said.

'Daft Wullie is right,' he said quietly. 'This is her safe place. She holds the land, she has it in her eye. The creature can ne'er touch her here. *Here,* she has power. But 'twill be a jail hoose for her here unless she fights the monster. She'd be locked in here and watch her life gae doon the cludgie. She'll look oot at the world like a pris'ner at a tiny window, and see hersel' hated and feared. So we'll fetch the beast in here against its will, and here it will die!'

The Feegles cheered. They weren't sure what was going on, but they liked the sound of it.

'How?' said Awf'ly Wee Billy.

'Ye had to gae and ask that, eh?' said Rob Anybody bitterly. 'An' I wuz doin' sae weel wi' the thinkin'—'

He turned. There was a scratching noise on the door above him.

Up there, across the rows and rows of half rubbed-out markings, freshly chalked letters were appearing one by one, as if an invisible hand was writing them.

'Worrds,' said Rob Anybody. 'She's tryin' tae tell us somethin'!'

'Yes, they say—' Billy began.

'I ken weel what they say!' snapped Rob Anybody. 'I ha' the knowin' of the readin'! They say—'

He looked up again. 'OK, they say . . . that's the snake, an' that's the kinda like a gate letter, an' the comb on its side, two o' that, an' the fat man standin' still, an' the snake again, and then there's whut we calls a "space" and then there's the letter like a saw's teeth, and two o' the letters that's roound like the sun, and the letter that's a man sittin' doon, and onna next line we ha' . . . the man wi' his arms oot, and the letter that's you, an' ha, the fat man again but noo he's walkin, an' next he's standin' still again, an' next is the comb, an' the up-an'-doon ziggy-zaggy letter, and the man's got his arms oot, and then there's me, and that ziggy-zaggy and we end the line with the comb again . . . an' on the *next* line we starts wi' the bendy hook, that's the letter roound as the sun, them's twa' men sittin' doon, there's the letter reaching ooot tae the sky, then there's a space 'cos there's nae letter, then there's the snaky again, an' the letter like a hoose frame, and then there's the letter that's me, aye, an' another fella sitting doon, an' another big roound letter, and, ha, oor ol' friend, the fat man walkin'! The End!'

He stood back, hands on hips, and demanded: 'There! Is that readin' I just did, or wuz it no'?'

There was a cheer from the Feegles, and some applause.

Awf'ly Wee Billy looked up at the chalked words:

And then he looked at Rob Anybody's expression.

'Aye, aye,' he said, 'Ye're doin great, Mr Rob. Sheep's wool, turpentine and Jolly Sailor tobacco.'

'Ach, weel, anyone can read it all in one go,' said Rob Anybody, dismissively. 'But youse gotta be *guid* to break it doon intae all the tricksie letters. And *veera* guid to have the knowin' o' the meanin' o' the whole.'

'What is that?' said Awf'ly Wee Billy.

'The meaning, gonnagle, is that you are gonna' go *stealin'*!' There was a cheer from the rest of the Feegles. They hadn't been keeping up very well, but they recognized *that* word all right.

'An' it's gonna be a stealin' tae remember!' Rob yelled, to another cheer. 'Daft Wullie!'

'Aye!'

'Ye'll be in charge! Ye ha' not got the brains o' a beetle, brother o' mine, but when it comes tae the thievin' ye hae no equal in this wurld! Ye've got tae fetch turpentine and fresh ship wool and some o' the Jolly Sailor baccy! Ye got tae get them to the big hag wi' twa' bodies! Tell her she must mak' the hiver *smell* them, right? It'll bring it here! And ye'd best be quick, because that sun is movin' down the sky. Ye'll be stealin' fra' Time itself – aye? Ye have a question?'

Daft Wullie had raised a finger.

'Point o' order, Rob,' he said, 'but it was a wee bittie hurtful there for you to say I dinnae hae the brains of a beetle . . .'

Rob hesitated, but only for a moment. 'Aye, Daft Wullie, ye are right in whut ye say. It was unricht o' me to say that. It was the heat o' the moment, an' I am full sorry for it. As I stand here before ye now, I will say: Daft Wullie, ye *do* hae the brains o' a beetle, an' I'll fight any scunner who says different!'

Daft Wullie's face broke into a huge smile, then crinkled into a frown. 'But ye are the leader, Rob,' he said.

'No' on this raid, Wullie. A'm staying here. I have every confidence that ye'll be a fiiinne leader on this raid an' not totally mess it up like ye did the last seventeen times!'

There was a general groan from the crowd.

'Look at the sun, will ye!' said Rob, pointing. 'It's moved since we've been talkin'! Someone's got tae stay wi' her! I will no' ha' it said we left her tae die alone! Now, get movin', ye scunners, or feel the flat o' my blade!'

He raised his sword and growled. They fled.

Rob Anybody laid his sword down with care, then sat on the step of the shepherding hut to watch the sun.

After a while, he was aware of something else . . .

Hamish the aviator gave Miss Level's broomstick a doubtful look. It hung a few feet above the ground and it worried him.

He hitched up the bundle on his back that contained his parachute, although it was technically the 'paradrawers', since it was made of string and an old pair of Tiffany's best Sunday drawers, well washed. They still had flowers on, but there was nothing like them for getting a Feegle safely to the ground. He had a feeling it (or they) were going to be needed.

'It's no' got feathers,' he complained.

'Look, we dinnae ha' time to argue!' said Daft Wullie. 'We're in a hurry, ye ken, an' you're the only one who knows how tae fly!'

'A broomstick isnae *flyin'*,' said Hamish. 'It's magic. It hasnae any wings! I dinnae ken that stuff!'

But Big Yan had already thrown a piece of string over the bristle end of the stick and was climbing up. Other Feegles followed.

'Besides, how do they steer these things?' Hamish went on.

'Weel, how do ye do it with wi' the birdies?' Daft Wullie demanded.

'Oh, that's easy. Ye just shift your weight, but—'

'Ach, ye'll learn as we go,' said Wullie. 'Flying cannae be that difficult. Even *ducks* can do it, and they have nae brains at a'.'

And there was really no point in arguing, which is why, a few minutes later, Hamish inched his way along the stick's handle. The rest of the Feegles clung to the bristles at the other end, chattering.

Firmly tied to the bristles was a bundle of what looked like sticks and rags, with a battered hat and the stolen beard on top of it.

At least this extra weight meant that the stick end was pointing up, towards a gap in the fruit trees. Hamish sighed, took a deep breath, pulled his goggles over his eyes and put a hand on a shiny area of stick just in front of him.

Gently, the stick began to move through the air. There was a cheer from the Feegles.

'See? Told yez ye'd be OK,' Daft Wullie called out. 'But can ye no' make it go a wee bit faster?'

Carefully, Hamish touched the shiny area again.

The stick shuddered, hung motionless for a moment, and then shot upwards trailing a noise very like *Arrrrrrrrggggggggggghhhhhhhhhhhhh* . . .

In the silent world of Tiffany's head, Rob Anybody picked up his sword again and crept across the darkening turf.

There was something there, small but moving.

It was a tiny thorn bush, growing so fast that its twigs visibly moved. Its shadow danced on the grass.

Rob Anybody stared at it. It had to mean something. He watched it carefully. Little bush, growing . . .

And then he remembered what the old kelda had told them when he'd been a wee boy.

Once, the land had been all forest, heavy and dark. Then men came and cut down trees. They let the sun in. The grass grew up in the clearings. The bigjobs brought in sheep, which ate the grass, and also what grew in the grass: *tree seedlings.* And so the dark forests died. There hadn't been much life in them, not once the tree trunks closed in behind you; it had been dark as the bottom of the sea in there, the leaves far above keeping out the light. Sometimes there was the crash of a branch, or the rattle and patter as acorns the squirrels had missed bounced down, from branch to branch, into the gloom. Mostly it was just hot and silent. Around the edges of the forest were the homes of many creatures. Deep inside the forest, the everlasting forest, was the home of wood.

But the turf *lived* in the sun, with its hundreds of grasses and flowers and birds and insects. The Nac Mac Feegle knew that better than most, being so much closer to it. What looked like a green desert at a distance was a tiny, thriving, roaring *jungle* . . .

'Ach,' said Rob Anybody. 'So that's yer game, izzit?

Weel, ye're no' takin' over in here too!'

He chopped at the spindly thing with his sword, and stood back.

The rustling of leaves behind him made him turn.

There were two more saplings unfolding. And a third. He looked across the grass and saw a dozen, a hundred tiny trees beginning their race for the sky.

Worried though he was, and he was worried to his boots, Rob Anybody grinned. If there's one thing a Feegle likes, it's knowing that wherever you strike you're going to hit an enemy.

The sun was going down and the shadows were moving and the turf was dying.

Rob *charged*.

Arrrrrrrrgggggggggggghhhhhhhhhhhhh . . .

What happened during the Nac Mac Feegles' search for the right smell was remembered by several witnesses (quite apart from all the owls and bats who were left spinning in the air by a broomstick being navigated by a bunch of screaming little blue men).

One of them was Number 95, a ram owned by a not very imaginative farmer. But all he remembered was a sudden noise in the night and a draughty feeling on his back. That was about as exciting as it got for Number 95, so he went back to thinking about grass.

Arrrrrrrrgggggggggggghhhhhhhhhhhhh . . .

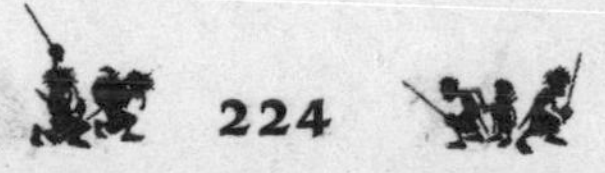

Then there was Mildred Pusher, aged seven, who was the daughter of the farmer who owned Number 95. One day, when she'd grown up and become a grandmother, she told her grandchildren about the night she came downstairs by candlelight for a drink of water and heard the noises under the sink . . .

'And there were these little voices, you see, and one said, "Ach, Wullie, you cannae drink that, look, it says 'Poison!!' on the bottle," and another voice said, "Aye, gonnagle, they put that on tae frighten a man from havin' a wee drink," and the *first* voice said, "Wullie, it's rat poison!" and the second voice said, "That's fine, then, 'cos I'm no' a rat!" And then I opened the cupboard under the sink and, what do you think, it was full of fairies! And they looked at me and I looked at them and one of them said, "Hey, this is a dream you're having, big wee girl!" and immediately they all agreed! And the first one said, "So, in this *dream* ye're having, big wee girl, you wouldna mind telling us where the turpentine is, wouldya?" And so I told them it was outside in the barn, and he said, "Aye? Then we're offski. But here's a wee gift fra' the fairies for a big wee girl who's gonna go right back tae sleep!" And then they were gone!'

One of her grandchildren, who'd been listening with his mouth open, said, 'What did they give you, Grandma?'

'This!' Mildred held up a silver spoon. 'And the

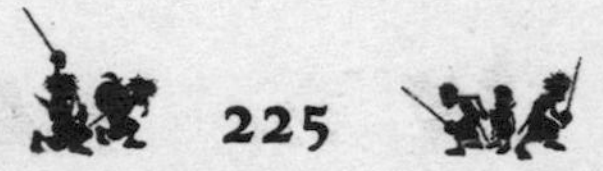

strange thing is, it's just like the ones my mother had, which vanished mysteriously from the drawer the very same night! I've kept it safe ever since!'

This was admired by all. Then one of the grandchildren asked: 'What were the fairies *like*, Grandma?'

Grandma Mildred thought about this. 'Not as pretty as you might expect,' she said at last. 'But definitely more smelly. And just after they'd gone there was a sound like—'

Arrrrrrrrggggggggggghhhhhhhhhhhh . . .

People in the King's Legs (the owner had noticed that there were lots of inns and pubs called the King's Head or the King's Arms, and spotted a gap in the market) looked up when they heard the noise outside.

After a minute or two the door burst open.

'Good night to ye, fellow bigjobs!' roared a figure in the doorway.

The room fell horribly silent. Awkwardly, legs going in every direction, the scarecrow figure wove unsteadily towards the bar and grabbed it thankfully, hanging on as it sagged onto its knees.

'A big huge wee drop o' yer finest whisky, me fine fellow barman fellow,' it said from somewhere under the hat.

'It seems to me that you've already had enough to drink, friend,' said the barman, whose hand had crept to the cudgel he kept under the bar for special customers.

'Who're ye calling "friend", pal?' roared the figure, trying to pull itself up. 'That's fightin' talk, that is! And I havenae had enough to drink, pal, 'cos if I have, why've I still got all this money, eh? Answer me that!'

A hand sagged into a coat pocket, came out jerkily and slammed down onto the top of the bar. Ancient gold coins rolled in every direction and a couple of silver spoons dropped out of the sleeve.

The silence of the bar became a lot deeper. Dozens of eyes watched the shiny discs as they spun off the bar and rolled across the floor.

'An' I want an ounce o' Jolly Sailor baccy,' said the figure.

'Why, certainly, sir,' said the barman, who had been brought up to be respectful to gold coins. He felt under the bar and his expression changed.

'Oh. I'm sorry, sir, we've sold out. Very popular, Jolly Sailor. But we've got plenty of—'

The figure had already turned round to face the rest of the room.

'OK, I'll gi'e a handful o' gold to the first scunner who gi'es me a pipeful o' Jolly Sailor!' it yelled.

The room erupted. Tables scraped. Chairs overturned.

The scarecrow man grabbed the first pipe and threw the coins into the air. As fights immediately broke out, he turned back to the bar and said:

'And I'll ha' that wee drop o' whisky before I go, barman. Ach, no you willnae, Big Yan! *Shame on ye!* Hey, youse legs can shut up right noo! A wee pint of whisky'll do us no harm! Oh, aye? *Who deid and made ye Big Man, eh?* Listen, ye scunner, oor Rob is in there! *Aye, and he'd have a wee drink, too!*'

The customers stopped pushing one another out of the way to get at the coins, and got up to face a whole body arguing with itself.

'Anywa', I'm in the heid, right? The heid's in charge. I dinnae ha' tae listen to a bunch o' knees! *I said this wuz a bad idea, Wullie, ye ken we ha' trouble getting oot of pubs!* Well, speaking on behalf o' the legs, we're not gonna stand by and watch the heid get pished, thank ye so veerae much!'

To the horror of the customers the entire bottom half of the figure turned round and started to walk towards the door, causing the top half to fall forward. It gripped the edge of the bar desperately, managed to say, 'OK! Is a deep-fried pickled egg totally oot o' the question?' and then the figure –

– tore itself in half. The legs staggered a few steps towards the door, and fell over.

In the shocked silence a voice from somewhere in the trousers said: 'Crivens! Time for offski!'

The air blurred for a moment and the door slammed.

After a while one of the customers stepped forward cautiously and prodded the heap of old clothes and sticks that was all that remained of the visitor. The hat rolled off and he jumped back.

A glove that was still hanging onto the bar fell onto the floor with a *thwap!* that sounded very loud.

'Well, look at it this way,' said the barman. 'Whatever it was, at least it's left its pockets—'

From outside came the sound of:

Arrrrrrrrggggggggggghhhhhhhhhhhh . . .

The broomstick hit the thatched roof of Miss Level's cottage hard, and stuck in it. Feegles fell off, still fighting.

In a struggling, punching mass they rolled into the cottage, conducted guerrilla warfare all the way up the stairs and ended up in a head-butting, kicking heap in Tiffany's bedroom, where those who'd been left behind to guard the sleeping girl and Miss Level joined in out of interest.

Gradually, the fighters became aware of a sound. It was the skirl of the mousepipes, cutting through the battle like a sword. Hands stopped gripping throats, fists stopped in mid-punch, kicks hovered in mid-air.

Tears ran down Awf'ly Wee Billy's face as he played *The Bonny Flowers*, the saddest song in the world. It was about home, and mothers, and good times gone past, and faces no longer there. The Feegles let go of one another and stared down at their feet as the forlorn notes wound about them, speaking of betrayal and treachery and the breaking of promises—

'Shame on ye!' screamed Awf'ly Wee Billy, letting the pipe drop out of his mouth. 'Shame on ye! Traitors! Betrayers! Ye shame hearth and hame! Your hag is fightin' for her verra soul! Have ye no honour?' He flung down the mousepipes, which wailed into silence. 'I curse my feets that let me stand here in front o' ye! Ye shame the verra sun shinin' on ye! Ye shame the kelda that birthed ye! Traitors! Scuggans! What ha' I done to be among this parcel o' rogues? Any man here want tae fight? Then fight me! Aye, *fight me!* An' I swear by the harp o' bones I'll tak' him tae the deeps o' the sea an' then kick him tae the craters o' the moon an' see him ride tae the Pit o' Heel itself on a saddle made o' hedgehogs! I tell ye, my rage is the strength of the storm that tears mountains intae sand! Who among ye will stand agin me?'

Big Yan, who was almost three times the size of Awf'ly Wee Billy, cowered back as the little gonnagle stood in front of him. Not a Feegle would have raised a hand at that moment, for fear of his life. The rage of a gonnagle was a dreadful thing to see. A gonnagle could use words like swords.

Daft Wullie shuffled forward.

'I can see ye're upset, gonnagle,' he mumbled. ''Tis me that's at fault, on account o' being daft. I shoulda remembered aboout us and pubs.'

He looked so dejected that Awf'ly Wee Billy calmed down a little.

'Very well then,' he said, but rather coldly because

you can't lose that much anger all at once. 'We'll not talk aboot this again. But we *will* remember it, right?' He pointed to the sleeping shape of Tiffany. 'Now pick up that wool, and the tobacco, and the turpentine, understand? Someone tak' the top off the turpentine bottle and pour a wee drop onto a bit o' cloth. And no one, let me mak' myself clear, is tae drink *any* of it!'

The Feegles fell over themselves to obey. There was a ripping noise as 'the bit o' cloth' was obtained from the bottom of Miss Level's dress.

'Right,' said Awf'ly Wee Billy. 'Daft Wullie, you tak' all the three things and put them up on the big wee hag's chest, where she can smell them.'

'How can she smell them when she's oot cold like that?' said Wullie.

'The nose disnae sleep,' said the gonnagle flatly.

The three smells of the shepherding hut were laid reverentially just below Tiffany's chin.

'Noo we wait,' said Awf'ly Wee Billy. 'We wait, and hope.'

It was hot in the little bedroom with the sleeping witches and a crowd of Feegles. It wasn't long before the smells of sheep's wool, turpentine and tobacco rose and twined and filled the air . . .

Tiffany's nose twitched.

The nose is a big thinker. It's good at memory – very good. So good that a smell can take you back in memory so hard that it hurts. The brain can't stop it.

The brain has nothing to do with it. The hiver could control brains, but it couldn't control a stomach that threw up when it was flown on a broomstick. And it was *useless* at noses . . .

The smell of sheep's wool, turpentine and Jolly Sailor tobacco could carry a mind away, all the way to a silent place that was warm and safe and free from harm . . .

The hiver opened its eyes and looked around.

'The shepherding hut?' it said.

It sat up. Red light shone in through the open door, and through the trunks of the saplings growing everywhere. Many of them were quite big now and cast long shadows, putting the setting sun behind bars. Around the shepherding hut, though, they had been cut down.

'This is a trick,' it said. 'It won't work. We are you. We think like you. We're better at thinking like you than you are.'

Nothing happened.

The hiver looked like Tiffany, although here it was slightly taller because Tiffany thought she was slightly taller than she really was. It stepped out of the hut and onto the turf.

'It's getting late,' it said to the silence. 'Look at the trees! This place is dying. We don't have to escape. Soon all this will be part of us. Everything that you really could be. You're proud of your little piece of ground. We can remember when there were no worlds! We— you could change things with a wave of your hand! You could make things right or make things wrong, and *you* could decide which is which! You will never die!'

'Then why are ye sweatin', ye big heap o' jobbies? Ach, what a scunner!' said a voice behind it.

For a moment the hiver wavered. Its shape changed, many times in the fractions of a second. There were bits of scales, fins, teeth, a pointy hat, claws . . . and then it was Tiffany again, smiling.

'Oh, Rob Anybody, we are glad to see you,' it said. 'Can you help us—?'

'Dinnae gi' me all that swiddle!' shouted Rob, bouncing up and down in rage. 'I know a hiver when I sees one! Crivens but ye're due a kickin'!'

The hiver changed again, became a lion with teeth the size of swords and roared at him.

'Ach, it's like that, is it?' said Rob Anybody. 'Dinnae go awa'!' He ran a few steps and vanished.

The hiver changed back to its Tiffany shape again.

'Your little friend has gone,' it said. 'Come out now. Come out *now*. Why fear us? We *are* you. You won't be like the rest, the dumb animals, the stupid kings, the greedy wizards. Together—'

Rob Anybody returned, followed by . . . well, everyone.

'Ye cannae die,' he yelled. 'But we'll make ye wish ye could!'

They charged.

The Feegles had the advantage in most fights

because they were small and fought big enemies. If you're small and fast you're hard to hit. The hiver fought back by changing shape, all the time. Swords clanged on scales, heads butted fangs – it whirled across the turf, growling and screaming, calling up past shapes to counter every attack. But Feegles were hard to kill. They bounced when thrown, sprang back when trodden on and easily dodged teeth and claws. They fought –

– and the ground shook so suddenly that even the hiver lost its footing.

The shepherding hut creaked and began to settle into the turf, which opened up around it as easily as butter. The saplings trembled and began to fall over, one after the other, as if their roots were being cut under the grass.

The land . . . rose.

Rolling down the shifting slope, the Feegles saw the hills climbing towards the sky. What was there, what had always been there, become more plain.

Rising into the dark sky was a head, shoulders, a chest . . . Someone who had been lying down, growing turf, their arms and legs the hills and valleys of the downland, was sitting up. They moved with great stony slowness, millions of tons of hill shifting and creaking around them. What had looked like two long mounds in the shape of a cross became giant green arms, unfolding.

A hand with fingers longer than houses reached down, picked up the hiver and lifted it up into the air.

Far off, something thumped three times. The sound seemed to be coming from outside the world. The Feegles, turning and watching from the small hill that was one of the knees of the giant girl, ignored them.

'She tells the land whut it is, and it tells her who she is,' said Awf'ly Wee Billy, tears running down his face. 'I cannae write a song aboot this! I'm nae good enough!'

'Is that the big wee hag dreamin' she's the hills or the hills dreamin' they're the big wee hag?' said Daft Wullie.

'Both, mebbe,' said Rob Anybody. They watched the huge hand close and winced.

'But ye cannae kill a hiver,' said Daft Wullie.

'Aye, but ye can frit it awa',' said Rob Anybody. 'It's a big wee universe oot there. If I was it, I'd no' think o' tryin' *her* again!'

There were three more booms in the distance, louder this time.

'I think,' he went on, 'that's it's time we were offski.'

In Miss Level's cottage, someone was knocking heavily on the front door. *Thump. Thump. Thump.*

Chapter 9

Soul and Centre

Tiffany opened her eyes, remembered, and thought: Was that a dream, or was that real?

And the next thought was: How do I know I'm me? Suppose I'm not me but just think I'm me? How can I tell if I'm me or not? Who's the 'me' that's asking the question? Am I thinking these thoughts? How would I know if it wasn't?

'Dinnae ask me,' said a voice by her head. 'Is this one of them tricksie ones?'

It was Daft Wullie. He was sitting on her pillow.

Tiffany squinted down. She was in bed in Miss Level's cottage. A green quilt stretched out in front of her. A quilt. Green. Not turf, not hills . . . but it looked like the downland, from here.

'Did I say all that aloud?' she asked.

'Oh, aye.'

'Er . . . it did all happen, didn't it?' said Tiffany.

'Oh, aye,' said Daft Wullie cheerfully. 'The big hag

wuz up here till just noo, but she said ye probably wasnae gonna wake up a monster.'

More bits of memory landed in Tiffany's memory like red-hot rocks landing on a peaceful planet.

'Are you all right?'

'Oh, aye,' said Daft Wullie.

'And Miss Level?'

And this rock of memory was huge, a flaming mountain that'd make a million dinosaurs flee for their lives. Tiffany's hands flew to her mouth.

'I killed her!' she said.

'Noo, then, ye didnae—'

'I did! I felt my mind thinking it. She made me angry! I just waved my hand like this' – a dozen Nac Mac Feegle dived for cover – 'and she just exploded into nothing! It was *me*! I remember!'

'Aye, but the big hag o' hags said it wuz usin' your mind tae think with—' Daft Wullie began.

'I've got the memories! It was *me*, with this hand!' The Feegles who had raised their heads ducked back down again. 'And . . . the memories I've got . . . I remember dust, turning into stars . . . things . . . the heat . . . blood . . . the taste of blood . . . I remember . . . I remember the see-me trick! Oh, no! I practically *invited* it in! I killed Miss Level!'

Shadows were closing in around her vision, and there was a ringing in her ears. Tiffany heard the door swing open and hands picked her up as though she was as light as a bubble. She was slung over a shoulder and carried swiftly down the stairs and out into the bright morning, where she was swung down onto the ground.

'. . . And all of us . . . we killed her . . . take one crucible of silver . . .' she mumbled.

A hand slapped her sharply across the face. She stared through inner mists at the tall dark figure in front of her. A bucket handle was pressed firmly into her hand.

'Milk the goats now, Tiffany! Now, Tiffany, d'you hear! The trusting creatures look to you! They wait for you! Tiffany milks the goats. Do it, Tiffany! The hands know how, the mind *will* remember and grow stronger, Tiffany!'

She was thrust down onto the milking stool and, through the mist in her head, made out the cowering shape of . . . of . . . Black Meg.

The hands remembered. They placed the pail, grasped a teat and then, as Meg raised a leg to play the foot-in-the-bucket game, grabbed it and forced it safely back down onto the milking platform.

She worked slowly, her head full of hot fog, letting her hands have their way. Buckets were filled and emptied, milked goats got a bucket of feed from the bin . . .

Sensibility Bustle was rather puzzled that his hands were milking a goat. He stopped.

'What is your name?' said a voice behind him.

'Bustle. Sensibil—'

'No! That was the wizard, Tiffany! He was the

strongest echo, but you're not him! Get into the dairy, TIFFANY!'

She stumbled into the cool room under the command of that voice and the world focused. There was a foul cheese on the slab, sweating and stinking.

'Who put this here?' she asked.

'The hiver did, Tiffany. Tried to make a cheese by magic, Tiffany. Hah!' said the voice. 'And you are not it, Tiffany! You *know* how to make cheese the right way, don't you, Tiffany? Indeed you do! What is your name?'

. . . all was confusion and strange smells. In panic, she roared—

Her face was slapped again.

'No, that was the sabre-toothed tiger, Tiffany! They're all just old memories the hiver left behind, Tiffany! It's worn a lot of creatures but they are not you! Come forward, Tiffany!'

She heard the words without really understanding them. They were just out there somewhere, between people who were just shadows. But it was unthinkable to disobey them.

'Drat!' said the hazy tall figure. 'Where's that little blue feller? Mister Anyone?'

'Here, mistress. It's Rob Anybody, mistress. I beg o' ye not tae turn me intae somethin' unnatural, mistress!'

'You said she had a box of keepsakes. Fetch it down here this minute. I feared this might happen. I *hates* doin' it this way!'

Tiffany was turned round and once again looked into the blurry face while strong hands gripped her arms. Two blue eyes stared into hers. They shone in the mist like sapphires.

'What's your name, Tiffany?' said the voice.

'Tiffany!'

The eyes bored into her. 'Is it? Really? Sing me the first song you ever learned, Tiffany! *Now!*'

'Hzan, hzana, m'taza—'

'Stop! That was never learned on a chalk hill! You ain't Tiffany! I reckon you're that desert queen who killed twelve of her husbands with scorpion sandwiches! Tiffany is the one I'm after! Back into the dark with you!'

Things went blurry again. She could hear whispered discussions through the fog and the voice said: 'Well, that might work. What's your name, pictsie?'

'Awf'ly Wee Billy Bigchin Mac Feegle, mistress.'

'You're *very* small, aren't you?'

'Only for my height, mistress.'

The grip tightened on Tiffany's arms again. The blue eyes glinted.

'What does your name mean in the Old Speech of the Nac Mac Feegle, Tiffany? Think . . .'

It rose from the depths of her mind, trailing the fog behind it. It came up through the clamouring voices and lifted her beyond the reach of ghostly hands. Ahead, the clouds parted.

'My name is Land Under Wave,' said Tiffany and slumped forward.

'No, no, none of that, we can't have that,' said the figure holding her. 'You've slept enough. Good, you know who you are! Now you must be up and doing! You must be Tiffany as hard as you may, and the other voices *will* leave you alone, depend on it. Although it might be a good idea if you don't make sandwiches for a while.'

She did feel better. She'd said her name. The clamouring in her head had calmed down, although it was still a chatter that made it hard to think straight. But now at least she could see clearly. The black-dressed figure holding her wasn't tall, but she was so good at acting as if she was that it tended to fool most people.

'Oh . . . you're . . . *Mistress Weatherwax?*'

Mistress Weatherwax pushed her down gently into a chair. From every flat surface in the kitchen, the Nac Mac Feegles watched Tiffany.

'I am. And a fine mess we have here. Rest for a moment and then we must be up and doing—'

'Good morning, ladies. Er, how is she?'

Tiffany turned her head. Miss Level stood in the door. She looked pale and she was walking with a stick.

'I was lying in bed and I thought, Well, there's no reason to stay up here feeling sorry for myself,' she said.

Tiffany stood up. 'I'm so sor—' she began, but Miss Level waved a hand vaguely.

'Not your fault,' she said, sitting down heavily at

the table. 'How are you? And, for that matter, *who* are you?'

Tiffany blushed. 'Still me, I think,' she mumbled.

'I got here last night and saw to Miss Level,' said Mistress Weatherwax. 'Watched over you, too, girl. You talked in your sleep or, rather, Sensibility Bustle did, what's left of him. That ol' wizard was quite helpful, for something that's nothing much more'n a bunch of memories and habits.'

'I don't understand about the wizard,' said Tiffany. 'Or the desert queen.'

'Don't you?' said the witch. 'Well, a hiver collects people. Tries to add them to itself, you might say, use them to think with. Dr Bustle was studying them hundreds of years ago, and set a trap to catch one. It got him instead, silly fool. It killed him in the end. It gets 'em all killed in the end. They go mad, one way or the other, they stop remembering what they shouldn't do. But it keeps a sort of . . . pale copy of them, a sort of living memory . . .' She looked at Tiffany's puzzled expression and shrugged. 'Something like a ghost,' she said.

'And it's left *ghosts* in my head?'

'More like ghosts of ghosts, really,' said Mistress Weatherwax. 'Something we don't have a word for, maybe.'

Miss Level shuddered. 'Well, thank goodness you've got rid of the thing, at least,' she quavered. 'Would anyone like a nice cup of tea?'

'Ach, leave that tae us!' shouted Rob Anybody, leaping up. 'Daft Wullie, you an' the boys mak' some tea for the ladies!'

'Thank you,' said Miss Level weakly, as a clattering began behind her. 'I feel so clum— *what?* I thought you broke all the teacups when you did the washing up!'

'Oh, aye,' said Rob cheerfully. 'But Wullie found a whole load o' old ones shut awa' in a cupboard—'

'That very valuable bone china was left to me by a very dear friend!' shouted Miss Level. She sprang to her feet and turned towards the sink. With amazing speed for someone who was partly dead she snatched teapot, cup and saucer from the surprised pictsies and held them up as high as she could.

'Crivens!' said Rob Anybody, staring at the crockery. 'Now that's what I call hagglin'!'

'I'm sorry to be rude, but they're of great sentimental value!' said Miss Level.

'Mister Anybody, you and your men will kindly get away from Miss Level and *shut up*!' said Mistress Weatherwax quickly. 'Pray do not disturb Miss Level while she's making tea!'

'But she's holding—' Tiffany began, in amazement.

'And let her get on with it without your chatter either, girl!' the witch snapped.

'Aye, but she picked up yon teapot wi'oot—' a voice began.

The old witch's head spun round. Feegles backed away like trees bending to a gale.

'Daft William,' she said coldly, 'there's room in my well for one more frog, except that you don't have the brains of one!'

'Ahahaha, that's wholly correct, mistress,' said Daft Wullie, sticking out his chin with pride. 'I fooled you there! I ha' the brains o' a beetle!'

Mistress Weatherwax glared at him, then turned back to Tiffany.

'*I* turned someone into a frog!' Tiffany said. 'It was dreadful! He didn't all fit in so there was this sort of huge pink—'

'Never mind that right now,' said Mistress Weatherwax in a voice that was suddenly so nice and ordinary that it tinkled like a bell. 'I expect you finds things a bit different here than they were at home, eh?'

'What? Well, yes, at home I never turned—' Tiffany began in surprise, then saw that just above her lap the old woman was making frantic circular hand motions that somehow meant *Keep going as if nothing has happened.*

So they chatted madly about sheep and Mistress Weatherwax said they were very woolly, weren't they, and Tiffany said that they were, extremely so, and Mistress Weatherwax said extremely woolly was what she'd heard . . . while every eye in the room watched Miss Level –

– making tea using four arms, two of which did not exist, and not realizing it.

The black kettle sailed across the room and

apparently tipped itself into the pot. Cups and saucers and spoons and the sugar bowl floated with a purpose.

Mistress Weatherwax leaned across to Tiffany.

'I hope you're still feeling . . . alone?' she whispered.

'Yes, thank you. I mean, I can . . . sort of . . . feel them there, but they're not getting in the way . . . er . . . sooner or later she's going to realize . . . I mean, isn't she?'

'Very funny thing, the human mind,' whispered the old woman. 'I once had to see to a poor young man who had a tree fall on his legs. Lost both legs from the knee down. Had to have wooden legs made. Still, they were made out of that tree, which I suppose was some comfort, and he gets about pretty well. But I remember him saying, "Mistress Weatherwax, I can still feel my toes sometimes." It's like the head don't accept what's happened. And it's not like she's . . . your everyday kind of person to start with, I mean, she's used to havin' arms she can't see—'

'Here we are,' said Miss Level, bustling over with three cups and saucers and the sugar bowl. 'One for you, one for you, and one for— Oh . . .'

The sugar bowl dropped from an invisible hand and spilled its sugar onto the table. Miss Level stared at it in horror while, in the other hand that wasn't there, a cup and saucer wobbled without visible means of support.

'Shut your eyes, Miss Level!' And there was something in the voice, some edge or strange tone that made Tiffany shut her eyes too.

'Right! Now, you *know* the cup's there, you can *feel* your arm,' said Mistress Weatherwax, standing up. 'Trust it! Your eyes are not in possession of all the facts! Now put the cup down gently . . . thaaat's right. You can open your eyes now, but what I wants you to do, right, as a favour to me, is *put the hands that you can see flat down on the table*. Right. Good. Now, without takin' those hands away, just go over to the dresser and fetch me that blue biscuit tin, will you? I'm always partial to a biscuit with my tea. Thank you very much.'

'But . . . but I can't do that now—'

'Get past "I can't", Miss Level,' Mistress Weatherwax snapped. 'Don't think about it, just do it! My tea's getting cold!'

So *this* is witchcraft too, Tiffany thought. It's like Granny Aching talking to animals. It's in the voice! Sharp and soft by turns, and you use little words of command and encouragement and you *keep* talking, making the words fill the creature's world, so that the sheepdogs obey you and the nervous sheep are calmed . . .

The biscuit tin floated away from the dresser. As it neared the old woman the lid unscrewed and hovered in the air beside it. She reached in delicately.

'Ooh, store-bought Teatime Assortment,' she said,

taking four biscuits and quickly putting three of them in her pocket. 'Very posh.'

'It's terribly difficult to do this!' Miss Level moaned. 'It's like trying not to think of a pink rhinoceros!'

'Well?' said Mistress Weatherwax. 'What's so special about not thinking of a pink rhinoceros?'

'It's impossible not to think of one if someone tells you you mustn't,' Tiffany explained.

'No it ain't,' said Mistress Weatherwax, firmly. 'I ain't thinking of one right now, and I gives you my word on that. You want to take control of that brain of yours, Miss Level. So you've lost a spare body? What's another body when all's said and done? Just a lot of upkeep, another mouth to feed, wear and tear on the furniture . . . in a word, *fuss*. Get your mind right, Miss Level, and the world is your . . .' The old witch leaned down to Tiffany and whispered: 'What's that thing, lives in the sea, very small, folks eat it?'

'Shrimp?' Tiffany suggested, a bit puzzled.

'Shrimp? All right. The world is your shrimp, Miss Level. Not only will there be a great saving on clothes and food, which is not to be sneezed at in these difficult times, but when people see you moving things though the air, well, they'll say, "There's a witch and a half, and no mistake!" and they will be right. You just hold on to that skill, Miss Level. You maintain. Think on what I've said. And now you stay and rest. We'll see to what needs doing today. You just make a little list for me, and Tiffany'll know the way.'

'Well, indeed, I do feel . . . somewhat shaken,' said Miss Level, absent-mindedly brushing her hair out of her eyes with an invisible hand. 'Let me see . . . you could just drop in on Mr Umbril, and Mistress Turvy, and the young Raddle boy, and check on Mrs Towney's bruise, and take some Number Five ointment to Mr Drover, and pay a call on old Mrs Hunter at Saucy Corner and . . . now, who have I forgotten . . . ?'

Tiffany realized she was holding her breath. It had been a horrible day, and a dreadful night, but what was looming and queuing up for its place on Miss Level's tongue was, somehow, going to be worse than either.

'. . . Ah, yes, have a word with Miss Quickly at Uttercliff, and then probably you'll need to talk to Mrs Quickly, too, and there're a few packages to be dropped off on the way, they're in my basket, all marked up. And I think that's it . . . oh, no, silly me, I almost forgot . . . and you need to drop in on Mr Weavall, too.'

Tiffany breathed out. She really didn't want to. She'd rather not breathe ever again than face Mr Weavall and open an empty box.

'Are you sure you're . . . totally yourself, Tiffany?' said Miss Level, and Tiffany leaped for this lifesaving excuse not to go.

'Well, I do feel a bit—' she began, but Mistress Weatherwax interrupted with, 'She's fine, Miss

Level, apart from the echoes. The hiver has gone away from this house, I can assure you.'

'Really?' said Miss Level. 'I don't mean to be rude, but how can you be so certain?'

Mistress Weatherwax pointed down.

Grain by grain, the spilled sugar was rolling across the tabletop and leaping into the sugar bowl.

Miss Level clasped her hands together.

'Oh, *Oswald,'* she said, her face one huge smile, 'you've come back!'

Miss Level, and possibly Oswald, watched them go from the gate.

'She'll be fine with your little men keeping her company,' said Mistress Weatherwax as she and Tiffany turned away and took the lane through the woods. 'It could be the making of her, you know, being half dead.'

Tiffany was shocked. 'How can you be so cruel?'

'She'll get some respect when people see her moving stuff through the air. Respect is meat and drink to a witch. Without respect, you ain't got a thing. She doesn't get much respect, our Miss Level.'

That was true. People didn't respect Miss Level. They liked her, in an unthinking sort of way, and that was it. Mistress Weatherwax was right, and Tiffany wished she wasn't.

'Why did you and Miss Tick send me to her, then?' she said.

'Because she likes people,' said the witch, striding

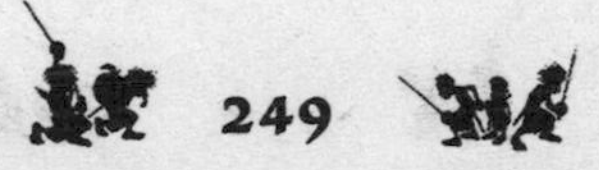

ahead. 'She cares about 'em. Even the stupid, mean, dribbling ones, the mothers with the runny babies and no sense, the feckless and the silly and the fools who treat her like some kind of a servant. Now *that's* what *I* call magic – seein' all that, dealin' with all that, and still goin' on. It's sittin' up all night with some poor old man who's leavin' the world, taking away such pain as you can, comfortin' their terror, seein' 'em safely on their way . . . and then cleanin' 'em up, layin' 'em out, making 'em neat for the funeral, and helpin' the weeping widow strip the bed and wash the sheets – which is, let me tell you, no errand for the faint-hearted – and stayin' up the *next* night to watch over the coffin before the funeral, and then going home and sitting down for five minutes before some shouting *angry* man comes bangin' on your door 'cos his wife's havin' difficulty givin' birth to their first child and the midwife's at her wits' end and then getting up and fetching your bag and going out again . . . We all do that, in our own way, and she does it better'n me, if I was to put my hand on my heart. *That* is the root and heart and soul and centre of witchcraft, that is. The soul and centre!' Mistress Weatherwax smacked her fist into her hand, hammering out her words. 'The . . . soul . . . and . . . *centre*!'

Echoes came back from the trees in the sudden silence. Even the grasshoppers by the side of the track had stopped sizzling.

'And Mrs Earwig,' said Mistress Weatherwax, her

voice sinking to a growl, '*Mrs Earwig* tells her girls it's about cosmic balances and stars and circles and colours and wands and . . . and *toys*, nothing but toys!' She sniffed. 'Oh, I daresay they're all very well as *decoration*, somethin' nice to look at while you're workin', somethin' for show, but the start and finish, *the start and finish*, is helpin' people when life is on the edge. Even people you don't like. Stars is easy, people is hard.'

She stopped talking. It was several seconds before birds began to sing again.

'Anyway, that's what I think,' she added in the tone of someone who suspects that they might have gone just a bit further than they meant to.

She turned round when Tiffany said nothing, and saw that she had stopped and was standing in the lane looking like a drowned hen.

'Are you all right, girl?' she said.

'It was me!' wailed Tiffany. 'The hiver *was* me! It wasn't thinking with my brain, it was using my thoughts! It was using what it found in my head! All those insults, all that . . .' She gulped. 'That . . . nastiness. All it was was me with—'

'– *without* the bit of you that was locked away,' said Mistress Weatherwax sharply. 'Remember that.'

'Yes, but supposing—' Tiffany began, struggling to get all the woe out.

'The locked-up bit was the important bit,' said Mistress Weatherwax. 'Learnin' how not to do things is as hard as learning *how* to do them. Harder, maybe.

There'd be a sight more frogs in this world if I didn't know how *not* to turn people into them. And big pink balloons, too.'

'Don't,' said Tiffany, shuddering.

'That's why we do all the tramping around and doctorin' and stuff,' said Mistress Weatherwax. 'Well, and because it makes people a bit better, of course. But doing it moves you into your centre, so's you don't wobble. It anchors you. Keeps you human, stops you cackling. Just like your granny with her sheep, which are to my mind as stupid and wayward and ungrateful as humans. You think you've had a sight of yourself and found out you're bad? Hah! I've seen bad, and you don't get near it. Now, are you going to stop grizzling?'

'What?' snapped Tiffany.

Mistress Weatherwax laughed, to Tiffany's sudden fury.

'Yes, you're a witch to your boots,' she said. 'You're sad, and behind that you're watching yourself being sad and thinking, Oh, poor me, and behind *that* you're angry with *me* for not going "There, there, poor dear." Let me talk to those Third Thoughts then, because I want to hear from the girl who went to fight a fairy queen armed with nothin' but a fryin' pan, not some child feelin' sorry for herself and wallowing in misery!'

'What? I am *not* wallowing in misery!' Tiffany shouted, striding up to her until they were inches apart. 'And what was all that about being nice to people, eh?' Overhead, leaves fell off the trees.

'That doesn't count when it's another witch, especially one like you!' Mistress Weatherwax snapped, prodding her in the chest with a finger as hard as wood.

'Oh? Oh? And what's that supposed to mean?' A deer galloped off through the woods. The wind got up.

'One who's not paying attention, child!'

'Why, what have I missed that *you've* seen . . . old woman?'

'Old woman I may be, but I'm tellin' you the hiver is still around! You only threw it out!' Mistress Weatherwax shouted. Birds rose from the trees in panic.

'I know!' screamed Tiffany.

'Oh yes? Really? And how do you know that?'

'Because there's a bit of me still in it! A bit of me I'd rather not know about, thank you! I can *feel* it out there! Anyway, how do *you* know!'

'Because I'm a bloody good witch, that's why,' snarled Mistress Weatherwax, as rabbits burrowed deeper to get out of the way. 'And what do you want me to do about the creature while you sit there snivellin', eh?'

'How dare you! How *dare* you! It's my responsibility! I'll deal with it, thank you so very much!'

'You? A hiver? It'll take more than a frying pan! They can't be killed!'

'I'll find a way! A witch deals with things!'

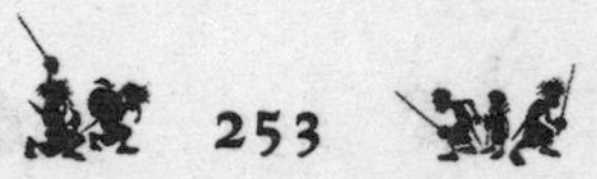

'Hah! I'd like to see you try!'

'I will!' shouted Tiffany. It started to rain.

'Oh? So you know how to attack it, do you?'

'Don't be silly! I can't! It can always keep out of my way! It can even sink into the ground! But it'll come looking for me, understand? *Me*, not anyone else! I *know* it! And this time I'll be ready!'

'Will you, indeed?' said Mistress Weatherwax, folding her arms.

'Yes!'

'*When?*'

'Now!'

'No!'

The old witch held up a hand.

'Peace be on this place,' she said, quietly. The wind dropped. The rain stopped. 'No, not yet,' she went on as peace once again descended. 'It's not attackin' yet. Don't you think that's odd? It'd be licking its wounds, if it had a tongue. And you're not ready yet, whatever you thinks. No, we've got somethin' else to do, haven't we?'

Tiffany was speechless. The tide of outrage inside her was so hot that it burned her ears. But Mistress Weatherwax was smiling. The two facts did not work well together.

Her first thoughts were: I've just had a blazing row with Mistress Weatherwax! They say that if you cut her with a knife she wouldn't bleed until she wanted to! They say that when some vampires bit *her* they all started to crave tea and sweet biscuits. She can do anything, be anywhere! And I called her an old woman!

Her Second Thoughts were: Well, she is.

Her Third Thoughts were: Yes, she *is* Mistress Weatherwax. And she's keeping you angry. If you're full of anger, there's no room left for fear.

'You hold that anger,' Mistress Weatherwax said, as if reading all of her mind. 'Cup it in your heart, remember where it came from, remember the shape of it, save it until you need it. But now the wolf is out there somewhere in the woods, and you need to see to the flock.'

It's the voice, Tiffany thought. She really does talk to people like Granny Aching talked to sheep, except she hardly cusses at all. But I feel . . . better.

'Thank you,' she said.

'And that includes Mr Weavall.'

'Yes,' said Tiffany. 'I know.'

Chapter 10

The Late Bloomer

It was an . . . interesting day. *Everyone* in the mountains had heard of Mistress Weatherwax. If you didn't have respect, she said, you didn't have anything. Today, she had it all. Some of it even rubbed off on Tiffany.

They were treated like royalty – not the sort who get dragged off to be beheaded or have something nasty done with a red-hot poker, but the other sort, when people walk away dazed, saying, 'She actually said hello to me, very graciously! I will never wash my hand again!'

Not that many people they dealt with washed their hands at all, Tiffany thought, with the primness of a dairy worker. But people crowded around outside the cottage doors, watching and listening, and people sidled up to Tiffany to say things like, 'Would she like a cup of tea? I've cleaned our cup!' And in the garden of every cottage they passed, Tiffany noticed, the beehives were suddenly bustling with activity.

She worked away, trying to stay calm, trying to think about what she was doing. You did the doctoring work as neatly as you could, and if it was on something oozy then you just thought about how nice things would be when you'd stopped doing it. She felt Mistress Weatherwax wouldn't approve of this attitude. But Tiffany didn't much like hers either. She lied all the— she *didn't tell the truth* all the time.

For example, there was the Raddles' privy. Miss Level had explained carefully to Mr and Mrs Raddle several times that it was far too close to the well, and so the drinking water was full of tiny, tiny creatures that were making their children sick. They'd listened very carefully, every time they heard the lecture, and still they never moved the privy. But Mistress Weatherwax told them it was caused by goblins who were attracted to the smell, and by the time they left that cottage Mr Raddle and three of his friends were already digging a new well the other end of the garden.

'It really *is* caused by tiny creatures, you know,' said Tiffany, who'd once handed over an egg to a travelling teacher so she could line up and look through his **'**Astounding Mikroscopical Device! A Zoo in Every Drop of Ditchwater!**'** She'd almost collapsed next day from not drinking. Some of those creatures were *hairy*.

'Is that so?' said Mistress Weatherwax sarcastically.

'Yes. It is. And Miss Level believes in telling them the truth!'

'Good. She's a fine, honest woman,' said Mistress Weatherwax. 'But what I say is, you have to tell people a story they can understand. Right now I reckon you'd have to change quite a lot of the world, and maybe bang Mr Raddle's stupid fat head against the wall a few times, before he'd believe that you can be sickened by drinking tiny invisible beasts. And while you're doing that, those kids of theirs will get sicker. But goblins, now, they makes sense *today*. A story gets things done. And when I see Miss Tick tomorrow I'll tell her it's about time them wandering teachers started coming up here.'

'All right,' said Tiffany reluctantly, 'but you told Mr Umbril the shoemaker that his chest pains will clear up if he walks to the waterfall at Tumble Crag every day for a month and throws three shiny pebbles into the pool for the water sprites! That's not doctoring!'

'No, but he thinks it is. The man spends too much time sitting hunched up. A five-mile walk in the fresh air every day for a month will see him as right as rain,' said Mistress Weatherwax.

'Oh,' said Tiffany. 'Another story?'

'If you like,' said Mistress Weatherwax, her eyes twinkling. 'And you never know, maybe the water sprites will be grateful for the pebbles.'

She glanced sidelong at Tiffany's expression, and patted her on the shoulder.

'Never mind, miss,' she said. 'Look at it this way. Tomorrow, your job is to change the world into a better place. Today, my job is to see that everyone gets there.'

'Well, I think—' Tiffany began, then stopped. She looked up at the line of woods between the small fields of the valleys and the steep meadows of the mountains.

'It's still there,' she said.

'I know,' said Mistress Weatherwax.

'It's moving around but it's keeping away from us.'

'I know,' said Mistress Weatherwax.

'What does it think it's doing?'

'It's got a bit of you in it. What do *you* think it's doing?'

Tiffany tried to think. Why wouldn't it attack? Oh, she'd be better prepared this time, but it was strong.

'Maybe it's waiting until I'm upset again,' she said. 'But I keep having a thought. It makes no sense. I keep thinking about . . . three wishes.'

'Wishes for what?'

'I don't know. It sounds silly.'

Mistress Weatherwax stopped. 'No, it's not,' she said. 'It's a deep part of you trying to send yourself a message. Just remember it. Because now—'

Tiffany sighed. 'Yes, I know. Mr Weavall.'

No dragon's cave was ever approached as carefully as the cottage in the overgrown garden.

Tiffany paused at the gate and looked back, but Mistress Weatherwax had diplomatically vanished. Probably she's found someone to give her a cup of tea and a sweet biscuit, she thought. She lives on them!

She opened the gate and walked up the path.

You couldn't say: It's not my fault. You couldn't say: It's not my responsibility.

You could say: I will deal with this.

You didn't have to want to. But you had to do it.

Tiffany took a deep breath and stepped into the dark cottage.

Mr Weavall, in his chair, was just inside the door and fast asleep, showing the world an open mouth full of yellow teeth.

'Um . . . hello, Mr Weavall,' Tiffany quavered, but perhaps not quite loud enough. 'Just, er, here to see that you, that everything is . . . is all right . . .'

There was a snort nonetheless, and he woke, smacking his lips to get the sleep out of his mouth.

'Oh, 'tis you,' he said. 'Good afternoon to ye.' He eased himself more upright and started to stare out of the doorway, ignoring her.

Maybe he won't ask, she thought as she washed up and dusted and plumped the cushions and, not to put too fine a point on it, emptied the commode. But she nearly yelped when the arm shot out and grabbed her wrist and the old man gave her his pleading look.

'Just check the box, Mary, will you? Before you go? Only I heard clinking noises last night, see. Could be one o' the sneaky thieves got in.'

'Yes, Mr Weavall,' said Tiffany, while she thought:

Idon'twanttobehereIdon'twanttobehere!

She pulled out the box. There was no choice.

It felt heavy. She stood up and lifted the lid.

After the creak of the hinges, there was silence.

'Are you all right, gel?' said Mr Weavall.

'Um . . .' said Tiffany.

'It's all there, ain't it?' said the old man anxiously.

Tiffany's mind was a puddle of goo.

'Um . . . it's all here,' she managed. 'Um . . . and now it's all *gold*, Mr Weavall.'

'Gold? Hah! Don't you pull my leg, gel. No gold ever came my way!'

Tiffany put the box on the old man's lap, as gently as she could, and he stared into it.

Tiffany recognized the worn coins. The pictsies ate off them in the mound. There had been pictures on them, but they were too worn to make out now.

But gold was gold, pictures or not.

She turned her head sharply and was certain she saw something small and red-headed vanish into the shadows.

'Well now,' said Mr Weavall. 'Well now.' And that seemed to exhaust his conversation for a while. Then he said, 'Far too much money here to pay for a buryin'. I don't recall savin' all this. I reckon you could bury a *king* for this amount of money.'

Tiffany swallowed. She couldn't leave things like this. She just couldn't.

'Mr Weavall, I've got something I must tell you,' she said. And she told him. She told him all of it, not just the good bits. He sat and listened carefully.

'Well, now, isn't that interesting,' he said when she'd finished.

'Um . . . I'm sorry,' said Tiffany. She couldn't think of anything else to say.

'So what you're *saying*, right, is 'cos that creature made you take my burying money, right, you think these fairy friends o' yourn filled my ol' box with gold so's you wouldn't get into trouble, right?'

'I think so,' said Tiffany.

'Well, it looks like I should thank you, then,' said Mr Weavall.

'What?'

'Well, it seems to I, if you hadn't ha' took the silver and copper, there wouldn't have been any room for all this gold, right?' said Mr Weavall. 'And I shouldn't reckon that ol' dead king up on yon hills needs it now.'

'Yes, but—'

Mr Weavall fumbled in the box and held up a gold coin that would have bought his cottage.

'A little something for you, then, girl,' he said. 'Buy yourself some ribbons or something . . .'

'No! I can't! That wouldn't be fair!' Tiffany protested, desperately. This was *completely* going wrong!

'Wouldn't it, now?' said Mr Weavall, and his bright eyes gave her a long, shrewd look. 'Well, then, let's call it payment for this little errand you're gonna run for I, eh? You're gonna run up they stairs, which I can't quite manage any more, and bring down the black suit that's hanging behind the door, and there's a clean shirt in the chest at the end of the bed. And you'll polish my boots and help I up, but I'm thinking I could prob'ly make it down the lane on my own. 'Cos, y'see, this is far too much money to buy a man's funeral, but I reckon it'll do fine to marry him off, so I am proposin' to propose to the Widow Tussy that she engages in matrimony with I!'

The last sentence took a little working out, and then Tiffany said, 'You *are*?'

'That I am,' said Mr Weavall, struggling to his feet. 'She's a fine woman who bakes a very reasonable steak-and-onion pie and she has all her own teeth. I know that because she showed I. Her youngest son got her a set of fancy store-bought teeth all the way from the big city, and very handsome she looks in 'em. She was kind enough to loan 'em to I one day when I had a difficult piece of pork to tackle, and a man doesn't forget a kindness like that.'

'Er . . . you don't think you ought to think about this, do you?' said Tiffany.

Mr Weavall laughed. 'Think? I got no business to be *thinking* about it, young lady! Who're you to tell me an old 'un like I that he ought to be thinking? I'm ninety-one, I am! Got to be up and doing! Besides, I have reason to believe by the twinkle in her eye that the Widow Tussy will not turn up her nose at my suggestion. I've seen a fair number of twinkles over the years, and that was a good'un. And I daresay that suddenly having a box of gold will fill in the corners, as my ol' dad would say.'

It took ten minutes for Mr Weavall to get changed, with a lot of struggling and bad language and no help from Tiffany, who was told to turn her back and put her hands over her ears. Then she had to help him out into the garden, where he threw away one walking stick and waggled a finger at the weeds.

'And I'll be chopping down the lot of you to-morrow!' he shouted triumphantly.

At the garden gate he grasped the post and pulled himself nearly vertical, panting.

'All right,' he said, just a little anxiously. 'It's now or never. I look OK, does I?'

'You look fine, Mr Weavall.'

'Everything clean? Everything done up?'

'Er . . . yes,' said Tiffany.

'How's my hair look?'

'Er . . . you don't have any, Mr Weavall,' she reminded him.

'Ah, right. Yes, 'tis true. I'll have to buy one o' the whatdyoucallem's, like a hat made of hair? Have I got enough money for that, d'you think?'

'A wig? You could buy thousands, Mr Weavall!'

'Hah! Right.' His gleaming eyes looked around the garden. 'Any flowers out? Can't see too well . . . Ah . . . speckatickles, I saw 'em once, made of glass, makes you see good as new. That's what I need . . . have I got enough for speckatickles?'

'Mr Weavall,' said Tiffany, 'you've got enough for *anything*.'

'Why, bless you!' said Mr Weavall. 'But right now I need a bow-kwet of flowers, girl. Can't go courtin' without flowers and I can't see none. Anythin' left?'

A few roses were hanging on among the weeds and briars in the garden. Tiffany fetched a knife from the kitchen and made them up into a bouquet.

'Ah, good,' he said. 'Late bloomers, just like I!' He held them tightly in his free hand, then suddenly frowned, fell silent and stood like a statue

'I wish my Toby and my Mary was goin' to be able to come to the weddin',' he said quietly. 'But they're dead, you know.'

'Yes,' said Tiffany. 'I know, Mr Weavall.'

'And I could wish that my Nancy was alive, too, although bein' as I hopes to be marryin' another lady that ain't a sensible wish, maybe. Hah! Nearly everyone I knows is dead.' Mr Weavall stared at the bunch of flowers for a while, and then straightened up again. 'Still, can't do nothin' about that, can we? Not even for a box full of gold!'

'No, Mr Weavall," said Tiffany hoarsely.

'Oh, don't cry, gel! The sun is shinin', the birds is singin' and what's past can't be mended, eh?' said Mr Weavall jovially. 'And the Widow Tussy is waitin'!'

For a moment he looked panicky, and then he cleared his throat.

'Don't *smell* too bad, do I?' he said.

'Er . . . only of mothballs, Mr Weavall.'

'Mothballs? Mothballs is OK. Right, then! Time's a wastin'!'

Using only the one stick, waving his other arm with the flowers in the air to keep his balance, Mr Weavall set off with surprising speed.

'Well,' said Mistress Weatherwax as, with jacket flying, he rounded the corner. 'That was nice, wasn't it?'

Tiffany looked around quickly. Mistress Weatherwax was still nowhere to be seen, but she was somewhere to be unseen. Tiffany squinted at what was definitely an old wall with some ivy growing up it, and it was only when the old witch moved that she spotted her. She hadn't done anything to her clothes, hadn't done any magic as far as Tiffany knew, but she'd simply . . . faded in.

'Er, yes,' said Tiffany, taking out a handkerchief and blowing her nose.

'But it worries you,' said the witch. 'You think it *shouldn't* have ended like that, right?'

'No!' said Tiffany hotly.

'It would have been better if he'd been buried in some ol' cheap coffin paid for by the village, you think?'

'*No!*' Tiffany twisted up her fingers. Mistress Weatherwax was sharper than a field of pins. 'But . . . all right, it just doesn't seem . . . fair. I mean, I wish the Feegles hadn't done that. I'm sure I could have . . . sorted it out somehow, saved up . . .'

'It's an unfair world, child. Be glad you have friends.'

Tiffany looked up at the tree line.

'Yes,' said Mistress Weatherwax. 'But not up there.'

'I'm going away,' said Tiffany. 'I've been thinking about it, and I'm going away.'

'Broomstick?' said Mistress Weatherwax. 'It don't move fast—'

'No! Where would I fly to? Home? I don't want to take it there! Anyway, I can't just fly off with it roaming around! When it . . . when I meet it, I don't want to be near people, you understand? I know what I . . . what *it* can do if it's angry! It half-killed Miss Level!'

'And if it follows you?'

'Good! I'll take it up there somewhere!' Tiffany waved at the mountains.

'All alone?'

'I don't have a choice, do I?'

Mistress Weatherwax gave her a look that went on too long.

'No,' she said. 'You don't. But neither have I. That's why I *will* come with you. Don't argue, miss. How would you stop me, eh? Oh, that reminds me . . . them mysterious bruises Mrs Towny gets is because Mr Towny beats her, and the father of Miss Quickly's baby is young Fred Turvey. You might mention that to Miss Level.'

As she spoke, a bee flew out of her ear.

Bait, thought Tiffany a few hours later, as they walked away from Miss Level's cottage and up towards the high moors. I wonder if I'm bait, just like in the old days when the hunters would tether a lamb or a baby goat to bring the wolves nearer?

She's got a plan to kill the hiver. I *know* it. She's worked something out. It'll come for me and she'll just wave a hand.

She must think I'm stupid.

They had argued, of course. But Mistress Weatherwax had made a nasty personal remark. It was: *You're eleven*. Just like that. You're eleven, and what is Miss Tick going to tell your parents? Sorry about Tiffany, but we let her go off by herself to fight an ancient monster that can't be killed and what's left of her is in this jar?

Miss Level had joined in at that part, almost in tears.

If Tiffany hadn't been a witch, she would have whined about everyone being so *unfair*!

In fact they were being fair. She knew they were being fair. They were not thinking just of her, but of other people, and Tiffany hated herself – well, slightly – because she hadn't. But it was sneaky of them to choose *this* moment to be fair. *That* was unfair.

No one had told her she was only nine when she went into Fairyland armed with just a frying pan. Admittedly, no one else had known she was going, except the Nac Mac Feegle, and she was much taller than they were. Would she have gone if she'd known what was in there? she wondered.

Yes. I would.

And you're going to face the hiver even though you don't know how to beat it?

Yes. I am. There's part of me still in it. I might be able to do something—

But aren't you just ever so slightly glad that Mistress Weatherwax and Miss Level won the argument and now you're going off very bravely but you happen to be accompanied, *completely* against your will, by the most powerful witch alive?

Tiffany sighed. It was dreadful when your own thoughts tried to gang up on you.

The Feegles hadn't objected to her going to find the hiver. They *did* object to not being allowed to come with her. They'd been insulted, she knew. But, as Mistress Weatherwax had said, this was true haggling and there was no place in it for Feegles. If the hiver came, out there, not in a dream but for real, it'd have nothing about it that could be kicked or head-butted.

Tiffany had tried to make a little speech, thanking them for their help, but Rob Anybody had folded his arms and turned his back. It had all gone wrong. But the old witch had been right. They could get hurt. The trouble was, explaining to a Feegle how dangerous things were going to be only got them more enthusiastic.

She left them arguing with one another. It had not gone well.

But now that was all behind her, in more ways

than one. The trees beside the track were less bushy and more pointy or, if Tiffany had known more about trees, she would have said that the oaks were giving way to evergreens.

She could feel the hiver. It was following them, but a long way back.

If you had to imagine a head witch, you wouldn't imagine Mistress Weatherwax. You might imagine Mrs Earwig, who glided across the floor as though she was on wheels, and had a dress as black as the darkness in a deep cellar, but Mistress Weatherwax was just an old woman with a lined face and rough hands in a dress as black as night, which is never as black as people think. It was dusty and ragged round the hem, too.

On the other hand, thought her Second Thoughts, *you once bought Granny Aching a china shepherdess, remember? All blue and white and sparkly?*

Her First Thoughts thought: Well, yes, but I was a lot younger then.

Her Second Thoughts thought: *Yes, but which one was the real shepherdess? The shiny lady in the nice clean dress and buckled shoes, or the old woman who stumped around in the snow with boots filled with straw and a sack across her shoulders?*

At which point, Mistress Weatherwax stumbled. She caught her balance very quickly.

'Dangerously loose stones on this path,' she said. 'Watch out for them.'

Tiffany looked down. There weren't that many

stones and they didn't seem very dangerous or particularly loose.

How old was Mistress Weatherwax? That was another question she wished she hadn't asked. She was skinny and wiry, just like Granny Aching, the kind of person who goes on and on – but one day Granny Aching had gone to bed and had never got up again, just like that . . .

The sun was setting. Tiffany could feel the hiver in the same way that you can sense that someone is looking at you. It was still in the woods that hugged the mountain like a scarf.

At last the witch stopped at a spot where rocks like pillars sprouted out of the turf. She sat down with her back to a big rock.

'This'll have to do,' she said. 'It'll be dark soon and you could turn an ankle on all this loose stone.'

There were huge boulders around them, house-sized, which had rolled down from the mountains in the past. The rock of the peaks began not far away, a wall of stone that seemed to hang above Tiffany like a wave. It was a desolate place. Every sound echoed.

She sat down by Mistress Weatherwax and opened the bag that Miss Level had packed for the journey.

Tiffany wasn't very experienced at things like this but, according to the book of fairy tales, the typical food for taking on an adventure was bread and cheese. Hard cheese, too.

Miss Level had made them ham sandwiches, with pickles, and she'd included napkins. That was kind of a strange thought to keep in your head: We're trying to find a way of killing a terrible creature, but at least we won't be covered in crumbs.

There was a bottle of cold tea, too, and a bag of biscuits. Miss Level knew Mistress Weatherwax.

'Shouldn't we light a fire?' Tiffany suggested.

'Why? It's a long way down to the tree line to get the firewood, and there'll be a fine half-moon up in twenty minutes. Your friend's keeping his distance and there nothing else that'll attack us up here.'

'Are you sure?'

'I walk safely in *my* mountains,' said Mistress Weatherwax.

'But aren't there trolls and wolves and things?'

'Oh, yes. Lots.'

'And they don't try to attack you?'

'Not any more,' said a self-satisfied voice in the dark. 'Pass me the biscuits, will you?'

'Here you are. Would you like some pickles?'

'Pickles gives me the wind something awful.'

'In that case—'

'Oh, I wasn't saying *no*,' said Mistress Weatherwax, taking two large pickled cucumbers.

Oh, *good*, Tiffany thought.

She'd brought three fresh eggs with her. Getting the hang of a shamble was taking too long. It was stupid. All the other girls were able to use them. She was sure she was doing everything right.

She'd filled her pocket with random things. Now

she pulled them out without looking, wove the thread around the egg like she'd done a hundred times before, grasped the pieces of wood and moved them so that . . .

Poc!

The egg cracked, and oozed.

'I told you,' said Mistress Weatherwax, who'd opened one eye. 'They're toys. Sticks and stones.'

'Have you ever *used* one?' said Tiffany.

'No. Couldn't get the hang of them. They got in the way.' Mistress Weatherwax yawned, wrapped the blanket around her, made a couple of *mnup, mnup* noises as she tried to get comfortable against the rock and, after a while, her breathing became deeper.

Tiffany waited in silence, her blanket around her, until the moon came up. She'd expected that to make things better, but it didn't. Before, there had just been darkness. Now there were shadows.

There was a snore beside her. It was one of those good solid ones, like ripping canvas.

Silence happened. It came across the night on silver wings, noiseless as the fall of a feather, silence made into a bird, which alighted on a rock close by. It swivelled its head to look at Tiffany.

There was more than just the curiosity of a bird in that look.

The old woman snored again. Tiffany reached out, still staring at the owl, and shook her gently. When that didn't work, she shook her hardly.

There was a sound like three pigs colliding and

Mistress Weatherwax opened one eye and said, 'Whoo?'

'There's an owl watching us! It's right up close!'

Suddenly the owl blinked, looked at Tiffany as if amazed to see her, spread its wings and glided off into the night.

Mistress Weatherwax gripped her throat, coughed once or twice, and then said hoarsely, 'Of course it was an owl, child! It took me ten minutes to lure it this close! Now just you be quiet while I starts again, otherwise I shall have to make do with a bat, and when I goes out on a bat for any time at all I ends up thinkin' I can see with my ears, which is no way for a decent woman to behave!'

'But you were snoring!'

'I was *not* snoring! I was just resting gently while I tickled an owl closer! If you hadn't shaken me and scared it away, I'd have been up there with this entire moor under my eye.'

'You . . . take over its *mind*?' said Tiffany nervously.

'No! I'm not one of your hivers! I just . . . borrows a lift from it, I just . . . nudges it now and again, it don't even know I'm there. Now try to rest!'

'But what if the hiver—?'

'If it comes anywhere near it'll be *me* that tells *you*!' Mistress Weatherwax hissed, and lay back. Then her head jerked up one more time. 'And I do *not* snore!' she added.

After half a minute, she started to snore again.

Minutes after that the owl came back, or perhaps

it was a different owl. It glided onto the same rock, settled there for a while and then sped away. The witch stopped snoring. In fact, she stopped breathing.

Tiffany leaned closer and finally lowered an ear to the skinny chest to see if there was a heartbeat.

Her own heart felt as if it was clenched like a fist –

– because of the day she'd found Granny Aching in the hut. She was lying peacefully on the narrow iron bed, but Tiffany had known something was wrong as soon as she had stepped inside—

Boom.

Tiffany counted to three.

Boom.

Well, it *was* a heartbeat.

Very slowly, like a twig growing, a stiff hand moved. It slid like a glacier into a pocket, and came up holding a large piece of card on which was written:

Tiffany decided she wasn't going to argue. But she pulled the blanket over the old woman and wrapped her own around herself.

By moonlight, she tried again with her shamble.

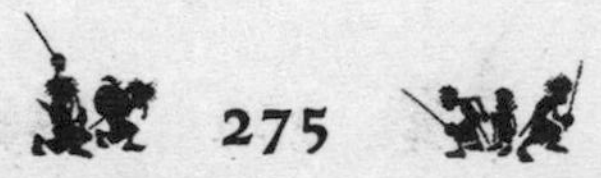

Surely she should be able to make it do *something*. Maybe if—

By moonlight, she very, very carefully—

Poc!

The egg cracked. The egg *always* cracked, and now there was only one left. Tiffany didn't dare try it with a beetle, even if she could find one. It would be too cruel.

She sat back and looked across the landscape of silver and black, and her Third Thoughts thought: *It's not going to come near*.

Why?

She thought, *I'm not sure why I know. But I know. It's keeping away. It knows Mistress Weatherwax is with me*.

She thought: How can it know that? It's not got a mind. It doesn't know what a Mistress Weatherwax *is*!

Still thinking, thought her Third Thoughts.

Tiffany slumped against the rock.

Sometimes her head was too . . . crowded . . .

And then it was morning, and sunlight, and dew on her hair, and mist coming off the ground like smoke . . . and an eagle sitting on the rock where the owl had been, eating something furry. She could see every feather on its wing.

It swallowed, glared at Tiffany with its mad bird eyes and flapped away, making the mist swirl.

Beside her, Mistress Weatherwax began to snore again, which Tiffany took to mean that she was in her body. She gave the old woman a nudge, and the sound that had been a regular *gnaaaargrgrgrgrg* suddenly became *blort*.

The old woman sat up, coughing, and waved a hand irritably at Tiffany to pass her the tea bottle. She didn't speak until she'd gulped half of it.

'Ah, say what you like, but rabbit tastes a lot better cooked,' she gasped, shoving the cork back in. 'And *without* the fur on!'

'You took— *borrowed* the eagle?' said Tiffany.

'O'course. I couldn't expect the poor ol' owl to fly around after daybreak, just to see who's about. It was hunting voles all night and, believe me, raw rabbit's better'n voles. Don't eat voles.'

'I won't,' said Tiffany, and meant it. 'Mistress Weatherwax, I *think* I know what the hiver's doing. It's thinking.'

'I thought it had no brains!'

Tiffany let her thoughts speak for themselves.

'But there's an echo of me in it, isn't there? There must be. It has an echo of everyone it's . . . been. There *must* be a bit of me in it. I know it's out there, and it knows I'm here with you. And it's keeping away.'

'Oh? Why's that, then?'

'Because it's frightened of you, I think.'

'Huh! And why's that?'

'Yes,' said Tiffany simply. 'It's because I am. A bit.'

'Oh dear. Are you?'

'Yes,' said Tiffany again. 'It's like a dog that's been

beaten but won't run away. It doesn't understand what it's done wrong. But . . . there's something about it that . . . there's a thought that I'm nearly having . . .'

Mistress Weatherwax said nothing. Her face went blank.

'Are you all right?' said Tiffany.

'I was just leavin' you time to have that thought,' said Mistress Weatherwax.

'Sorry. It's gone now. But . . . we're thinking about the hiver in the wrong way.'

'Oh, yes? And why's that?'

'Because . . .' Tiffany struggled with the idea. 'I think it's because we don't want to think about it the right way. It's something to do with . . . the third wish. And I don't know what that means.'

The witch said, 'Keep picking at that thought,' and then looked up and added, 'We've got company.'

It took Tiffany several seconds to spot what Mistress Weatherwax had seen – a shape at the edge of the woods, small and dark. It was coming closer, but rather uncertainly.

It resolved itself into the figure of Petulia, flying slowly and nervously a few feet above the heather. Sometimes she jumped down and wrenched the stick in a slightly different direction.

She got off again when she reached Tiffany and Mistress Weatherwax, grabbed the broom hastily and aimed it at a big rock. It hit it gently and hung there, trying to fly through stone.

'Um, sorry,' she panted. 'But I can't always stop it,

and this is better than having an anchor . . . Um.'

She started to bob a curtsy to Mistress Weatherwax, remembered she was a witch and tried to turn it into a bow halfway down, which was an event you'd pay money to see. She ended up bent double, and from somewhere in there came the little voice, 'Um, can someone help, please? I think my Octogram of Trimontane has got caught up on my Pouch of Nine Herbs . . .'

There was a tricky minute while they untangled her, with Mistress Weatherwax muttering 'Toys, just toys' as they unhooked bangles and necklaces.

Petulia stood upright, red in the face. She saw Mistress Weatherwax's expression, whipped off her pointy hat and held it in front on her. This was a mark of respect, but it did mean that a two-foot, sharp, pointy thing was being aimed at them.

'Um . . . I went to see Miss Level and she said you'd come up here after some horrible thing,' she said. 'Um . . . so I thought I'd better see how you were.'

'Um . . . that was very kind of you,' said Tiffany, but her treacherous Second Thoughts thought: And what would you have done if it had attacked us? She had a momentary picture of Petulia standing in front of some horrible raging thing, but it wasn't as funny as she'd first thought. Petulia *would* stand in front of it, shaking with terror, her useless amulets clattering, scared almost out of her mind . . . but not backing away. She'd thought there might be people facing something horrible here, and she'd come *anyway*.

'What's your name, my girl?' said Mistress Weatherwax.

'Um, Petulia Gristle, mistress. I'm learning with Gwinifer Blackcap.'

'Old Mother Blackcap?' said Mistress Weatherwax. 'Very sound. A good woman with pigs. You did well to come here.'

Petulia looked nervously at Tiffany. 'Um, are you all right? Miss Level said you'd been . . . ill.'

'I'm much better now, but thank you very much for asking, anyway,' said Tiffany wretchedly. 'Look, I'm sorry about—'

'Well, you were ill,' said Petulia.

And that was another thing about Petulia. She always wanted to think the best of everybody. This was sort of worrying if you knew that the person she was doing her best to think nice thoughts about was you.

'Are you going to go back to the cottage before the Trials?' Petulia went on.

'Trials?' said Tiffany, suddenly lost.

'The Witch Trials,' said Mistress Weatherwax.

'Today,' said Petulia.

'I'd forgotten all about them!' said Tiffany.

'I hadn't,' said the old witch calmly. 'I never miss a Trial. Never missed a Trial in sixty years. Would you do a poor old lady a favour, Miss Gristle, and ride that stick of yours back to Miss Level's place and tell her that Mistress Weatherwax presents her compliments and intends to head directly to the Trials. Was she well?'

'Um, she was juggling balls *without using her hands*!' said Petulia in wonderment. 'And, d'you know what? I saw a *fairy* in her garden! A blue one!'

'Really?' said Tiffany, her heart sinking.

'Yes! It was rather scruffy, though. And when I asked it if it really was a fairy, it said it was . . . um . . . "the big stinky horrible spiky iron stinging nettle fairy from the Land o' Tinkle", and called me a "scunner". Do you know what that means?'

Tiffany looked into that round, hopeful face. She opened her mouth to say, 'It means someone who likes fairies,' but stopped in time. That just wouldn't be fair. She sighed.

'Petulia, you saw a Nac Mac Feegle,' she said. 'It *is* a kind of fairy, but they're not the sweet kind. I'm sorry. They're good . . . well, more or less . . . but they're not entirely nice. And "scunner" is a kind of swearword. I don't think it's a particularly bad one though.'

Petulia's expression didn't change for a while. Then she said: 'So it *was* a fairy, then?'

'Well, yes. Technically.'

The round pink face smiled. 'Good, I did wonder, because it was, um, you know . . . having a wee up against one of Miss Level's garden gnomes?'

'*Definitely* a Feegle,' said Tiffany.

'Oh well, I suppose the big stinky horrible spiky iron stinging nettle needs a fairy, just like every other plant,' said Petulia.

Chapter 11

Arthur

When Petulia had gone, Mistress Weatherwax stamped her feet and said, 'Let's go, young lady. It's about eight miles to Sheercliff. They'll have started before we get there.'

'What about the hiver?'

'Oh, it can come if it likes.' Mistress Weatherwax smiled. 'Oh, don't frown like that. There'll be more'n three hundred witches at the Trials, and they're right out in the country. It'll be as safe as anything. Or do you want to meet the hiver *now*? We could probably do that. It don't seem to move fast.'

'No!' said Tiffany, louder than she'd intended. 'No, because . . . things aren't what they seem. We'd do things wrong. Er . . . I can't explain it. It's because of the third wish.'

'Which you don't know what it is?'

'Yes. But I will soon, I hope.'

The witch stared at her. 'Yes, I hope so, too,' she

said. 'Well, no point in standing around. Let's get moving.' And with that the witch picked up her blanket and set off as though being pulled by a string.

'We haven't even had anything to eat!' said Tiffany, running after her.

'I had a lot of voles last night,' said Mistress Weatherwax over her shoulder.

'Yes, but *you* didn't actually eat them, did you?' said Tiffany. 'It was the owl that *actually* ate them.'

'Technic'ly, yes,' Mistress Weatherwax admitted. 'But if you think you've been eating voles all night you'd be amazed how much you don't want to eat anything next morning. Or ever again.'

She nodded at the distant, departing figure of Petulia.

'Friend of yours?' she said, as they set out.

'Er . . . if she is, I don't deserve it,' said Tiffany.

'Hmm,' said Mistress Weatherwax. 'Well, sometimes we get what we don't deserve.'

For an old woman Mistress Weatherwax could move quite fast. She strode over the moors as if distance was a personal insult. But she was good at something else too.

She knew about silence. There was the swish of her long skirt as it snagged the heathers, but somehow that became part of the background noise.

In the silence, as she walked, Tiffany could still hear the memories. There were hundreds of them left behind by the hiver. Most of them were so faint that they were nothing more than a slight uncomfortable feeling in her head, but the ancient tiger still burned brightly in the back of her brain, and behind that was the giant lizard. They'd been killing machines, the most powerful creatures in their world – once. The hiver had taken them both. And then they'd died fighting.

Always taking fresh bodies, always driving the owners mad with the urge for power which would always end with getting them killed . . . and just as Tiffany wondered *why*, a memory said: *Because it is frightened.*

Frightened of what? Tiffany thought. It's so powerful!

Who knows? But it's mad with terror. Completely binkers!

'You're Simplicity Bustle, aren't you,' said Tiffany, and then her ears informed her that she'd said this aloud.

'Talkative, ain't he,' said Mistress Weatherwax. 'He talked in your sleep the other night. Used to have a very high opinion of himself. I reckon that's why his memories held together for so long.'

'He doesn't know binkers from bonkers, though,' said Tiffany.

'Well, memory fades,' said Mistress Weatherwax. She stopped and leaned against a rock. She sounded out of breath.

'Are you all right, mistress?' said Tiffany.

'Sound as a bell,' said Mistress Weatherwax, wheezing slightly. 'Just getting my second wind.

Anyway, it's only another six miles.'

'I notice you're limping a bit,' said Tiffany.

'Do you, indeed? Then stop noticing!'

The shout echoed off the cliffs, full of command.

Mistress Weatherwax coughed, when the echo had died away. Tiffany had gone pale.

'It seems to me,' said the old witch, 'that I might just've been a shade on the sharp side there. It was prob'ly the voles.' She coughed again. 'Them as knows me, or has earned it one way or the other, calls me Granny Weatherwax. I shall not take it amiss if you did the same.'

'*Granny* Weatherwax?' said Tiffany, shocked out of her shock by this new shock.

'Not *technic'ly,*' said Mistress Weatherwax quickly. 'It's what they call a honorific, like Old Mother So-and-so, or Goodie Thingy, or Nanny Whatshername. To show that a witch has . . . is fully . . . has been—'

Tiffany didn't know whether to laugh or burst into tears. 'I *know,*' she said.

'You do?'

'Like Granny Aching,' said Tiffany. 'She *was* my granny, but everyone on the Chalk called her Granny Aching.'

'Mrs Aching' wouldn't have worked, she knew. You needed a big, warm, billowing, open kind of word. Granny Aching was there for everybody.

'It's like being everyone's grandmother,' she added. And didn't add: *who tells them stories!*

'Well, then. Perhaps so. Granny Weatherwax it is,'

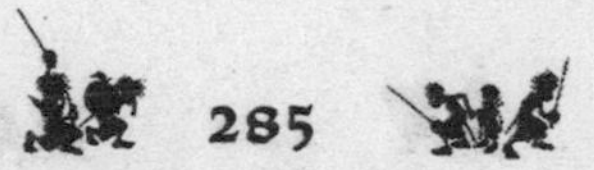

said Granny Weatherwax, and added quickly, 'but not *technic'ly*. Now we're best be moving.'

She straightened up and set off again.

Granny Weatherwax. Tiffany tried it out in her head. She'd never known her other grandmother, who'd died before she was born. Calling someone else Granny was strange but, oddly, it seemed right. And you *could* have two.

The hiver followed them. Tiffany could feel it. But it was still keeping its distance. Well, there's a trick to take to the Trials, she thought. Granny – her brain tingled as she thought the word – Granny has got a plan. She must have.

But . . . things weren't right. There was another thought she wasn't quite having; it ducked out of sight every time she thought she had it. The hiver wasn't acting right.

She made sure she kept up with Granny Weatherwax.

As they got nearer to the Trials, there were clues. Tiffany saw at least three broomsticks in the air, heading the same way. They reached a proper track, too, and groups of people were travelling in the same direction; there were a few pointy hats amongst them, which was a definite clue. The track dropped on down through some woods, came up in a patchwork of little fields and headed for a tall hedge, from behind which came the sound of a brass band playing a medley of Songs from the Shows, although by the sound of it no two musicians could agree on what Song or which Show.

Tiffany jumped when she saw a balloon sail up above the trees, catch the wind and swoop away, but it turned out to be just a balloon and not a lump of excess Brian. She could tell this because it was followed by a long scream of rage mixed with a roar of complaint: 'AAaargwannawannaaaagongongonaargggaaaa BLOON!' which is the traditional sound of a very small child learning that with balloons, as with life itself, it is important to know *when not to let go of the string*. The whole point of balloons is to teach small children this.

However, on this occasion a broomstick with a pointy-hatted passenger rose above the trees, caught up with the balloon and towed it back down to the Trials ground.

'Didn't used to be like this,' Granny Weatherwax grumbled as they reached a gate. 'When I was a girl, we just used to meet up in some meadow somewhere, all by ourselves. But now, oh no, it has to be a Grand Day Out For All The Family. Hah!'

There had been a crowd around the gate leading into the field, but there was something about that 'Hah!' The crowd parted, as if by magic, and the women pulled their children a little closer to them as Granny walked right up to the gate.

There was a boy there, selling tickets and wishing, now, that he'd never been born.

Granny Weatherwax stared at him. Tiffany saw his ears go red.

'Two tickets, young man,' said Granny. Little bits of ice tinkled off her words.

'That'll, er, be, er . . . one child and one senior citizen?' the young man quavered.

Granny leaned forward and said: '*What* is a senior citizen, young man?'

'It's like . . . you know . . . old folks,' the boy mumbled. Now his hands were shaking.

Granny leaned further forward. The boy really, really wanted to step back but his feet were rooted to the ground. All he could do was bend backwards.

'Young man,' said Granny, 'I am not now, nor shall I ever be, an "old folk". We'll take two tickets, which I see on that board there is a penny apiece.' Her hand shot out, fast as an adder. The boy made a noise like *gneeee* as he leaped back.

'Here's tuppence,' said Granny Weatherwax.

Tiffany looked at Granny's hand. The first finger and thumb were held together, but there did not appear to be any coins between them.

Nevertheless, the young man, grinning horribly, took the total absence of coins very carefully between *his* thumb and finger. Granny twitched two tickets out of his other hand.

'Thank you, young man,' she said, and walked into the field. Tiffany ran after her.

'What did—?' she began, but Granny Weatherwax raised a finger to her lips, grasped Tiffany's shoulder and swivelled her round.

The ticket-seller was still staring at his fingers. He even rubbed them together. Then he shrugged, held them over his leather moneybag and let go.

Clink, clink . . .

The crowd around the gate gave a gasp, and one or two of them started to applaud. The boy looked around with a sick kind of grin, as if *of course* he'd expected that to happen.

'Ah, right,' said Granny Weatherwax happily. 'And now I could just do with a cup of tea and maybe a sweet biscuit.'

'Granny, there are children here! Not just witches!'

People were looking at them. Granny Weatherwax jerked Tiffany's chin up so that she could look into her eyes.

'Look around, eh? You can't move down here for amulets and wands and whatnot! It'll be *bound* to keep away, eh?'

Tiffany turned to look. There were sideshows all around the field. A lot of them were funfair stuff that she'd seen before at agricultural shows around the Chalk: Roll-a-Penny, Lucky Dip, Bobbing for Piranhas, that sort of thing. The Ducking Stool was very popular among young children on such a hot day. There wasn't a fortune-telling tent, because no fortune-teller would turn up at an event where so many visitors were qualified to argue and answer back, but there were a number of witch stalls. Zakzak's had a huge tent, with a display dummy outside wearing a Sky Scraper hat and a Zephyr Billow cloak, which had drawn a crowd of admirers. The other stalls were smaller, but they were thick with things that glittered and tinkled and they were doing a brisk trade amongst the younger witches. There were whole stalls full of dream-catchers and curse-nets, including the new self-emptying ones. It was odd to think of witches buying them, though. It was like fish buying umbrellas.

Surely a hiver wouldn't come here, with all these witches?

She turned to Granny Weatherwax.

Granny Weatherwax wasn't there.

It is hard to find a witch at the Witch Trials. That is, it is too *easy* to find a witch at the Witch Trials, but very hard to find the one you're looking for, especially if you suddenly feel lost and all alone and you can feel panic starting to open inside you like a fern.

Most of the older witches were sitting at trestle tables in a huge roped-off area. They were drinking tea. Pointy hats bobbed as tongues wagged. Every woman seemed capable of talking while listening to all the others on the table at the same time, although this talent isn't confined to witches. It was no place to search for an old woman in black with a pointy hat.

The sun was quite high in the sky now. The field was filling up. Witches were circling to land at the far end, and more and more people were pouring in through the gateway. The noise was intense.

Everywhere Tiffany turned, black hats were scurrying.

Pushing her way through the throng, she looked desperately for a friendly face, like Miss Tick or Miss Level or Petulia. If it came to it, an unfriendly one would do – even Mrs Earwig.

And she tried not to think. She tried not to think that she was terrified and alone in this huge crowd, and that up on the hill, invisible, the hiver now knew this because just a tiny part of it was her.

She felt the hiver stir. She felt it begin to move.

Tiffany stumbled through a chattering group of witches, their voices sounding shrill and unpleasant. She felt ill, as though she'd been in the sun too long. The world was spinning.

A remarkable thing about a hiver, a reedy voice began, somewhere in the back of her head, *is that its hunting pattern mimics that of the common shark, among other creatures—*

'I do not want a lecture, Mr Bustle,' Tiffany mumbled. 'I do not want you in my head!'

But the memory of Simplicity Bustle had never taken much notice of other people when he was alive and it wasn't going to begin now. It went on in its self-satisfied squeak: – *in that, once it has selected its prey, it will completely ignore other attractive targets—*

She could see right across the Trials field, and something *was* coming. It moved through the crowd like the wind through a field of grass. You could plot its progress by the people. Some fainted, some yelped and turned round, some ran. Witches stopped their gossip, chairs were overturned and the shouting started. But it wasn't attacking anything. It was only interested in Tiffany.

Like a shark, thought Tiffany. The killer of the sea, where worse things happened.

Tiffany backed away, the panic filling her up. She bumped into witches hurrying towards the commotion and shouted at them:

'You can't stop it! You don't know what it is! You'll flail at it and wave glittery sticks and it will keep coming! It will keep coming!'

She put her hands into her pockets and touched the lucky stone. And the string. And the piece of chalk.

If this was a story, she thought bitterly, I'd trust in my heart and follow my star and all that other stuff and it would all turn out all right, right now, by tinkly Magikkkk. But you're never in a story when you need to be.

Story, story, story . . .

The third wish. The Third Wish. The third wish is the important one.

In stories the genie or the witch or the magic cat . . . offers you three wishes.

Three wishes . . .

She grabbed a hurrying witch and looked into the face of Annagramma, who stared at her in terror and tried to cower away.

'Please don't do anything to me! Please!' she cried. 'I'm your *friend,* aren't I?'

'If you like, but that wasn't me and I'm better now,' said Tiffany, knowing she was lying. It *had* been her, and that was important. She had to remember that. 'Quick, Annagramma! What's the third wish? Quickly! When you get three wishes, what's the third wish!'

Annagramma's face screwed up into the affronted frown she wore when something had the nerve not to be understandable. 'But why do—?'

'Don't think about it, please! Just answer!'

'Well, er . . . it could be anything . . . being invisible or . . . or blonde, or anything—' Annagramma burbled, her mind coming apart at the seams.

Tiffany shook her head and let her go. She ran to an old witch who was staring at the commotion.

'Please, mistress, this is important! In stories, what's the third wish! Don't ask me why, please! Just remember!'

'Er . . . happiness. It's happiness, isn't it?' said the old lady. 'Yes, definitely. Health, wealth and happiness. Now if I was you I'd—'

'Happiness? Happiness . . . thank you,' said Tiffany, and looked around desperately for someone else. It wasn't happiness, she knew that in her boots. You couldn't get happiness by magic, and *that* was another clue right there.

There was Miss Tick, hurrying between the tents. There was no time for half-measures. Tiffany pulled her round and shouted: 'HelloMissTickYesI'mFineI HopeYouAreWellTooWhatIsTheThirdWishQuickly

ThisIsImportantPleaseDon'tArgueOrAskQuestions ThereIsn'tTime!'

Miss Tick, to her credit, hesitated only for a moment or two. 'To have a hundred more wishes, isn't it?' she said.

Tiffany stared at her and then said, 'Thank you. It isn't, but that's a clue, too.'

'Tiffany, there's a—' Miss Tick began.

But Tiffany had seen Granny Weatherwax.

She was standing in the middle of the field, in a big square that had been roped off for some reason. No one seemed to notice her. She was watching the frantic witches around the hiver, where there was an occasional flash and sparkle of magic. She had a calm, faraway look.

Tiffany brushed Miss Tick's arm away, ducked under the rope and ran up to her.

'Granny!'

The blue eyes turned to her.

'Yes?'

'*In stories,* where the genie or the magic frog or the fairy godmother gives you three wishes . . . what's the third wish?'

'Ah, *stories,*' said Granny. 'That's easy. In any story worth the tellin', that knows about the way of the world, *the third wish is the one that undoes the harm the first two wishes caused.*'

'Yes! That's it! That's it!' shouted Tiffany, and the words piling up behind the question poured out. 'It's not evil! It can't be! It hasn't got a mind of its own!

This is all about wishes! *Our* wishes! It's like in the stories, where they—'

'Calm down. Take a deep breath,' said Granny. She took Tiffany by the shoulders so that she faced the panicking crowd.

'You got frightened for a moment, and now it's comin' and it's not going to turn back, not now, 'cos it's desperate. It don't even *see* the crowd, they don't mean a thing to it. It's you it wants. It's you it's after. You should be the one who faces it. Are you ready?'

'But supposing I lose—'

'I never got where I am today by supposin' I was goin' to lose, young lady. You beat it once, you can do it again!'

'But I could turn into something terrible!'

'Then you'll face me,' said Granny. 'You'll face me, on my ground. But that won't happen, will it? You were fed up with grubby babies and silly women? Then this is . . . the other stuff. It's noon now. They should've started the Trials proper, but, hah, it looks as though people have forgotten. Now, then . . . do you have it in you to be a witch by noonlight, far away from your hills?'

'Yes!' There was no other answer, not to Granny Weatherwax.

Granny Weatherwax bowed low and then took a few steps back.

'In your own time, then, madam,' she said.

Wishes, wishes, wishes, thought Tiffany, distracted, fumbling in her pockets for the bits to make a shamble. It's not evil. *It gives us what we think we want!* And what do people ask for? More wishes!

You couldn't say: A monster got into my head and made me do it. She'd wished the money was hers. The hiver just took her at her thought.

You couldn't say: Yes, but I'd *never* have really taken it! The hiver used what it found – the little secret wishes, the desires, the moments of rage, all the things that real humans knew how to ignore! It didn't let you ignore them!

Then, as she fumbled to tie the pieces together, the egg flipped out of her hands, trusted in gravity and smashed on the toe of her boot.

She stared at it, the blackness of despair darkening the noonlight. Why did I try this? I've never made a shamble that worked, so why did I try? Because I believed it had to work this time, that's why. Like in a story. Suddenly it would all be . . . all right.

But this isn't a story, and there are no more eggs . . .

There was a scream but it was high up and the sound of it took Tiffany home in the bounce of a heartbeat. It was a buzzard, in the eye of the sun, getting bigger in its plunge towards the field.

It soared up again as it passed over Tiffany's head, fast as an arrow, and as it did so, something small let go its hold on the buzzard's talons with a cry of 'Crivens!'

Rob Anybody dropped like a stone, but there was a *thwap!* and suddenly a balloon of cloth snapped open above him. Two balloons, in fact, or to put it another way, Rob Anybody had 'borrowed' Hamish's parachute.

He let go of them as soon as they'd slowed him down, and dropped neatly into the shamble.

'Did ye think we'd leave ye?' he shouted, holding onto the strings. 'I'm under a geas, me! Get on wi' it, right noo!'

'What? I can't!' said Tiffany, trying to shake him off. 'Not with you! I'll kill you! I always crack the eggs! What goose?'

'Dinnae argue!' shouted Rob, bouncing up and down in the strings. 'Do it! Or ye're no' the hag of the hills! An' I know ye are!'

People were running past now. Tiffany glanced up. She thought she could *see* the hiver now as a moving shape in the dust.

She looked at the tangle in her hands and at Rob's grinning face.

The moment twanged.

A witch deals with things, said her Second Thoughts. Get past the 'I can't.'

O-K . . .

Why hasn't it ever worked before? Because there was no reason for it to work. I didn't *need* it to work.

I need it to help me now. No. I need *me* to help me.

So *think* about it. Ignore the noise, ignore the hiver rolling towards her over the trodden grass . . .

She'd use the things she'd had, so that was right. Calm down. Slow down. Look at the shamble. Think about the moment. There were all the things from home . . .

No. Not all the things. Not all the things at all. This time, she felt the shape of what wasn't there –

– and tugged at the silver horse around her neck, breaking its chain, then hanging it in the threads.

Suddenly her thoughts were as cool and clear as ice, as bright and shiny as they needed to be. Let's see . . . that looks better there . . . and that needs to be pulled *this* way . . .

The movement jerked the silver horse into life. Then it spun gently, passing through the threads *and* Rob Anybody, who said, 'Didnae hurt a bit! Keep goin'!'

Tiffany felt a tingle in her feet. The horse gleamed as it turned.

'I dinnae want to hurry ye!' said Rob Anybody. 'But hurry!'

I'm far from home, thought Tiffany, in the same clear way, but I have it in my eye. Now I open my eyes. Now I open my eyes again—

Ahh . . .

Can I be a witch away from my hills? Of course I can. I never really leave you, Land Under Wave . . .

Shepherds on the Chalk felt the ground shake, like thunder under the turf. Birds scattered from the bushes. The sheep looked up.

Again, the ground trembled.

Some people said a shadow crossed the sun. Some

people said they heard the sound of hooves.

And a boy trying to catch hares in the little valley of the Horse said the hillside had burst and a horse had leaped out like a wave as high as the sky, with a mane like the wave of the sea and a coat as white as chalk. He said it had galloped into the air like rising mist, and flew towards the mountains like a storm.

He got punished for telling stories, of course, but he thought it was worth it.

The shamble glowed. Silver coursed along the threads. It was coming from Tiffany's hands, sparking like stars.

In that light, she saw the hiver reach her and spread out until it was all around her, invisibility made visible. It rippled and reflected the light oddly. In those glints and sparkles there were faces, wavering and stretching like reflections in water.

Time was going slowly. She could see, beyond the wall of hiver, witches staring at her. One had lost her hat in the commotion, but it was hanging in the air. It hadn't had time to fall yet.

Tiffany's fingers moved. The hiver shimmered in the air, disturbed like a pond when a pebble has been dropped into it. Tendrils of it reached towards her. She felt its panic, felt its terror as it found itself caught—

'Welcome,' said Tiffany.

Welcome? said the hiver in Tiffany's own voice.

'Yes. You are welcome in this place. You are safe here.'

No! We are never safe!

'You are safe here,' Tiffany repeated.

Please! said the hiver. *Shelter us!*

'The wizard was nearly right about you,' said Tiffany. 'You hid in other creatures. But he didn't wonder *why*. What are you hiding from?'

Everything, said the hiver.

'I *think* I know what you mean,' said Tiffany.

Do you? Do you know what it feels like to be aware of every star, every blade of grass? Yes. You do. You call it 'opening your eyes again'. But you do it for a moment. We have done it for eternity. No sleep, no rest, just endless . . . endless experience, endless awareness. Of everything. All the time. *How we envy you,* envy you! *Lucky humans, who can close your minds to the endless cold deeps of space! You have this thing you call . . . boredom? That is the rarest talent in the universe! We heard a song, it went 'Twinkle twinkle little star . . .' What power! What wondrous power! You can take a billion trillion tons of flaming matter, a furnace of unimaginable strength, and turn it into a little song for children! You build little worlds, little stories, little shells around your minds and that keeps infinity at bay and allows you to wake up in the morning without screaming!*

Completely binkers! said a cheerful voice at the back of Tiffany's memory. You just couldn't keep Dr Bustle down.

Pity us, yes, pity us, said the voices of the hiver. *No shield for us, no rest for us, no sanctuary. But you, you withstood us. We saw that in you. You have minds within minds. Hide us!*

'You want silence?' said Tiffany.

Yes, and more than silence, said the voice of the hiver. *You humans are so good at ignoring things. You are almost blind and almost deaf. You look at a tree and see . . . just a tree, a stiff weed. You don't see its history, feel the pumping of the sap, hear every insect in the bark, sense the chemistry of the leaves, notice the hundred shades of green, the tiny movements to follow the sun, the subtle growth of the wood . . .*

'But you don't understand us,' said Tiffany. 'I don't think any human could survive you. You give us what you think we want, as soon as we want it, just like in fairy stories. And the wishes always go wrong.'

Yes. We know that now. We have an echo of you now. We have . . . understanding, said the hiver. *So now we come to you with a wish. It is the wish that puts the others right.*

'Yes,' said Tiffany. 'That's always the last wish, the third wish. It's the one that says "Make this not have happened".'

Teach us the way to die, said the voices of the hiver.

'I don't know it!'

All humans know the way, said the voices of the hiver. *You walk it every day of your short, short lives. You know it. We envy you your knowledge. You know how to* end. *You are very talented.*

I *must* know how to die, Tiffany thought. Somewhere deep down. Let me think. Let me get past the 'I can't' . . .

She held up the glittering shamble. Shafts of light

still spun off it, but she didn't need it any more. She could hold the power in the centre of herself. It was all a matter of balance.

The light died. Rob Anybody was still hanging in the threads, but all his hair had come unplaited and stood out from his head in a great red ball. He looked stunned.

'I could just *murrrder* a kebab,' he said.

Tiffany lowered him to the ground, where he swayed slightly, then she put the rest of the shamble in her pocket.

'Thank you, Rob,' she said. 'But I want you to go now. It could get . . . serious.'

It was, of course, the wrong thing to say.

'I'm no' leavin'!' he snapped. 'I promised Jeannie to keep ye safe! Let's get on wi' it!'

There was no arguing. Rob was standing in that half-crouch of his, fists bunched, chin out, ready for anything and burning with defiance.

'Thank you,' said Tiffany, and straightened up.

Death is right behind us, she thought. Life ends, and there's death, waiting. So . . . it must be close. Very close.

It would be . . . a door. Yes. An old door, old wood. Dark, too.

She turned. Behind her, there was a black door in the air.

The hinges would creak, she thought.

When she pushed it open, they did.

So-oo . . . she thought, this isn't exactly *real*. I'm

telling myself a story I can understand, about doors, and I'm fooling myself just enough for it all to work. I just have to keep balanced on that edge for it to go on working, too. And that's as hard as not thinking about a pink rhinoceros. And if Granny Weatherwax can do that, I can too.

Beyond the door, black sand stretched away under a sky of pale stars. There were some mountains on the distant horizon.

You must help us through, said the voices of the hiver.

'If you'll tak' my advice, you'll no' do that,' said Rob Anybody from Tiffany's ankle. 'I dinnae trust the scunner one wee bitty!'

'There's part of me in there. I trust that,' she said. 'I did say you don't have to come, Rob.'

'Oh, aye? An' I'm ta' see you go through there alone, am I? Ye'll not find me leavin' you now!'

'You've got a clan and a wife, Rob!'

'Aye, an' so I willnae dishonour them by lettin' yer step across Death's threshold alone,' said Rob Anybody firmly.

So, thought Tiffany as she stared through the doorway, *this* is what we do. We live on the edges. We help those who can't find the way . . .

She took a deep breath and stepped across.

Nothing much changed. The sand felt gritty underfoot and crunched when she walked over it, as she expected, but when it was kicked up it fell back as slowly as thistledown, and she hadn't expected that.

The air wasn't cold, but it was thin and prickly to breathe.

The door shut softly behind her.

Thank you, said the voices of the hiver. *What do we do now?*

Tiffany looked around her, and up at the stars. They weren't ones that she recognized.

'You die, I think,' she said.

But there is no 'me' to die, said the voices of the hiver. *There is only us.*

Tiffany took a deep breath. This was about words, and she knew about words. 'Here is a story to believe,' she said. 'Once we were blobs in the sea, and then fishes, and then lizards and rats and then monkeys, and hundreds of things in between. This hand was once a fin, this hand once had claws! In my human mouth I have the pointy teeth of a wolf and the chisel teeth of a rabbit and the grinding teeth of a cow! Our blood is as salty as the sea we used to live in! When we're frightened the hair on our skins stands up, just like it did when we had fur. We *are* history! Everything we've ever been on the way to becoming us, we still are. Would you like the rest of the story?'

Tell us, said the hiver.

'I'm made up of the memories of my parents and grandparents, all my ancestors. They're in the way I look, in the colour of my hair. And I'm made up of everyone I've ever met who's changed the way I think. So who is "me"?'

The piece that just told us that story, said the hiver. *The piece that's truly* you.

'Well . . . yes. But you must have that too. You know you say you're "us" – who is it saying it? Who is saying you're not you? You're not different from us. We're just much, much better at forgetting. And we know when not to listen to the monkey.'

You've just puzzled us, said the hiver.

'The old bit of our brains that wants to be head monkey, and attacks when it's surprised,' said Tiffany. 'It reacts. It doesn't think. Being human is knowing when not to be the monkey or the lizard or any of the other old echoes. But when *you* take people over, you silence the human part. You listen to the monkey. The monkey doesn't know what it needs, only what it wants. No, you are not an "us". You are an "I".'

I, me, said the hiver. *I.* Who *am I?*

'Do you want a name? That helps.'

Yes. A name . . .

'I've always liked Arthur, as a name.'

Arthur, said the hiver. *I like Arthur, too. And if I am, I can stop. What happens next?*

'The creatures you . . . took over, didn't they die?'

Yes, said the Arthur. *But we – but I didn't see what happened. They just stopped being here.*

Tiffany looked around at the endless sand. She couldn't see anybody, but there was something out there that suggested movement. It was the occasional change in the light, perhaps, as if she was catching glimpses of something she was not supposed to see.

'I think,' she said, 'that you have to cross the desert.'

What's on the other side? said Arthur.

Tiffany hesitated. 'Some people think you go to a better world,' she said. 'Some people think you come back to this one in a different body. And some think there's just nothing. They think you just stop.'

And what do you think? Arthur asked.

'I think that there are no words to describe it,' said Tiffany.

Is that true? said Arthur.

'I think that's why you have to cross the desert,' said Tiffany. 'To find out.'

I will look forward to it. Thank you.

'Goodbye . . . Arthur.'

She felt the hiver fall away. There wasn't much sign of it – a movement of a few sand grains, a sizzle in the air – but it slid away slowly across the black sand.

'An' bad cess an' good riddance ta' ye!' Rob Anybody shouted after it.

'No,' said Tiffany. 'Don't say that.'

'Aye, but it killed folk to stay alive.'

'It didn't want to. It didn't know how people work.'

'That was a fine load of o' blethers ye gave it, at any rate,' said Rob admiringly. 'Not even a gonnagle could make up a load o' blethers like that.'

Tiffany wondered if it had been. Once, when the wandering teachers had come to the village, she had paid half a dozen eggs for a morning's education on *****Wonders of the Univers!!***** That was expensive, for education, but it had been thoroughly worth it. The teacher had been a little bit crazy, even for a teacher, but what he'd said had seemed to make absolute sense. One of the most amazing things about the universe, he had said, was that, sooner or later, everything is made of everything else, although it'll probably take millions and millions of years for this to happen. The other children had giggled or argued, but Tiffany knew that what had once been tiny living creatures was now the chalk of the hills. Everything went round, even stars.

That had been a very good morning, especially since she'd been refunded half an egg for pointing out that 'Universe' had been spelled wrong.

Was it true? Maybe that didn't matter. Maybe it just had to be true enough for Arthur.

Her eyes, the inner eyes that opened twice, were beginning to close. She could feel the power draining away. You couldn't stay in that state for long. You became so aware of the universe that you stopped being aware of you. How clever of humans to have learned how to close their minds. Was there anything so amazing in the universe as boredom?

She sat down, just for a moment, and picked up a handful of the sand. It rose above her hand, twisting like smoke, reflecting the starlight, then settled back as if it had all the time in the world.

She had never felt this tired.

She still heard the inner voices. The hiver had left memories behind, just a few. She could remember when there had been no stars and when there had been no such thing as 'yesterday'. She knew what was beyond the sky and beneath the grass. But she couldn't remember when she had last slept, properly *slept*, in a *bed*. Being unconscious didn't count. She closed her eyes, and closed her eyes again—

Someone kicked her hard on the foot.

'Dinnae gae to sleep!' Rob Anybody shouted. 'Not here! Ye cannae gae to sleep *here*! Rise an' shine!'

Still feeling muzzy, Tiffany pushed herself back onto her feet, through gentle swirls of rising dust, and turned to the dark door.

It wasn't there.

There were her footprints in the sand, but they went only a few feet and, anyway, were slowly disappearing. There was nothing around her but dead desert, for ever.

She turned back to look towards the distant mountains, but her view was blocked by a tall figure, all in black, holding a scythe. It hadn't been there before.

GOOD AFTERNOON, said Death.

Chapter 12

The Egress

Tiffany stared up into a black hood. There was a skull in it, but the eye sockets glowed blue.

At least bones had never frightened Tiffany. They were only chalk that had walked around.

'Are you—?' she began, but Rob Anybody gave a yell and leaped straight for the hood.

There was a thud. Death took a step backwards and raised a skeletal hand to his cowl. He pulled out Rob Anybody by his hair and held him at arm's length while the Nac Mac Feegle cursed and kicked.

IS THIS YOURS? Death asked Tiffany. The voice was heavy and all around her, like thunder.

'No. Er . . . he's his.'

I WAS NOT EXPECTING A NAC MAC FEEGLE TODAY, said Death. OTHERWISE I WOULD HAVE WORN PROTECTIVE CLOTHING, HA HA.

'They do fight a lot,' Tiffany admitted. 'You *are*

Death, aren't you? I know this might sound a silly question.'

YOU ARE NOT AFRAID?

'Not yet. But, er . . . which way to the egress, please?'

There was a pause. Then Death said, in a puzzled voice: ISN'T THAT A FEMALE EAGLE?

'No,' said Tiffany. 'Everyone thinks that. Actually, it's the way out. The exit.'

Death pointed, with the hand that still held the incandescently angry Rob Anybody.

THAT WAY. YOU HAVE TO WALK THE DESERT.

'All the way to the mountains?'

YES. BUT ONLY THE DEAD CAN TAKE THAT WAY.

'Ye've got ta' let me go sooner or later, ye big 'natomy!' yelled Rob Anybody. 'And then ye're gonna get sich a kickin'!'

'There was a door here!' said Tiffany.

AH YES, said Death. BUT THERE ARE RULES. THAT WAS A WAY *IN*, YOU SEE.

'What's the difference?'

A FAIRLY IMPORTANT ONE, I'M SORRY TO SAY. YOU WILL HAVE TO SEE YOURSELVES OUT. DO NOT FALL ASLEEP HERE. SLEEP HERE NEVER ENDS.

Death vanished. Rob Anybody dropped to the sand and came up ready to fight, but they were alone.

'Ye'll have to make a door oot,' he said.

'I don't know how! Rob, I told you not to come with me. Can't *you* get out?'

'Aye. Probably. But I've got to see ye safe. The

kelda put a geas on me. I must save the hag o' the hills.'

'*Jeannie* told you that?'

'Aye. She was verra *definite,*' said Rob Anybody.

Tiffany slumped down onto the sand again. It fountained up around her.

'I'll never get out,' she said. How to get in, yes, *that* wasn't hard . . .

She looked around. They weren't obvious, but there were occasional changes in the light, and little puffs of dust.

People she couldn't see were walking past her. People were crossing the desert. Dead people, going to find out what was beyond the mountains . . .

I'm eleven, she thought. People will be upset. She thought about the farm, and how her mother and father would react. But there wouldn't be a body, would there? So people would hope and hope that she'd come back and was just . . . missing, like old Mrs Happens in the village, who lit a candle in the window every night for her son who'd been lost at sea thirty years ago.

She wondered if Rob could send a message, but what could she say? 'I'm not dead, I'm just stuck'?

'I should have thought of other people,' she said aloud.

'Aye, weel, ye did,' said Rob, sitting down by her foot. 'Yon Arthur went off happy, and ye saved other folk fra' being killed. Ye did what ye had to do.'

Yes, thought Tiffany. That's what we have to do.

And there's no one to protect you, because *you're* the one who's supposed to do that sort of thing.

But her Second Thoughts said: I'm *glad* I did it. I'd do it again. I stopped the hiver killing anyone else, even though we led it right into the Trials. And that thought was followed by a space. There should have been another thought, but she was too tired to have it. It had been important.

'Thank you for coming, Rob,' she said. 'But when . . . you can leave, you must go straight back to Jeannie, understand? And tell her I'm grateful she sent you. Say I wish we'd had a chance to get to know one another better.'

'Oh, aye. I've sent the lads back anyway. Hamish is waitin' for me.'

At which point the door appeared, and opened.

Granny Weatherwax stepped through and beckoned urgently.

'Some people don't have the sense they were born with! Come on, right now!' she commanded. Behind her, the door started to swing shut, but she swung round savagely and rammed her boot against the jamb, shouting, 'Oh, no you don't, you sly devil!'

'But . . . I thought there were rules!' said Tiffany, getting up and hurrying forward, all tiredness suddenly gone. Even a tired body wants to survive.

'Oh? Really?' said Granny. 'Did you sign anything? Did you take any kind of oath? No? Then they weren't *your* rules! Quickly, now! And you, Mr Anyone!'

Rob Anybody jumped onto her boot just before she pulled it away. The door shut with another click, disappeared and left them in . . . dead light, it seemed, a space of grey air.

'Won't take long,' said Granny Weatherwax. 'It doesn't usually. It's the world getting back into line. Oh, don't look like that. You showed it the Way, right? Out of pity. Well, I know this path already. You'll tread it again, no doubt, for some other poor soul, open the door for them as can't find it. But we don't talk about it, understand?'

'Miss Level never—'

'We don't talk about it, I said,' said Granny Weatherwax. 'Do you know what a part of being a witch is? It's making the choices that have to be made. The hard choices. But you did . . . quite well. There's no shame in pity.'

She brushed some grass seed off her dress.

'I hope Mrs Ogg has arrived,' she said. 'I need her recipe for apple chutney. Oh . . . when we arrive you might feel a bit dizzy. I'd better warn you.'

'Granny?' said Tiffany, as the light began to grow brighter. It brought back tiredness with it, too.

'Yes?'

'What *exactly* happened just then?'

'What do you think happened?'

Light burst in upon them.

Someone was wiping Tiffany's forehead with a damp cloth.

She lay, feeling the beautiful coolness. There were voices around her, and she recognized the chronic-complainer's tones of Annagramma:

'. . . And she was really making a fuss in Zakzak's. Honestly, I don't think she's quite right in the head! I think she's literally gone cuckoo! She was shouting things and using some kind of, oh, I don't know, some peasant trick to make us think she'd turned that fool Brian into a frog. Well, of course, she didn't fool *me* for one minute—'

Tiffany opened her eyes and saw the round pink face of Petulia, screwed up with concern.

'Um, she's awake!' said the girl.

The space between Tiffany and the ceiling filled up with pointy hats. They drew back, reluctantly, as she sat up. From above, it must have looked like a dark daisy, closing and opening.

'Where is this?' she said.

'Um, the First Aid and Lost Children's Tent,' said Petulia. 'Um . . . you fainted when Mistress Weatherwax brought you back from . . . from wherever you'd gone. *Everyone's* been in to see you!'

'She said you'd, like, *dragged* the monster into, like, the Next World!' Lucy Warbeck said, her eyes gleaming. 'Mistress Weatherwax told everyone all about it!'

'Well, it wasn't quite—' Tiffany began. She felt something prod her in the back. She reached behind her, and her hand came back holding a pointy hat. It was almost grey with age and quite battered. Zakzak wouldn't have dared try to sell something like this, but the other girls stared it like starving dogs watching a butcher's hand.

'Um, Mistress Weatherwax gave you her *hat,*' breathed Petulia. 'Her actual *hat.*'

'She said you were a born witch and no witch should be without a hat!' said Dimity Hubbub, watching.

'That's nice,' said Tiffany. She was used to second-hand clothes.

'It's only an old hat,' said Annagramma.

Tiffany looked up at the tall girl and let herself smile slowly.

'Annagramma?' she said, raising a hand with the fingers open.

Annagramma backed away. 'Oh no,' she said. 'Don't you do that! *Don't* you do that! Someone stop her doing that!'

'Do you want a *balloon,* Annagramma?' said Tiffany, sliding off the table.

'No! Please!' Annagramma took another step back, holding her arms in front of her face, and fell over a bench. Tiffany picked her up and patted her cheerfully on a cheek.

'Then I shan't buy you one,' she said. 'But *please* learn what "literally" really means, will you?'

Annagramma smiled in a frozen kind of way. 'Er, yes,' she managed.

'Good. And then we will be friends.'

She left the girl standing there, and went back to pick up the hat.

'Um, you're probably still a bit woozy,' said Petulia. 'You probably don't understand.'

'Ha, I wasn't *actually* frightened, you know,' said Annagramma. 'It was all for fun, of course.' No one paid any attention.

'Understand what?' said Tiffany.

'It's her actual *hat*!' the girls chorused.

'It's, like, if that hat could talk, what stories it would have to, you know, tell,' said Lucy Warbeck.

'It was just a joke,' said Annagramma to anyone who was listening.

Tiffany looked at the hat. It was very battered, and not extremely clean. If that hat could talk, it would probably mutter.

'Where's Granny Weatherwax now?' she said.

There was a gasp from the girls. This was nearly as impressive as the hat.

'Um . . . she doesn't mind you calling her that?' said Petulia.

'She invited me to,' said Tiffany.

'Only we heard you had to have known her for, like, a hundred years before she let you call her that . . .' said Lucy Warbeck.

Tiffany shrugged. 'Well, anyway,' she said. 'Do you know where she is?'

'Oh, having tea with the other old witches and yakking on about chutney and how witches today aren't what they were when she was a girl,' said Lulu Darling.

'What?' said Tiffany. 'Just having *tea*?'

The young witches looked at one another in puzzlement.

'Um, there's buns too,' said Petulia. 'If that's important.'

'But she opened the door for me. The door into – out of the . . . the desert! You can't just sit down after that and have *buns*!'

'Um, the ones I saw had icing on,' Petulia ventured, nervously. 'They weren't just home-made—'

'Look,' said Lucy Warbeck, 'we didn't really, you know, *see* anything? You were just standing there with this, like, *glow* around you and we couldn't get in and then Gran— Mistress Weatherwax walked up and stepped right in and you both, you know, *stood* there? And then the glow went *zip* and vanished and you, like, fell over.'

'What Lucy's failing to say very accurately,' said Annagramma, 'is that we didn't actually see you go anywhere. I'm telling you this as a friend, of course. There was just this glow, which could have been *anything*.'

Annagramma was going to be a good witch, Tiffany considered. She could tell herself stories that she literally believed. And she could bounce back like a ball.

'Don't forget, I saw the horse,' said Harrieta Bilk.

Annagramma rolled her eyes. 'Oh yes, Harrieta thinks she saw some kind of horse in the sky. Except it didn't look like a horse, she says. She says it looked like a horse would look if you took the actual horse away and just left the horsiness, right, Harrieta?'

'I didn't say that!' snapped Harrieta.

'Well, pardon *me*. That's what it sounded like.'

'Um, and some people said they saw a white horse grazing in the next field, too, said Petulia. 'And a lot of the older witches said they felt a tremendous amount of—'

'Yes, some people thought they saw a horse in a field but it isn't there any more,' said Annagramma in the singsong voice she used when she thought it was all stupid. 'That must be very rare in the country, seeing horses in fields. Anyway, if there really *was* a white horse, it was grey.'

Tiffany sat on the edge of the table, staring at her knees. Anger at Annagramma had jolted her to life, but now the tiredness was creeping back.

'I suppose none of you saw a little blue man, about six inches high, with red hair?' she said quietly.

'Anyone?' said Annagramma, with malicious cheerfulness. There was a general mumbling of 'no'.

'Sorry, Tiffany,' said Lucy.

'Don't worry,' said Annagramma. 'He probably just rode away on his white horse!'

This is going to be like Fairyland all over again, thought Tiffany. Even I can't remember if it was real. Why should anyone believe me? But she had to try.

'There was a dark doorway,' she said slowly, 'and beyond it was a desert of black sand and it was quite light although there were stars in the sky, and Death was there. I spoke to him . . .'

'You spoke to him, did you?' said Annagramma. 'And what did he say, pray?'

'He didn't say "pray",' said Tiffany. 'We didn't talk about much. But he didn't know what an egress was.'

'It's a small type of heron, isn't it?' said Harrieta.

There was silence, except for the noise of the Trials outside.

'It's not your fault,' said Annagramma in what was, for her, almost a friendly voice. 'It's like I said: Mistress Weatherwax messes with people's heads.'

'What about the glow?' said Lucy.

'That was probably ball lightning,' said Annagramma. 'That's very strange stuff.'

'But people were, like, hammering on it! It was as hard as ice!'

'Ah, well, it probably *felt* like that,' said Annagramma, 'but it was . . . probably affecting people's muscles, maybe. I'm only trying to be helpful here,' she added. 'You've got to be sensible. She just stood there. You saw her. There weren't any doors or deserts. There was just her.'

Tiffany sighed. She just felt tired. She just wanted to crawl off somewhere. She just wanted to go home. She'd walk there now if her boots weren't suddenly so uncomfortable.

While the girls argued, she undid the laces and tugged one off.

Silver-black dust poured out. When it hit the ground it bounced, slowly, curving up into the air again like mist.

The girls turned, watching in silence. Then Petulia reached down and caught some of the dust. When she lifted her hand, the fine stuff flowed between her fingers. It fell as slowly as feathers.

'Sometimes things go wrong,' she said, in a far-away voice. 'Mistress Blackcap told me. Haven't any of you been there when old folk are dying?' There were one or two nods, but everyone was watching the dust.

'Sometimes things go wrong,' said Petulia again. 'Sometimes they're dying but they can't leave because they don't know the Way. She said that's when they need you to be there, close to them, to help them find the door so they don't get lost in the dark.'

'Petulia, we're not supposed to talk about this,' said Harrieta, gently.

'No!' said Petulia, her face red. 'It is a time to talk about it, just here, just us! Because she said it's the last thing you can do for someone. She said there's a dark desert they have to cross, where the sand—'

'Hah! Mrs Earwig says that sort of thing is black magic,' said Annagramma, her voice as sharp and sudden as a knife.

'Does she?' said Petulia dreamily as the sand poured down. 'Well, Mistress Blackcap said that sometimes the moon is light and sometimes it's in shadow but you should always remember it's the same moon. And . . . Annagramma?'

'Yes?'

Petulia took a deep breath.

'Don't you *ever* dare interrupt me again as long as you live. Don't you dare. Don't you *dare*! I mean it.'

Chapter 13

The Witch Trials

And then . . . there were the Trials themselves. That was the point of the day, wasn't it? But Tiffany, stepping out with the girls around her, sensed the buzz in the air. It said: Was there any point *now*? After what had happened?

Still, people had put up the rope square again, and a lot of the older witches dragged their chairs to the edge of it, and it seemed that it was going to happen after all. Tiffany wandered up to the rope, found a space and sat down on the grass with Granny Weatherwax's hat in front of her.

She was aware of the other girls behind her, and also a buzz or susurration of whispering spreading out into the crowd.

'*. . . She really did do it, too . . . no, really . . . all the way to the desert . . . saw the dust . . . her boots were full, they say . . .*'

Gossip spreads faster among witches than a bad

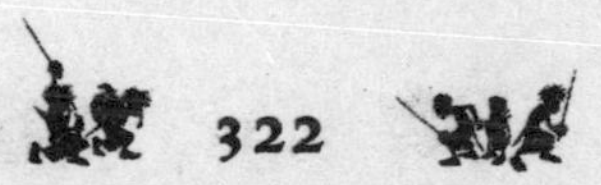

cold. Witches gossip like starlings.

There were no judges, and no prizes. The Trials weren't like that, as Petulia had said. The point was to show what you could do, to show what you'd become, so that people would go away thinking things like 'That Caramella Bottlethwaite, she's coming along nicely.' It wasn't a competition, honestly. No one *won*.

And if you believed *that* you'd believe that the moon is pushed around the sky by a goblin called Wilberforce.

What *was* true was that one of the older witches generally opened the thing with some competent but not surprising trick which everyone had seen before but still appreciated. That broke the ice. This year it was old Goodie Trample and her collection of singing mice.

But Tiffany wasn't paying attention. On the other side of the roped-off square, sitting on a chair and surrounded by older witches like a queen on her throne, was Granny Weatherwax.

The whispering went on. Maybe opening her eyes had opened her ears, too, because Tiffany felt she could hear the whispers all around the square.

'. . . Di'n't have no trainin', just did it . . . did you see that horse? . . . I never saw no horse! . . . Di'n't just open the door, she stepped right in! . . . Yeah, but who was it fetched her back? Esme Weatherwax, that's who! . . . Yes, that's what I'm sayin', any little fool could've opened the door by luck, but it takes a real witch to bring her back, that's a winner,

that is . . . fought the thing, left it there! . . . I didn't see you *doing anything, Violet Pulsimone! That child . . . Was there a horse or not? . . . Was going to do my dancing broom trick, but that'd be wasted now, of course . . . Why did Mistress Weatherwax give the girl her hat, eh? What's she want us to think? She never takes off her hat to no one!'*

You could feel the tension, crackling from pointy hat to pointy hat like summer lightning.

The mice did their best with *I'm Forever Blowing Bubbles* but it was easy to see that their minds weren't on it. Mice are highly strung and very temperamental.

Now people were leaning down beside Granny Weatherwax. Tiffany could see some animated conversations going on.

'You know, Tiffany,' said Lucy Warbeck, behind her, 'all you've got to do is, like, stand up and admit it. Everyone knows you did it. I mean, no one's ever, like, done something like *that* at the Trials!'

'And it's about time the old bully lost,' said Annagramma.

But she's not a bully, Tiffany thought. She's tough, and she expects other witches to be tough, because the edge is no place for people who break. Everything with her is a kind of test. And her Third Thoughts handed over the thought that had not quite made it back in the tent: *Granny Weatherwax, you* knew *the hiver would only come for me, didn't you? You talked to Dr Bustle, you told me. Did you just turn me into your trick for today? How much did you guess? Or know?*

'You'd win,' said Dimity Hubbub. 'Even some of the older ones would like to see her taken down a peg. They know big magic happened. There's not a whole shamble for *miles*.'

So I'd win because some people don't like somebody else? Tiffany thought. Oh, *yes*, that'd *really* be something to be proud of . . .

'You can bet *she'll* stand up,' said Annagramma. 'You watch. She'll explain how the poor child got dragged into the Next World by a monster, and she brought her back. That's what I'd do, if I was her.'

I expect you would, Tiffany thought. But you're not, and you're not me, either.

She stared at Granny Weatherwax, who was waving away a couple of elderly witches.

I wonder, she thought, if they've been saying things like 'This girl needs taking down a peg, Mistress Weatherwax.' And as she thought that, Granny turned back and caught her eye—

The mice stopped singing, mostly in embarrassment. There was a pause, and then people started to clap, because it was the sort of thing you had to do.

A witch, someone Tiffany didn't know, stepped out into the square, still clapping in that fluttery, hands-held-close-together-at shoulder-height way that people use when they want to encourage the audience to go on applauding just that little bit longer.

'Very well done, Doris, excellent work, as ever,' she trilled. 'They've come on marvellously since last year, thank you very much, wonderful, well done . . . ahem . . .'

The woman hesitated, while behind her Doris Trample crawled around on hands and knees trying to urge her mice back into their box. One of them was having hysterics.

'And now, perhaps . . . some lady would like to, er . . . take the, er . . . stage?' said the mistress of ceremonies, as brightly as a glass ball about to shatter. 'Anyone?'

There was stillness, and silence.

'Don't be shy, ladies!' The voice of the mistress of ceremonies was getting more strained by the second. It's no fun trying to organize a field full of born organizers. 'Modesty does not become us! Anyone?'

Tiffany *felt* the pointy hats turning, some towards her, some towards Granny Weatherwax. Away across the few yards of grass, Granny reached up and brushed someone's hand from her shoulder, sharply, without breaking eye contact with Tiffany. *And we're not wearing hats,* thought Tiffany. *You gave me a virtual hat once, Granny Weatherwax, and I thank you for it. But I don't need it today. Today, I know I'm a witch.*

'Oh, come now, ladies!' said the mistress of ceremonies, now almost frantic. 'This is the Trials! A place for friendly and instructive contestation in an atmosphere of fraternity and goodwill! Surely some lady . . . or young lady, perhaps . . . ?

Tiffany smiled. It should be 'sorority', not 'fraternity'. We're sisters, mistress, not brothers.

'Come *on*, Tiffany!' Dimity urged. 'They *know* you're good!'

Tiffany shook her head.

'Oh, well, that's it,' said Annagramma, rolling her eyes. 'The old baggage has messed with the girl's head, *as usual*—'

'I don't know who's messed with whose head,' snapped Petulia, rolling up her sleeves. 'But *I'm* going to do the pig trick.' She got to her feet and there was a general stir in the crowd.

'Oh, I see it's going to be— Oh, it's you, Petulia,' said the mistress of ceremonies, slightly disappointed.

'Yes, Miss Casement, and I intend to perform the pig trick,' said Petulia loudly.

'But, er, you don't seem to have brought a pig with you,' said Miss Casement, taken aback.

'Yes, Miss Casement. I shall perform the pig trick . . . *without a pig!*'

This caused a sensation, and cries of 'Impossible!' and 'There are children here, you know!'

Miss Casement looked around for assistance and found none. 'Oh well,' she said, helpless. 'If you are sure, dear . . .'

'Yes. I am. I shall use . . . a sausage!' said Petulia, producing one from a pocket and holding it up. There was another sensation.

Tiffany didn't see the trick. Nor did Granny Weatherwax. Their gaze was like an iron bar, and even Miss Casement instinctively didn't step into it.

But Tiffany heard the squeal, and the gasp of amazement, and then the thunder of applause. People would have applauded anything at that point, in the same way that pent-up water would take any route out of a dam.

And *then* witches got up. Miss Level juggled balls that stopped and reversed direction in mid-air. A middle-aged witch demonstrated a new way to stop people choking, which doesn't even sound magical until you understand that a way of turning nearly-dead people into fully-alive people is worth a dozen spells that just go *twing!* And other women and girls came up one at a time, with big tricks and handy tips and things that went *wheee!* or stopped toothache or, in one case, exploded –

– and then there were no more entries.

Miss Casement walked back into the centre of the field, almost drunk with relief that there *had* been a Trials, and made one final invitation to any ladies *'or, indeed, young ladies'* who might like to come forward.

There was a silence so thick you could have stuck pins in it.

And then she said: 'Oh, well . . . in that case, I declare the Trials well and truly closed. Tea will be in the big tent!'

Tiffany and Granny stood up at the same time, to the second, and bowed to one another. Then Granny turned away and joined the stampede towards the teas. It was interesting to see how the crowd parted, all unaware, to let her through, like the sea in front a particularly good prophet.

Petulia was surrounded by other young witches. The pig trick had gone down very well. Tiffany queued up to give her a hug.

'But *you* could have won!' said Petulia, red in the face with happiness and worry.

'That doesn't matter. It really doesn't,' said Tiffany.

'You gave it away,' said a sharp voice behind her. *'You had it in your hand, and you gave it all away. How do you feel about that, Tiffany? Do you have a taste for humble pie?'*

'Now you listen to me, Annagramma,' Petulia began, pointing a furious finger.

Tiffany reached out and lowered the girl's arm. Then she turned and smiled so happily at Annagramma that it was disturbing.

What she wanted to say was: 'Where I come from, Annagramma, they have the Sheepdog Trials. Shepherds travel there from all over to show off their dogs. And there're silver crooks and belts with silver buckles and prizes of all kinds, Annagramma, but do you know what the big prize was? No, you wouldn't. Oh, there were judges, but they didn't count, not for the *big* prize. There is— There *was* a little old lady who was always at the front of the crowd, leaning on the hurdles with her pipe in her mouth with the two finest sheepdogs ever pupped sitting at her feet. Their names were Thunder and Lightning and they moved so fast they set the air on fire and their coats outshone the sun, but she never, ever put them in the Trials. She knew more about sheep than even sheep know. And what every young shepherd wanted, really *wanted*, wasn't some silly cup or belt but to see her take her pipe out of her mouth as he left the arena and quietly say "That'll do" because that meant he was a *real* shepherd and all the other shepherds would know it, too. And if you'd told him he had to challenge her, he'd cuss at you and stamp his foot and tell you he'd sooner spit the sun dark. How could he ever win? She *was* shepherding. It was the whole of her life. What you took away from her you'd take away from yourself. You don't understand that, do you? But it's the heart and soul and centre of it! The soul . . . and . . . centre!'

But it would be wasted, so what she said was: 'Oh, just shut up, Annagramma. Let's see if there's any buns left, shall we?'

Overhead, a buzzard screamed. She looked up.

The bird turned on the wind and, racing through the air as it began the long glide, headed back towards home.

They were always there.

Beside her cauldron, Jeannie opened her eyes.

'He's comin' hame!' she said, scrambling to her feet. She waved a hand urgently at the watching Feegles. 'Don't ye just stand there gawping!' she commanded. 'Catch some rabbits to roast! Build up the fire! Boil up a load o' water, 'cos I'm takin' a bath! Look at this place, 'tis like a midden! Get it cleaned up! I want it sparkling for the Big Man! Go an' steal some Special Sheep Liniment! Cut some green boughs, holly or yew, mebbe! Shine up the golden plates! The place must sparkle! What're ye all standin' there for?'

'Er, what did ye want us to do first, Kelda,' said a Feegle nervously.

'All of it!'

In her chamber they filled the kelda's soup-bowl bath and she scrubbed, using one of Tiffany's old toothbrushes, while outside there were the sounds of Feegles working hard at cross-purposes. The smell of roasting rabbit began to fill the mound.

Jeannie dressed herself in her best dress, did her hair, picked up her shawl and climbed out of the hole. She stood there watching the mountains until, after about an hour, a dot in the sky got bigger and bigger.

As a kelda, she would welcome home a warrior. As a wife, she would kiss her husband and scold him for being so long away. As a woman, she thought she would melt with relief, thankfulness and joy.

Chapter 14

Queen of the Bees

And, one afternoon about a week later, Tiffany went to see Granny Weatherwax.

It was only fifteen miles as the broomstick flies, and as Tiffany still didn't like flying a broomstick, Miss Level took her.

It was the invisible part of Miss Level. Tiffany just lay flat on the stick, holding on with arms and legs and knees and ears if possible, and took along a paper bag to be sick into, because no one likes anonymous sick dropping out of the sky. She was also holding a large hessian sack, which she handled with care.

She didn't open her eyes until the rushing noises had stopped and the sounds around her told her she was probably very close to the ground. In fact Miss Level had been very kind. When she fell off, because of the cramp in her legs, the broomstick was just above some quite thick moss.

'Thank you,' said Tiffany as she got up, because it

always pays to mind your manners around invisible people.

She had a new dress. It was green, like the last one. The complex world of favours and obligations and gifts that Miss Level lived and moved in had thrown up four yards of nice material (for the trouble-free birth of Miss Quickly's baby boy) and a few hours' dressmaking (Mrs Hunter's bad leg feeling a lot better, thank you). She'd given the black one away. When I'm old I shall wear midnight, she'd decided. But, for now, she'd had enough of darkness.

She looked around at this clearing on the side of a hill, surrounded by oak and sycamore on three sides but open on the downhill side with a wide view of the countryside below. The sycamores were shedding their spinning seeds, which whirled down lazily across a patch of garden. It was unfenced, even though some goats were grazing nearby. If you wondered why it was the goats weren't eating the garden, it was because you'd forgotten who lived here. There was a well. And, of course, a cottage.

Mrs Earwig would definitely have objected to the cottage. It was out of a storybook. The walls leaned against one another for support, the thatched roof was slipping off like a bad wig, and the chimneys were corkscrewed. If you thought a gingerbread cottage would be too fattening, this was the next worst thing.

In a cottage deep in the forest lived the Wicked Old Witch . . .

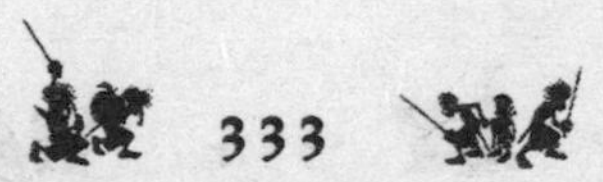

It was a cottage out of the nastier kind of fairy tale.

Granny Weatherwax's beehives were tucked away down one side of the cottage. Some were the old straw kind, most were patched-up wooden ones. They thundered with activity, even this late in the year.

Tiffany turned aside to look at them, and the bees poured out in a dark stream. They swarmed towards Tiffany, formed a column and—

She laughed. They'd made a witch of bees in front of her, thousands of them all holding station in the air. She raised her right hand. With a rise in the level of buzzing, the bee-witch raised its right hand. She turned around. It turned around, the bees carefully copying every swirl and flutter of her dress, the ones on the very edge buzzing desperately because they had furthest to fly.

She carefully put down the big sack and reached out towards the figure. With another roar of wings it went shapeless for a moment, and then re-formed a little way away, but with a hand outstretched towards her. The bee that was the tip of its forefinger hovered just in front of Tiffany's fingernail.

'Shall we dance?' said Tiffany.

In the clearing full of spinning seeds, she circled the swarm. It kept up pretty well, moving fingertip to buzzing tip, turning when she turned, although there were always a few bees racing to catch up.

Then it raised both its arms and twirled in the opposite direction, the bees in the 'skirt' spreading out again as it spun. It was learning.

Tiffany laughed and did the same thing. Swarm and girl whirled across the clearing.

She felt happy and wondered if she'd ever felt this happy before. The gold light, the falling bracts, the dancing bees . . . it was all one thing. This was the opposite of the dark desert. Here, light was everywhere and filled her up inside. She could feel herself here but see herself from above, twirling with a buzzing shadow that sparkled golden as the light struck the bees. Moments like this paid for it all.

Then the witch made of bees leaned closer to Tiffany, as if staring at her with its thousands of little jewelled eyes. There was a faint piping noise from inside the figure and the bee-witch exploded into a spreading, buzzing cloud of insects which raced away across the clearing and disappeared. The only movement now was the whirring fall of the sycamore seeds.

Tiffany breathed out.

'Now, some people would have found that scary,' said a voice behind her.

Tiffany didn't turn round immediately. First she said, 'Good afternoon, Granny Weatherwax.' *Then* she turned round.

'Have *you* ever done this?' she demanded, still half-drunk with delight.

'It's rude to start with questions. You'd better come in and have a cup of tea,' said Granny Weatherwax.

You'd barely know that anyone *lived* in the

cottage. There were two chairs by the fire, one of them a rocking chair, and by the table were two chairs that didn't rock but *did* wobble because of the uneven stone floor. There was a dresser, and a rag-rug in front of the huge hearth. A broomstick leaned against the wall in one corner, next to something mysterious and pointy, under a cloth. There was a very narrow and dark flight of stairs. And that was it. There was nothing shiny, nothing new and nothing unnecessary.

'To what do I owe the pleasure of this visit?' said Granny Weatherwax, taking a sooty black kettle off the fire and filling an equally black teapot.

Tiffany opened the sack she had brought with her. 'I've come to bring you your hat back,' she said.

'Ah,' said Granny Weatherwax. 'Have you? And why?'

'Because it's *your* hat,' said Tiffany, putting it on the table. 'Thank you for the loan of it, though.'

'I dare say there's plenty of young witches who'd give their high teeth for an ol' hat of mine,' said Granny, lifting up the battered hat.

'There are,' said Tiffany, and did *not* add 'and it's *eye* teeth, actually'. What she did add was: 'But I think everyone has to find their own hat. The right hat for them, I mean.'

'I see you're now wearing a shop-bought one, then,' said Granny Weatherwax. 'One of them Sky Scrapers. With *stars*,' she added, and there was so much acid in the word 'stars' that it would've melted copper and then dropped through the table and the floor and melted more copper in the cellar below. 'Think that makes it more magical, do you? *Stars?*'

'I . . . did when I bought it. And it'll do for now.'

'Until you find the right hat,' said Granny Weatherwax.

'Yes.'

'Which ain't mine?'

'No.'

'Good.'

The old witch walked across the room and tugged the cloth off the thing in the corner. It turned out to be a big wooden spike, just about the size of a pointy hat on a tall stand. A hat was being . . . *constructed* on it, with thin strips of willow and pins and stiff black cloth.

'I make my own,' she said. 'Every year. There's no hat like the hat you make yourself. Take my advice. I stiffens the calico and makes it waterproof with special jollop. It's amazing what you can put into a hat you make yourself. But you didn't come to talk about hats.'

Tiffany let the question out at last.

'Was it real?'

Granny Weatherwax poured the tea, picked up her cup and saucer, then carefully poured some of the tea out of the cup and into the saucer. She held this up and, with care, like someone dealing with an important and delicate task, blew gently on it. She did this slowly and calmly, while Tiffany tried hard to conceal her impatience.

'The hiver's not around any more?' said Granny.

'No. But—'

'And how did it all feel? When it was happenin'? Did it *feel* real?'

'No,' said Tiffany. 'It felt more than real.'

'Well, there you are, then,' said Granny Weatherwax, taking a sip from the saucer. 'And the answer is: If it wasn't real, it wasn't *false*.'

'It was like a dream where you've nearly woken up and can control it, you know?' said Tiffany. 'If I was careful, it worked. It was like making myself rise up in the air by pulling hard on my bootlaces. It was like telling myself a story—'

Granny nodded. 'There's always a story,' she said. 'It's all stories, really. The sun coming up every day is a story. Everything's got a story in it. Change the story, change the world.'

'And what was your plan to beat the hiver?' said Tiffany. 'Please? I've got to know!'

'My plan?' said Granny Weatherwax innocently. 'My plan was to let you deal with it.'

'Really? So what would you have done if I'd lost?'

'The best I can,' said Granny calmly. 'I always do.'

'Would you have killed me if I'd become the hiver again?'

The saucer was steady in the old witch's hand. She looked reflectively at the tea.

'I would have spared you if I could,' she said. 'But I didn't have to, right? The Trials was the best place to be. Believe me, witches can act together if they must. It's harder'n herding cats, but it can be done.'

'It's just that I think we . . . turned it all into a little show,' said Tiffany.

'Hah, no. We made it into a *big* show!' said Granny Weatherwax with great satisfaction. 'Thunder and lightning and white horses and wonderful rescues! Good value, eh, for a penny? And you'll learn, my girl, that a bit of a show every now and again does no harm to your reputation. I daresay Miss Level's findin' that out already, now she can juggle balls and raise her hat at the same time! Depend upon what I say!'

She delicately drank her tea out of the saucer, then nodded at the old hat on the table.

'Your grandmother,' she said, 'did *she* wear a hat?'

'What? Oh . . . not usually,' said Tiffany, still thinking about the big show. 'She used to wear an old sack as a kind of bonnet when the weather was really bad. She said hats only blow away up on the hill.'

'She made the sky her hat, then,' said Granny Weatherwax. 'And did she wear a coat?'

'Hah, all the shepherds used to say that if you saw Granny Aching in a coat it'd mean it was blowing rocks!' said Tiffany proudly.

'Then she made the wind her coat, too,' said Granny Weatherwax. 'It's a skill. Rain don't fall on a witch if she doesn't want it to, although personally I prefer to get wet and be thankful.'

'Thankful for what?' said Tiffany.

'That I'll get dry later.' Granny Weatherwax put

down the cup and saucer. 'Child, you've come here to learn what's true and what's not but there's little I can teach you that you don't already know. You just don't know you know it, and you'll spend the rest of your life learning what's already in your bones. And that's the truth.'

She stared at Tiffany's hopeful face and sighed.

'Come outside then,' she said. 'I'll give you lesson one. It's the only lesson there is. It don't need writing down in no book with eyes on.'

She led the way to the well in her back garden, looked around on the ground and picked up a stick.

'Magic wand,' she said. 'See?' A green flame leaped out of it, making Tiffany jump. 'Now you try.'

It didn't work for Tiffany, no matter how much she shook it.

'Of course not,' said Granny. 'It's a stick. Now, maybe I made a flame come out of it, or maybe I made you *think* it did. That don't matter. It was *me* is what I'm sayin', not the stick. Get your mind right and you can make a stick your wand and the sky your hat and a puddle your magic . . . your magic . . . er, what're them fancy cups called?'

'Er . . . goblet,' said Tiffany.

'Right. Magic goblet. Things aren't important. People are.' Granny Weatherwax looked sidelong at Tiffany. 'And I could teach you how to run across those hills of yours with the hare, I could teach you how to fly above them with the buzzard. I could tell you the secrets of the bees. I could teach you all this and much more besides if you'd do just one thing, right here and now. One simple thing, easy to do.'

Tiffany nodded, eyes wide.

'You understand, then, that all the glittery stuff is just toys, and toys can lead you astray?'

'Yes!'

'Then take off that shiny horse you wear around your neck, girl, and drop it in the well.'

Obediently, half-hypnotized by the voice, Tiffany reached behind her neck and undid the clasp.

The pieces of the silver horse shone as she held it over the water.

She stared at it as if she was seeing it for the first time. And then . . .

She tests people, she thought. *All the time.*

'Well?' said the old witch.

'No,' said Tiffany. 'I can't.'

'Can't or won't?' said Granny sharply.

'Can't,' said Tiffany and stuck out her chin. '*And* won't!'

She drew her hand back and fastened the necklace again, glaring defiantly at Granny Weatherwax

The witch smiled. 'Well done,' she said quietly. 'If you don't know when to be a human being, you don't know when to be a witch. And if you're too afraid of goin' astray, you won't go anywhere. May I see it, please?'

Tiffany looked into those blue eyes. Then she undid the clasp and handed over the necklace. Granny held it up.

'Funny, ain't it, that it seems to gallop when the light hits it,' said the witch, watching it twist this way and that. 'Well-made thing. O'course, it's not what a horse looks like, but it's certainly what a horse *is*.'

Tiffany stared at her with her mouth open. For a moment Granny Aching stood there grinning, and then Granny Weatherwax was back. Did she do that, she wondered, or did I do it myself? And do I dare find out?

'I didn't just come to bring the hat back,' she managed to say. 'I brought you a present, too.'

'I'm sure there's no call for anyone to bring *me* a present,' said Granny Weatherwax, sniffing.

Tiffany ignored this, because her mind was still spinning. She fetched her sack again and handed over a small, soft parcel, which moved as it changed shape in her hands.

'I took most of the stuff back to Mr Stronginthearm,' she said. 'But I thought you might have a . . . a *use* for this.'

The old woman slowly unwrapped the white paper. The Zephyr Billow cloak unrolled itself under her fingers and filled the air like smoke.

'It's lovely, but I couldn't wear it,' said Tiffany as the cloak shaped itself over the gentle currents of the clearing. 'You need gravitas to carry off a cloak like that.'

'What's gravitarse?' said Granny Weatherwax sharply.

'Oh . . . dignity. Seniority. Wisdom. Those sort of things,' said Tiffany.

'Ah,' said Granny, relaxing a little. She stared at the gently rippling cloak and sniffed. It really was a wonderful creation. The wizards had got at least one thing right when they had made it. It was one of those items that fill a hole in your life that you didn't know was there until you'd seen it.

'Well, I suppose there's those as can wear a cloak like this, and those as can't,' she conceded. She let it curl around her neck and fastened it there with a crescent-shaped brooch. 'It's a bit too grand for the likes of me,' she said. 'A bit too fancy. I could look like a flibbertigibbet wearing something like this.' It was spoken like a statement but it had a curl like a question.

'No, it suits you, it really does,' said Tiffany cheerfully. 'If you don't know when to be a human being, you don't know when to be a witch.'

Birds stopped singing. Up in the trees, squirrels ran and hid. Even the sky seemed to darken for a moment.

'Er . . . that's what I heard,' said Tiffany, and added, 'From someone who knows these things.'

The blue eyes stared into hers. There were no secrets from Granny Weatherwax. Whatever you said, she watched what you meant.

'Perhaps you'll call again sometimes,' she said, turning slowly and watching the cloak curve in the air. 'It's always very quiet here.'

'I should like that,' said Tiffany. 'Shall I tell the bees before I come, so you can get the tea ready?'

For a moment Granny Weatherwax glared, and then the lines faded into a wry grin.

'Clever,' she said.

What's inside you? Tiffany thought. Who are you really, in there? Did you *want* me to take your hat? You pretend to be the big bad wicked witch, and you're not. You test people all the time, test, test, test, but you really want them to be clever enough to beat you. Because it must be hard, being the best. You're not allowed to stop. You can only be beaten, and you're too proud ever to lose. Pride! You've turned it into terrible strength, but it eats away at you. Are you afraid to laugh in case you hear an early cackle?

We'll meet again, one day. We both know it. We'll meet again, at the Witch Trials.

'I'm clever enough to know how you manage *not* to think of a pink rhinoceros if someone says "pink rhinoceros",' she managed to say aloud.

'Ah, that's deep magic, that is,' said Granny Weatherwax.

'No. It's not. You don't know what a rhinoceros looks like, do you?'

Sunlight filled the clearing as the old witch laughed, as clear as a downland stream.

'That's right!' she said.

Chapter 15

A Hat Full of Sky

It was one of those strange days in late February when it's a little warmer than it should be and, although there's wind, it seems to be all round the horizons and never quite where you are.

Tiffany climbed up onto the downs where, in the sheltered valleys, the early lambs had already found their legs and were running around in a gang in that strange jerky run that lambs have, which makes them look like woolly rocking horses.

Perhaps there was something about that day, because the old ewes joined in, too, and skipped with their lambs. They jumped and spun, half happy, half embarrassed, big winter fleeces bouncing up and down like a clown's trousers.

It had been an interesting winter. She'd learned a lot of things. One of them was that you could be a bridesmaid to two people who between them were over 170 years old. This time Mr Weavall, with his wig spinning on his head and his big spectacles gleaming, had *insisted* on giving one of the gold pieces to 'our little helper', which more than made up for the wages that she hadn't asked for and Miss Level couldn't afford. She'd used some of it to buy a really good brown cloak. It didn't billow, it didn't fly out behind her, but it was warm and thick and kept her dry.

She'd learned lots of other things too. As she walked past the sheep and their lambs, she gently touched their minds, so softly that they didn't notice . . .

Tiffany had stayed up in the mountains for Hogswatch, which officially marked the changing of the year. There'd been a lot to do there, and anyway it wasn't much celebrated on the Chalk. Miss Level had been happy to give her leave now, though, for the lambing festival, which the old people called Sheepbellies. It was when the shepherds' year began. The hag of the hills couldn't miss that. That was when, in warm nests of straw shielded from the wind by hurdles and barriers of cut furze, the future happened. She'd helped it happen, working with the shepherds by lantern light, dealing with the difficult births. She'd worked with the pointy hat on her head and had felt the shepherds watching her as, with knife and needle and thread and hands and soothing words, she'd saved ewes from the black doorway and helped new lambs into the light. You had to give them a show. You had to give them a story. And she'd walked back home proudly in the morning and bloody to the elbows, but it had been the blood of life.

Later, she had gone up to the Feegles' mound, and slid down the hole. She'd thought about this for some time, and had gone prepared – with clean torn-up handkerchiefs and some soapwort shampoo made to a recipe Miss Level had given her. She had a feeling that Jeannie would have a use for these. Miss Level always visited new mothers. It was what you did.

Jeannie had been pleased to see her. Lying on her stomach so that she could get part of her body into the kelda's chamber, Tiffany had been allowed to hold all eight of what she kept thinking of as the Roblets, born at the same time as the lambs. Seven of them were bawling and fighting one another. The eighth lay quietly, biding her time. The future happened.

It wasn't only Jeannie who thought of her differently. News had got around. The people of the Chalk hadn't liked witches. They had always come from outside. They had always come as strangers. But now here was *our* Tiffany, birthing the lambs like her granny did, and they say she's been learning witchery in the mountains! Ah, but that's still our Tiffany, that is. OK, I'll grant you that she's wearing a hat with big stars on it, but she makes good cheese and she knows about lambing and she's *Granny Aching's grand-daughter*, right? And they'd tap their noses, knowingly. Granny Aching's grand-daughter. Remember what the old woman could do? So if witch she be, then she's *our* witch. She knows about sheep, she does. Hah, and I heard they had a big sort of trial for witches up in them mountains and our Tiffany showed 'em what a girl from the Chalk can do. It's modern times, right? We got a witch now, and she's better'n anyone else's! No one's throwing Granny Aching's grand-daughter in a pond!

Tomorrow she'd go back to the mountains again. It had been a busy three weeks, quite apart from the lambing. Roland had invited her to tea at the castle. It had been a bit awkward, as these things are, but it was funny how, in a couple of years, he'd gone from a lumbering oaf into a nervous young man who forgot what he was talking about when she smiled at him. And they had *books* in the castle!

He'd shyly presented her with a Dictionary of Amazingly Uncommon Words, and she had been prepared enough to bring him a hunting knife made by Zakzak, who was excellent at blades even if he was rubbish at magic. The hat wasn't mentioned, very carefully. And when she'd got home she'd found a bookmark in the P section and a faint pencil underline under the words '**Plongeon**: a small curtsy, about one-third as deep as the traditional one. No longer used.' Alone in her bedroom, she'd blushed. It's always surprising to be reminded that while you're watching and thinking about people, all knowing and superior, they're watching and thinking about you, right back at you.

She written it down in her diary, which was a lot thicker now, what with all the pressed herbs and extra notes and bookmarks. It had been trodden on by cows, struck by lightning and dropped in tea. And it didn't have an eye on it. An eye would have got knocked off on day one. It was a *real* witch's diary.

Tiffany had stopped wearing the hat, except in public, because it kept getting bent by low doorways and completely crushed by her bedroom ceiling. She was wearing it today, though, clutching it occasionally whenever a gust tried to snatch it off her head.

She reached the place where four rusty iron wheels were half buried in the turf and a pot-bellied stove stood up from the grass. It made a useful seat.

Silence spread out around Tiffany, a living silence, while the sheep danced with their lambs and the world turned.

Why do you go away? So that you can come back. So that you can see the place you came from with new eyes and extra colours. And the people there see you differently, too. Coming back to where you started is not the same as never leaving.

The words ran through Tiffany's mind as she watched the sheep, and she found herself fill up with joy – at the new lambs, at life, at everything. Joy is to fun what the deep sea is to a puddle. It's a feeling inside that can hardly be contained. It came out as laughter.

'I've come back!' she announced, to the hills. 'Better than I went!'

She snatched off the hat with stars on it. It wasn't a bad hat, for show, although the stars made it look like a toy. But it was never *her* hat. It couldn't be. The only hat worth wearing was the one you made for yourself, not one you bought, not one you were given. Your own hat, for your own head. Your own future, not someone else's.

She hurled the starry hat up as high as she could. The wind there caught it neatly. It tumbled for a moment and then was lifted by a gust and, swooping and spinning, sailed away across the downs and vanished for ever.

Then Tiffany made a hat out of the sky and sat on the old pot-bellied stove, listening to the wind around the horizons while the sun went down.

As the shadows lengthened, many small shapes crept out of the nearby mound and joined her in the sacred place, to watch.

The sun set, which is everyday magic, and warm night came.

The hat filled up with stars . . .

Author's Note

The Doctrine of Signatures mentioned on page 90 really exists in this world, although now it's better known by historians than doctors. For hundreds of years, perhaps thousands, people believed that God, who of course had made everything, had 'signed' each thing in a way that showed humanity what it could be used for. For example, goldenrod is yellow so 'must' be good for jaundice, which turns the skin yellow (a certain amount of guesswork was involved, but sometimes patients survived).

By an amazing coincidence, the Horse carved on the Chalk is remarkably similar to the Uffington White Horse, which in this world is carved on the downlands near the village of Uffington in south-west Oxfordshire. It's 374 feet long, several thousand years old and carved on the hill in such a way that you can only see all of it in one go from the air. This suggests that: a) it was carved for the gods to see; or,

b) flying was invented a lot earlier that we thought; or, c) people used to be much, much taller.

Oh, and this world had Witch Trials, too. They were not fun.